What reviewers are saying about the stories in

A Changeling for All Seasons

Angela Knight, A Vampire Christmas

"A Vampire Christmas is a great short story, with all the elements of a great tale: hot sex, emotional yearning, and a great ending."
– *Enchanted in Romance*

Sahara Kelly, Now Playing: A Christmas Pageant

"If you're looking for something to warm up your nights and keep you in the holiday spirit, look no further than Now Playing: A Christmas Pageant."
– *Jennifer Bishop, Romance Reviews Today*

Judy Mays, Jingle Balls

"With its humor-filled plotline, captivating characters, and some of the most amusing scenes I've ever read, this is one story that readers will enjoy for sure."
– *Sinclair Reid, Romance Reviews Today*

Marteeka Karland, Sealed with a Kiss

"This is one of the best short stories I have read… sweet enough for the most jaded of Valentine's Day naysayer."
– *Marina, Mon Boudoir*

Kate Douglas, My Valentine

"Easily the most emotional, beautiful and unforgettable novella I've read this year, My Valentine is simply breathtaking."
– *Ayden Delacroix, In the Library Reviews*

Changeling Press LLC

www.ChangelingPress.com

A Changeling For All Seasons

Angela Knight – A Vampire Christmas
Sahara Kelly – A Christmas Pageant
Judy Mays – Jingle Balls
Marteeka Karland – Sealed With A Kiss
Kate Douglas – My Valentine
Shelby Morgen – Changeling
Willa Okati – Elven Enchantment
Kate Hill – Jolene's Pooka
Lacey Savage – Chemistry to Burn
Shelby Morgen – Troll Under The Bridge

Publisher:
Changeling Press LLC
PO Box 1561
Shepherdstown, WV 25443-1561
www.ChangelingPress.com

Printed in the U.S.A.
Lightning Source, Inc.
1246 Heil Quaker Blvd
La Vergne TN 37086
www.lightningsource.com

Anthology Editor: Margaret Riley
Cover Artist: Bryan Keller

The individual stories in this anthology have been previously released in E-Book format.

A Vampire Christmas
Angela Knight

Chapter One

Amelia Patton clattered up the beige stairs of the apartment complex, the plastic dress bag hooked over one shoulder. It had been a long shift at the hospital, but the prospect of showing David her purchase had put a bounce back in her step. The gown was every little girl's fairytale dream – seed pearls, white lace, and yards and yards of satin skirt, with a train that would reach halfway down the church aisle. The lace veil alone had her inner eight-year-old sighing in bliss.

Clutching her precious dress with one hand, she juggled the keys until she found the right one and inserted it into the lock. The door swung open, revealing the living room that had made real strides in livability over the past two months. When she'd first moved in, David's furniture had consisted of a couch he'd bought at Goodwill and a really tacky table made from a cable spool. The big screen television and entertainment center were worth more than all the rest of the furniture in the apartment. God love the man, he was too butch for taste.

Amelia had coaxed him into replacing the castoffs with a lovely cream living room set, colorful pastel sketches, and a pretty floor lamp with a stained glass shade. She made good money as a nurse, she argued. They could afford it.

"Honey, I'm home!" God, she loved saying that.

No answer. She frowned. It was well after midnight; David would be home from his shift with the Atlanta Police. Unless something had happened… A frisson of fear slid up her spine, but she forced it away. "Hey, Dave! I went by the mall on my dinner break and picked up that gown I told you about. Wait 'til you see it…"

The bedsprings creaked from the next room. "Amelia." His voice sounded hoarse.

"Hey, babe, you okay? Did you get into another fight?" That was how they'd met. David had come by the ER after a drug dealer resisted arrest with a little too much enthusiasm. She'd been smearing antibiotic cream across those sculpted ribs when he'd asked her to dinner. Amelia had looked into those crystalline blue eyes, and fallen helplessly in lust. She hadn't been able to say no to him since.

A year later, she still lusted for him – but she'd also come to know and love his wicked sense of humor, strong character, and clever mind.

"Come here." David normally reserved that cold, demanding tone for the prisoners he brought to the hospital after they'd tried to bust his head. He'd never before used it with her.

"David, what's wrong?" Worried, Amelia hurried into the bedroom, the dress slung over her shoulder.

They'd bought the massive iron bedstead in an antique store when she'd moved in with him. David had teased her that its tall, ornate posts were perfect for bondage.

She'd still never expected to find him naked and shackled spread-eagle to it like a beefcake buffet.

David was a big man, as dark as she was blonde, broad shouldered and narrow hipped. He spent a couple of hours in the department gym four days a week, building the layers of rippling muscle he considered an occupational necessity for a beat cop. Adding to the impression of overwhelming masculinity, a dark ruff of hair spread across his chest and arrowed down his cobblestone belly toward his thick cock.

His face was just as broad and angular as his tough body, with prominent cheekbones and a regal nose, straight and narrow. His mouth added the only note of sensual vulnerability about him with its full lower lip and lush upper curve. A hint of a dimple graced one corner, giving his smile a boyish charm.

"Yum," Amelia purred, grinning at the sight of him spread out in chains. "For me?"

"What do you think?" His cock stirred hungrily, and he stared at her like a cat watching a caged canary.

She rocked back on the rubber heels of her shoes and grinned. "This is an interesting switch. Usually I'm the one tied to that bed."

"Come here," he said again. His blue eyes blazed with lust.

Smiling wickedly, Amelia paused just long enough to hang the dress in the closet. Then, reaching for the hem of her scrubs, she started toward him. But before she could reach his side, she realized something was wrong. He was far too pale, in the way she'd come to associate with massive blood loss, and his face was drawn. She let the hem drop. "David, are you okay?"

"I said *come here!*" he roared, peeling his lips back from his teeth in a savage snarl.

He had fangs.

Sharp, white, damn near two inches long, they made his handsome, sensual mouth look alien and threatening.

They couldn't possibly be real.

She gave him an uncertain smile. This must be some kind of new sex game, and yet... "What's with the Count Dracula dental work? Halloween isn't for three months."

"Get over here!" He lunged at her so hard the bed danced on the floor, but he couldn't break the chains. The iron posts began to bend.

Amelia jumped back, sick horror creeping over her with the knowledge this was no joke. Strong as he was, there was no way he should be able to bend the solid iron headboard. "Jesus, David! What the hell is going on?"

"What are you doing here?" a female voice demanded. Amelia whirled as a woman she'd never seen before stepped into the room. The stranger barely came up to her shoulder, a petite brunette with a wealth of sable hair and a small, heart-shaped face. She wore jeans and a black knit top that made the most of impressive breasts. Her frown was ferocious as she glared up at Amelia. "You don't belong here, it's too dangerous. You must leave until this is finished." She stalked past on booted feet, pulling a familiar plastic bag out of her purse. Before Amelia could ask where the hell she'd gotten a unit of whole blood, she snatched a pair of scissors off the table, clipped the top off the bag, and thrust it into David's mouth. He began to drink thirstily.

Blood. *He was drinking blood.*

Like some kind of vampire.

A sense of unreality crashed in. Amelia took a step back. David. Naked. With a strange woman. Chained to a bed. Drinking blood. "Who the hell are you? Will somebody please tell me what's going on?"

"Get out!" the brunette snapped. She had an exotic accent, clipped and Slavic. "If he breaks loose from these chains, he'll kill you. Go! When he is sane again, I will tell you." She had fangs too.

Amelia's jaw dropped. "You're a vampire!"

The brunette shot her a glare. "Congratulations. Your grasp of the obvious is stunning. Now use those dubious wits and get out while you still can."

Still drinking, David rolled his blue eyes in her direction. The depths of his eyes glinted red. There was nothing at all sane in his gaze.

Amelia whirled and ran.

She moved in with one of her nurse coworkers the next day. She never went back to the apartment; she was too spooked. Instead she bought new clothes and uniforms, changed her cell number, and did her best to disappear, broken heart and all.

Two weeks later, Amelia learned from another officer that David had resigned from the force.

She tried very hard not to think about him otherwise. She didn't dare.

Yet for months it felt as if somebody had dug bloody chunks out of her heart with an ice cream scoop. The ache never went away, but in time she got better at ignoring it.

At least until the day five months after she left him, when the phone rang at the ER nursing desk. Amelia was closest, so she picked it up. "ER."

"Amelia."

It was like hearing the voice of a ghost. Her entire body flushed hot, then went ice cold. "David."

"I'm… sorry. About what happened that night. The Change drove me a little crazy. You have no idea what it's like becoming a…" He broke off. "But I'm back to normal. Or as close as I can come to it, without you in my life. God, Amelia, I miss you. I want to see you again. Please…"

Amelia hung up the phone and walked into the women's bathroom. Sagging against the wall, she began crying in deep, ragged sobs.

The man she loved was a monster. And she didn't dare see him again.

Christmas Eve

A brutally cold wind whipped through the hospital parking lot, and Amelia hunched deeper in her coat as she walked toward her car. She'd worked a double shift tonight, and she was exhausted. But she figured it was worth it. After all, her fellow nurses had families to celebrate Christmas with. Children. Husbands. Taking two shifts meant one of them got more time with the people who loved her.

And tired Amelia out too much to think.

Enough that she could face going home to the empty apartment she'd moved into four months ago. At least no tinsel and colored lights waited there to torment her with memories. Last year, David had tied her up and banged her brains out under the Christmas tree. She hadn't been able to even look at holiday decorations this year without feeling a fist clench around her heart.

As she headed toward her car, a flicker of interest penetrated her depression. There was a black limo parked next to her car. A tall blond man stood next to it, his arm around a woman who was bundled against the cold. The two had their heads together, whispering.

A memory ambushed Amelia. David, standing with her in that same pose, his arms strong and warm around her. She caught her breath in pain and turned her face away from the pair. Trying to ignore them, she stepped between the cars and clicked her key fob to unlock the Honda.

"Amelia?" The man's voice was deep, with a faint Slavic accent.

Automatically, she turned. "Yes?"

And froze, instantly recognizing the woman who stood beside him. It was the petite dark-haired woman who'd been with David that night.

The vampire.

Staring into those dark eyes, the world spun around her, propelled by raw terror.

"Turn around and put your wrists behind you," the vampire said.

Like hell, Amelia thought. But to her horror, she felt her body turn, as if she was no longer in control of it. Fighting her rebellious arms as they obediently extended behind her, she gasped. "What? What the hell...? What are you..."

"Silence," the woman snapped. "Dimitri?"

The blond man stepped up behind her. Amelia felt something cold close around her wrists. Handcuffs?

"Wait! Stop that!" Panicking, she tried to jerk away, but her body wouldn't obey.

The woman opened the door of the limo. "Get in."

"No!" Amelia wailed, even as her body mechanically slid into the car.

"Oh, do be quiet," the vampire snapped. "This is your own fault. Go to sleep."

Darkness crashed down.

* * *

Amelia regained consciousness to a metallic taste in her mouth. She was moving. Evidently they'd put her in that limo of theirs, since she could smell expensive leather. Her arms were twisted behind her in an uncomfortable pose.

"Are you ready to discuss this calmly?" a coldly familiar voice asked. The female vampire!

Fighting panic, Amelia lifted her head. By the looks of things, they were riding in the back of the limo she'd seen in the parking lot. The woman sat next to her. A man was driving; she could see nothing of him but broad shoulders and the dull gold gleam of his hair. The one the vampire had called Dimitri?

Amelia herself was belted in with her arms held behind her. She rolled her shoulders and discovered something cold – metal. That's right, they'd handcuffed her. "What is this?" she croaked. "Where are you taking me?" Fear rose, cold and tight in her chest. *They're kidnapping me!*

"Calm down," the woman said. "I have no intention of hurting you."

"Yeah?" Her voice cracked. Amelia grimaced, cleared her throat, and tried for a little more authority. "Just exactly what *do* you have in mind?"

Determination hardened her captor's coolly beautiful face. "We're going to put things back to rights."

"We owe David Tate a debt," the blond man said. Yes, that was definitely Dimitri. Amelia recognized the voice. "And we intend to pay it."

"What kind of debt?" There, that was better. Much better to be pissed off than terrified. "Who the hell are you, anyway?"

The woman's dark eyes fixed on her face. In the darkness of the car, there was a strange ruby glint in their depths, something not quite human. She nodded at the driver. "This is my husband, Dimitri. My name is Varina Karov. Your lover saved my life."

Amelia licked dry lips. "I thought it was you," she whispered. "You were with him that last night. You kept him from... hurting me."

Those unhuman eyes narrowed. "He was not himself."

"Yeah, I gathered that when he tried to rip out my throat."

"He's better now."

"I seriously doubt that."

Lush lips tightened with anger. Belatedly it occurred to Amelia that pissing off her captor wasn't a good idea. "He's through it now. He's recovered."

"As much as he can with you being so blindly stubborn," her husband rumbled from the front seat. "You've hurt him badly."

"*I* hurt *him*? He tried to *kill* me, mister!" Amelia glared at him, then turned to the woman beside her. "Where are you taking me?"

"To see him." It was Dimitri who spoke.

"So he can kill me?" She wanted to scream.

Varina's creepy ruby eyes flicked toward her. "Don't be a fool. If I saved you six months ago, would I let him kill you now?"

"I don't know. Would you?"

"We do not kill, no matter what your peasant superstitions say."

"That's not what you said six months ago."

"He'd just made the transformation. It's a dangerous time for us. But he has adjusted to his new nature. He's come back to himself, and he wants to see you."

"Well, I don't want to see him." Amelia turned her head away, surprised at the bitter jealousy she felt. David had spent the past six months – or longer – with this beautiful vampire. And *now* he wanted a reunion? She didn't think so. "I told him I wanted nothing to do with him when he called."

Not that her desires mattered, since she was evidently on her way to see him anyway. The thought of what he might do to her made Amelia feel faint and sick.

"He's not a monster, Ms. Patton," Varina said. "And neither am I."

"Yeah, well, the whole kidnapping thing is not exactly a gesture of good faith."

"*We do not kill.* We don't even need that much blood. A pint or so, perhaps. Most of us take it from lovers, but he hasn't touched another woman since you left. He drinks from blood bags."

"Yeah? *You* obviously touched him plenty." There it was again, that bitter stab of jealousy. This woman was so petite and delicate, she made tall, blonde Amelia feel like a cow.

"I was dying. I had no choice." Varina's lush mouth tightened in frustration. They were headed out of Atlanta, the lights of the city falling behind them. "And as I said, I'm married."

"Happily married," Dimitri growled. "I would have lost her if it hadn't been for David."

Despite the dictates of common sense, some aching part of Amelia had to know. "What happened?"

"Dimitri was out of town on business," the vampire said. "I was hunting drug dealers..."

"*Drug dealers?*"

Varina shrugged and smiled slightly. "I get bored. I get hungry. And when Dimitri is out of town..." She stopped and sighed. "But it was stupid. I see that now. If I'd died, my husband would have died too."

"What? Why?"

"We are linked in a blood bond," Dimitri explained. "It's a kind of psychic union we formed by sharing blood. She feeds from me, and though I am not a vampire, I drink a small amount from her. Her blood makes me immortal, while mine sustains her. But if one of us died..."

"The death would kill the other," Varina finished grimly.

"So David..."

"Saved both of us," Dimitri said.

Amelia licked her lips and turned her attention to the vampire. "So what happened?"

She hesitated a moment, gathering her thoughts. "That night I had my eye on a group of young dealers. They'd been the bane of their neighborhood, terrorizing elderly people and young families. I wanted to get them under control. If I drank from them, I could establish psychic dominance over the lot and stop them."

"You didn't drink from me, and yet you seem able to tell me what to do," Amelia interrupted bitterly.

Varina shot her an irritated glance. "I'm in your presence. To control a group after I leave them, I must drink." She shrugged. "But no sooner had I approached them than a rival group staged a drive-by shooting. I took a shotgun blast in the chest, and the dealers scattered."

Amelia frowned. "But I thought it took a stake in the heart to kill a vampire."

"Superstition," Dimitri told her, meeting her gaze in the rearview mirror. "If you damage the heart badly enough, a vampire cannot heal."

"I lay in that alley, bleeding out my life, when David found me. He bent over me." Varina looked away, staring out the window at the darkness beyond. "I could smell the life in him. And I went... a little mad. I took him."

"You *attacked* him?" Amelia's jealous imaginings of vampire seduction vanished in a poof of sympathy. David had tried to help someone, and had had his life ripped away for his efforts. In a moment, he'd lost both his job and the woman he loved.

Varina nodded bleakly. "I lost control. By the time I regained myself, it was too late. He was dying. There was only one way to save him, and that was by making him a vampire."

Amelia felt sick. If Varina was telling the truth, David hadn't cheated on her – he'd been victimized through no fault of his own.

God, she wanted to believe that. But how could she trust anything Varina said? She wasn't even human. How could Amelia even trust her own need to believe? What if Varina was using her powers to trick her?

Besides, no matter how he got that way, David was a vampire now. None of these people could be trusted. "Okay, fine. If David wants to call me and talk, I'll listen. But in the meantime, *stop the car and let me out!*" That last emerged as a scream of mingled rage and fear.

The vampire shot Amelia a hard look, her pretty face impatient. "No." She ground her teeth in frustration. "Eh, I'm wasting my time. I'll let David explain – or whatever he cares to do to you." Ruby eyes met hers. It was like falling into a crimson sea. "Sleep, you stubborn, jealous little fool."

And for the second time that night, everything went black.

Chapter Two

Amelia opened her eyes to meet the gaze of a sweetly smiling angel peeking out from pine needles. She blinked and jerked, instantly realizing two things. First, the crystal angel was hanging from the branch of a Christmas tree, and second, she was bound and naked under the tree in question.

Frowning, she looked down her body at her bare breasts. Pine needles brushed her nipples, and some smartass had tied a red bow around her neck, as if she were a puppy.

She was pretty sure she knew who the smartass was.

"Bitch," Amelia growled, and squirmed, testing her bonds. Her wrists were bound together at the small of her back, and her ankles were circled by some kind of leather cuffs attached to either end of what felt like a bar. The arrangement arched her breasts upward and spread her thighs.

She lifted her head. Several small, neatly wrapped packages surrounded her in an artistic pile. Her eye fell on a little card attached to the bow around her throat. The tiny envelope read *To David*.

"Perfect, just perfect," Amelia muttered, as her heart began to pound. "I'm Christmas dinner!"

Her traitorous nipples hardened as a wash of longing took her by surprise.

"Cut that out," she growled at them. "He's a freakin' monster." Pain slid into her heart like an icepick. Her handsome, seductive David was now a vampire. The man she'd have trusted with her life six months ago might well kill her before the sun came up.

Unless Varina had told the truth, and David was the man he'd always been.

But hanging around to find out could get her killed. She'd try contacting him again on her own terms; the thing to do now was get the hell out. The question was, how?

Obviously the first step was to free her hands, which meant rolling off her bound wrists. Gingerly, Amelia began to wiggle her way out from beneath the tree. At the same time, she shot a look around the room, trying to figure out where she was.

Damn, the Vampire Queen had money.

The room was huge, with a soaring cathedral ceiling dominated by an immense chandelier. A thick Persian carpet spread over the honey gleam of the hardwood, providing a soft cushion for her bare back. Nearby, a marble fireplace dominated one end of the room, decorated in swags of fresh pine. A set of French doors and floor-to-ceiling windows lined the other wall, inset with stained glass in swirling abstract patterns.

An elegant couch, loveseat, and two armchairs upholstered in rich, vibrant red stood before the blazing fire, and scarlet candles stood here and there, casting a warm golden light over the room. The air was full of a Christmasy blend of spices – cinnamon, nutmeg, and peppermint. Carols played in the background, a soft, blues arrangement featuring lots of sax and somebody with a really nice baritone.

None of which was enough to get Amelia to hang around.

She worked her way a little further out from under the tree, decided she was clear enough to work, and rolled onto her side for a go at whatever it was around her wrists.

Amelia was hoping for Velcro cuffs like the ones she used to wear during the bondage games she and David once played, but no such luck. These cuffs felt like tough leather, linked by a short, thick length of chain. Twisting her hands awkwardly, she searched for a way to unfasten them.

She was just starting to panic when the French doors opened at the other end of the room, admitting a draft of cool night air – and David.

He stopped short in surprise, blue eyes widening. Despite the dictates of common sense, Amelia found herself staring at him with starved longing. His dark hair was longer than she remembered, as if growing out of the stern cut he'd affected as a cop. He wasn't as deadly pale and drawn as the last time she'd seen him. If anything, he looked even more tough and fit, and those broad shoulders looked even wider.

Then again, it might have been all the black. David was dressed in a black turtleneck and black trousers, with a long leather duster swirling around his booted feet. The clothing looked so expensive and well-cut, Amelia wondered if Varina had bought them for him. The thought was accompanied by another stab of irrational jealousy that made her grind her teeth. Her inner green-eyed monster didn't seem to care that Varina was married.

It was easy to see why anybody would want to cheat with such a stud. David had one of those starkly masculine faces, broad across the cheekbones and wide at the jaw, with intriguing hollows here and there. His nose was a trifle long and hawkish for a true GQ male beauty, but his mouth made up for it, with a full lower lip and a hint of a dimple. He'd hated those dimples, though they, along with those dark-lashed blue eyes, made him irresistible to anything female.

Including vampires, apparently.

God knew Amelia had never been able to resist him. And still couldn't. Despite everything, pain and need lodged in her heart.

It had been so long.

As she gazed at him in besotted fascination, he smiled slowly. Amelia realized that while she'd been checking him out, he'd been returning the favor. And since she was stark naked, his view was a hell of a lot more comprehensive.

"Well, well," David purred finally. "Look what Santa dragged in." He started toward her in a seductive male swagger, his eyes fixed on her breasts with an intensity that made her nipples peak.

"Touch me and I'll scream," Amelia managed. Her voice was embarrassingly hoarse.

His smile was wicked and starkly erotic. "You always were a responsive little thing."

"I meant I'll scream for the police," she gritted.

David shrugged. "Go ahead. In the unlikely event that anybody hears you, I'll send them away."

The same way Varina had made her get in the car. "You really do have psychic powers?"

He sank gracefully to one knee beside her, his eyes very hot and blue. "Vampirism has its privileges – one of which is undisturbed quality time with naked blonde Christmas presents."

Before she could shrink back, he reached for the bow around her neck and plucked free the card. Amelia watched his long, strong hands as he opened it and read. Her heart was pounding as if she'd run a marathon. She couldn't seem to keep the plea between her teeth. "Don't hurt me."

Blue eyes flicked to her face. "Don't be insulting. Besides, the terrified captive act would be a lot more convincing if your pussy wasn't wet."

"It is not!"

He reached between her thighs. As Amelia gasped in outrage, a long, strong finger thrust into her sex, sliding easily into her slick depths. The jolt of pleasure that zipped through her almost tore a humiliating moan from her lips.

David's eyes blazed hot and blue. Slowly, he drew the finger back and pushed it deep again. "You do realize I haven't had a woman in six months."

Her gaze flicked below his belt. The bulge in those expensive slacks was a vivid testament to his hunger. She sneered anyway. "What about the Queen of the Damned?"

"The Queen of the –" His brows flew upward as he withdrew that deliciously probing finger. She suppressed her groan of disappointment ruthlessly. "You mean Varina?"

"Yeah, 'Varina'." She felt remarkably petty even as the words left her mouth. "This is her house, right? And unless I miss my guess, she paid for that Armani you're wearing. Have you got a threesome going with her and the blond, or what?"

Male satisfaction lit his gaze, and he rocked back on his heels. "Jealous, darling?"

"Of a bloodsucking monster?"

David flinched. Such stark pain flashed across his face, she caught her breath. Then he looked away and picked up one of the wrapped presents. "Is that why you hung up on me – you don't talk to bloodsucking monsters?"

Amelia hesitated, thrown off-balance by that moment of anguished vulnerability. He started ripping the paper off the gift, his big hands quick with anger. Cautiously she said, "I didn't think there was anything to say."

Blue eyes flashed up to meet hers. "Evidently not." Flipping the lid off the box he'd unwrapped, David glanced inside. His eyes widened. "Well, what have we here?" He withdrew a tube from the box and read the label aloud. "Ass Master Lube." He smirked, glancing down at the card. "And it's from Dimitri. I don't think he likes you, darling."

She stared at the tube like a bird at a snake. *Ohboy.*

"As I recall," he drawled, "you once said you'd had fantasies about my buttfucking you. I wonder why the hell I said no. God knows I was seriously tempted."

Amelia licked her lips. "You were afraid of hurting me."

David shrugged those broad shoulders. "I've got a big dick." Eyeing her bound and naked body, he gave her a deliberate leer. "Luckily for me, bloodsucking monsters don't worry about the damage they do to tight little virgin assholes."

Her mouth went dry even as her sex clenched in hungry anticipation. It seemed her body didn't share her mind's fear.

His dark smile broadened as he made a show of inhaling. "And judging by the smell of that pussy, I don't think you're worried about it either."

"Bastard."

David shrugged. "Of course. Comes with the whole bloodsucking monster package. And speaking of packages..." He picked up another gift and tore it open with a flourish. Lifting the lid, he grinned into it. "Ahhh. Perfect. Nipple clamps." He gave her a toothy smile. "Varina doesn't seem to like you much either."

"It's mutual." As Amelia watched, he slipped one of the clamps onto his own pinky, then winced and adjusted a tiny screw. "What are you doing?"

He glanced down at her. "Tightening it, of course. I want to make sure it gives those little nips a good bite."

She frowned. It had looked to her like he'd loosened the screw. Which was completely in character for David – but not for the soulless undead thing she'd thought he'd become.

Had Dimitri and Varina been telling the truth? Could David be the same man he'd always been?

No. She hadn't imagined the bloodlust in his eyes that first night. Whatever he was now, he wasn't the man she loved.

Amelia was still wrestling with that thought when he suddenly bent down and enclosed her nipple in the wet heat of his mouth. Remembering those deadly fangs, she tried to twist away. "No! Don't hurt me!"

David's head jerked up, and once again she saw that flash of pained vulnerability. "I have no intention of hurting you, sweet – yet." One big hand came up to cup her breast, cupping her gently. His fingers were very warm as he caressed her stiffened nipple. "I just want these pretty pink nips nice and hard."

Despite her fear, pleasure rose in a warm, tingling wave as he skillfully twisted and pinched the sensitive tips. Watching her face, he smiled, slow and male.

He lowered his head again. This time she felt too much anticipation to protest.

David flicked his tongue tip over a blushing point, once, then again. Then he gave her a slow, sampling swirl before settling down to suck until hot lust danced along her nerves like sparks from a campfire.

God, he was so good at that. He always had been.

Despite her fears, her body insisted this was her David, her lover, the man she'd ached for every day of the past six months.

The man she loved.

Still suckling her right breast, he reached for her left with his free hand. Cool metal brushed over the hot peak. Closed tight.

Amelia arched against him, gasping in a shivering blend of arousal and pleasure and just the slightest hint of fear.

He'd put the clamp on her.

Instinctively, she tried to pull it off, only to realize again that her wrists were still bound. She was helpless. Amelia moaned, the sound half protest, half pleasure.

This was nuts. He was a vampire. If he hadn't been bound to the bed that night all those months ago, she had no doubt he'd have killed her.

Yet here she lay, trussed up under the Christmas tree while he tormented her tits, her arms going to sleep even as her pussy grew steadily more creamy. She knew good and damned well he planned to bang her ass with that big cock of his. And when he was done with that, he'd bite her on the neck and drink her blood. He could easily kill her.

Except...

She didn't really believe it. Oh, Amelia had no doubt she was in for an anal grudge fuck that would make it impossible to sit for a week, yet she didn't believe David would really hurt her. He'd always loved playing dominant as much as she'd loved playing submissive, but there wasn't a cruel bone in his body.

At least, there hadn't been when he'd been human, Amelia reminded herself. He wasn't human anymore. She didn't really know what he was capable of now.

But it looked like she was going to find out.

Chapter Three

David was twisting the clamp now while he licked and suckled her breast. Reaching between her thighs, he slipped a strong finger into her core, tearing a gasp of pleasure from her mouth. "Mmmm," he purred. "You are wet, aren't you? Too bad, really."

"What?" She sounded pleasure-drugged even to her own ears. "What do you...?"

He flashed his fangs at her. "It's not your pussy I'm gonna fuck, Amelia." Sliding his index finger from her slick core, he pressed it to her anus and began working his way inside. Amelia caught her breath. The sensation of being slowly stretched was both painful and unbearably arousing. "Oh, yeah," he breathed. "I'm in the mood for a tight little asshole. And given those six months of celibacy, you're in for a very rough ride."

She swallowed and made herself sneer. "Yeah, right."

His mouth tightened into a hard line. "Believe me or don't. Your ass is mine one way or another." Withdrawing his finger, he picked up the tube of lubricant and squirted a generous dollop into his hand.

Amelia watched helplessly as he reached between her spread thighs. Two fingers went in this time with a strong, hard thrust that made her gasp. She blinked up at him, heart pounding in reluctant, ferocious arousal as he pumped in deep.

"I'm going to fuck you hard, Amelia," he told her in a deep, rough rasp. "I'm going to grind my cock in your ass and make you come until you scream."

She licked her lips, fear and desire warring in her. "And then what?"

He bared his fangs. "What do you think? I'm going to drink your sweet blood."

Amelia shivered. This time it was definitely fear. "Don't... take too much. Please. If you ever cared anything about me..."

There it was again, that slight, telling flinch. A muscle flexed in his jaw. "I may be a bloodsucking monster, but I'm not a killer. It doesn't take that much to satisfy me."

David stood, rising to his feet to tower over her. Reaching for the hem of the black turtleneck, he pulled it off over his head. His chest was deliciously broad, tight and lean with sculpted muscle. He threw the sweater aside and balanced on one foot to pull off his boot. It dropped with a bang that made her jump. She watched breathlessly as he pulled off the other boot, then reached for his belt. The buckle rattled. His zipper hissed as he pulled it down and started stripping off his pants. His cock leaped free, thick and hungry, flushed dark with lust, so hard it angled upward. It looked even longer than she remembered.

And he was going to drive it into her virginal ass. Amelia whimpered softly in mingled fear and anticipation. God help her, she did want him.

He wasn't the only one who'd been celibate for six months.

David looked down at her, feet braced apart, cock jutting. Slowly, tauntingly, he stroked the massive shaft. "Yeah, whimper. I'm going to take my time with that tight little butt, baby. Slow, deep, and hard." He sank to his knees beside her bound body. "So I suppose the least I can do is make sure you're good and hot."

Amelia cleared her throat. "That's sweet of you."

Fangs flashed. "I'm a prince." He uncuffed her ankles from the spreader bar, then tossed it aside and settled between her legs. She caught her breath in anticipation as he draped her knees over his brawny shoulders and lowered his head.

Fingers spread her vaginal lips, giving him access to her helplessly creaming flesh. His first lick made her close her eyes and clench her teeth against a desperate moan. "Damn, baby," David breathed against her flesh, "you *are* wet. If I didn't know better, I'd think you were looking forward to getting your ass reamed by a bloodsucking monster." She flinched at the bitterness in those last two words.

Then his tongue swirled over her clit and between her lips, and she found it impossible to think about anything else. Even as he lapped and suckled with wicked skill, his fingers went to work on her ass, sliding deep, pumping slowly, stretching and preparing her for his cock. The thought of what he meant to do to her only added to the excitement.

But as her need spiraled higher and hotter, his stroking tongue slowed. No. Oh, please, she was close, so close, and so hot... Driven into a hot frenzy, Amelia began pumping her hips against his face. David drew back slightly, denying her the stimulation. With a frustrated groan, she circled her hips, grinding down on the two fingers impaling her ass. The penetration, painful as it was, was also intensely erotic. Imagining what his cock would feel like opening and stretching her, she shuddered in helpless hunger. "Fuck me!" The pleading in her own voice perversely added to her arousal. "God, David, fuck me!"

"Careful what you ask for, baby. You know where this cock is going, and it ain't your pussy."

She shut her eyes, shuddering. "Yes. Sweet Jesus, yes."

"Beg me."

"Fuck my ass, David. Please!"

David laughed, a note of hot male triumph in his voice as he sat up between her thighs and reached for the lube. "I hope you're not expecting mercy, Amelia. You're not getting any."

Dazed with raw lust, she lifted her head and watched him squirt a shining line of lube down the length of his cock. He stroked himself, getting the big shaft good and slick.

David grabbed one of her ankles and lifted it, pressing upward until her cheeks parted and her asshole lay undefended and ready for the thick head of his cock.

The shaft nuzzled the tiny hole gently, then sank forward slowly as he started forcing his way inside. Pain rose, cutting through Amelia's desperate arousal with the sensation of brutal impalement. She groaned. David's eyes blazed with hungry triumph and dark pleasure, and he panted as he drove deeper. "God," he growled, "that's good."

Amelia gritted her teeth. "It hurts!"

He stopped only halfway in. Startled, she looked up at him. Frustration and need tightened his face as he looked down into her eyes, reading her face. Delicately, he reached a big hand down and circled her slick clit with his thumb. The swirl of delight made her catch her breath. He began to pull out, slowly. After the pain of entry, the lush sensation of his exit was darkly seductive. It was the exact opposite of vaginal sex, when the pleasure was in the entry.

By the time only the head of his cock was still inside her, she was panting with lust, intrigued by the painful pleasure.

"Do you want me to stop?"

Startled, she met David's gaze and caught her breath. His eyes glowed with that odd ruby light she'd seen in Varina's. He clenched his teeth, as though against his own savage need, and his fangs curved down in stark reminder that he was no longer human. But the warm concern beneath the hunger was pure David. "Tell me to stop and I'll stop." His voice was low and strained with hunger.

"I thought you said I wasn't getting any mercy."

His smile flashed, a little bitter. "Seems us bloodsucking monsters talk a better game than we play. I can't stand to hurt you."

That's when Amelia knew.

It was him.

Relief poured through her. Despite the fangs, despite whatever he did or didn't drink, he was still the man she'd loved. Her resistance shattered as she realized how she must have hurt him. Yet he obviously still loved her. Hot tears stung her eyes. "David," she whispered. "God, David, I'm sorry."

His face closed. He pulled out and sat back on his knees, obviously about to stand up and walk away.

He thought she was rejecting him.

"No!" Amelia gasped. "Don't stop. Please, take me. Take my ass. Take me however you want."

David hesitated, searching her face. "Baby, my cock is too thick."

"I don't care!" And she didn't. It wasn't just the desire to atone for the pain she'd caused – it was a hunger to surrender herself to him in this hot, alien way. "I need you to fuck me. It felt good when you pulled out. I want more."

Indecision flashed over David's face, lust and fear and love battling in his eyes. Then he met her gaze, and whatever he saw there decided him. He knelt again.

To her surprise, he flipped her over onto her belly and did something to the cuffs. They sprang apart, and she gasped in relief as the tension vanished. Pins and needles raced across her skin as blood and sensation poured back.

"Now," David said, rolling her over onto her back once more. "Let's try this again." He lifted her legs until her heels rested against his shoulders, then presented the thick head of his cock to her ass once more. But this time, he started thrumming her clit with his thumb, sending a sweet surge of pleasure through her even as he pressed for entry.

Slowly, carefully, he sank inside. The sensation of being stretched and taken was still edged in pain, but it was offset by the delight he sent vibrating along her nerves with every stroke of his thumb. Panting, aroused, she watched him come down over her, his face dark and intent. He looked so damn big looming over her like this, all chiseled muscle between the spread vee of her thighs. His cock stretched her ass brutally wide in a slow, fiery possession as he took her one slow inch at a time. She writhed, maddened by the searing pleasure.

Until, finally, his balls rested heavy and full against her ass.

Carefully, David leaned down until he could brace his fists on the floor. The pose bent her double and seated his massive shaft that last fraction up her ass. Amelia panted, loving the sensation of being surrounded by his hard, hairy male body. Somehow it made her feel delicate and female and deliciously helpless.

"Jesus," she moaned, "I never realized how damn big you are."

"While you're so damn tiny." David threw back his head, his eyelashes fanning dark against his cheeks. The cords of his strong neck flexed with effort. "God, your ass feels good milking my dick like that. It's all I can do not to blow right now." Licking his lips, he started pulling out.

Amelia gasped. God, it felt even hotter this time than it had the first, a slick, sliding pleasure, wicked and darkly erotic. She whimpered, the sound stark with pleasure and lust.

When he pulled out to the tip, he stopped. "Push out this time," he growled. "Take it."

Biting her lip, she obeyed.

He sank in easier this time, though there was still a savage ache and fullness to his possession. "Ohhh, yeah," he growled. "That's right. Here I come, baby. I've wanted to fuck this perfect little ass for a long, long time. Every time you bent over, I'd get hard." He stopped to gasp. "But I was afraid of hurting you."

"You're not..." She sucked in a breath and shuttered her eyes. "You're not hurting me. More!"

"Oh, yeah." David braced his big hands on her helplessly bent thighs and started thrusting, picking up speed until he was grinding. She couldn't move, could barely breathe as he rode her, that big rod pistoning deep in her rectum, stretching and tormenting on the way in, pleasuring on the way out. And with every thrust, his pelvis ground against her sex, dragging her closer and closer to a hot, glittering orgasm.

She'd never felt so thoroughly fucked in her life. Or so hot.

Until suddenly he slammed in all the way to the balls and arched his back, roaring out his pleasure through bared fangs. The roll of his strong hips ground against her clit just right, and she exploded with a mindless shriek.

The pleasure tore through her like a glittering hurricane, on and on and on.

Endless moments later, he collapsed over her, then rolled off her with a groan, sliding free of her violated ass. Amelia whimpered with a combination of relief and regret. The whimper became a moan of pleasure as he drew her into his arms.

She lay there, unable to move, her body quivering and jumping in the aftermath of her savage orgasm. His chest worked like a bellows against her cheek, and his heart pounded. Wrapping her arms around his sweaty chest, she met his gaze. "You didn't bite me. You didn't feed."

David frowned, searching her gaze. "I didn't think you wanted me to."

Suddenly shy, Amelia had to look away. "Dimitri told me about the… the blood bond."

He went still. "And?"

"I hurt you, and I'm sorry for that. I was afraid, but I should have trusted you."

He sighed and shook his head. "Anybody would have been afraid, Amelia. For all you knew, I really had become a bloodsucking monster."

"But you didn't." She gazed into his handsome, beloved face with desperate hunger. If he said no… But she had to take the chance. "David, we should have been married by now. Let's do it. Right now. The blood bond first and then maybe a church." She broke off and bit her lip. "Unless you can't…"

David smiled reluctantly. "Churches and crosses don't bother me. I'm not undead." His smile broadened into a grin. "And I kept your wedding dress."

Her eyes widened as she remembered the beautiful gown she'd abandoned the night he turned. "You're kidding!"

He sobered. "It was all I had left of you."

For a long moment they gazed at one another, remembering the last lonely months. Finally Amelia said softly, "I never want to be separated from you like that again. I want us married in every sense of the word."

He searched her face. "You mean it? You really want the blood bond?"

"Yes."

"But Amelia – if anything happens to me, it would kill you. Literally."

"These past months without you, I might as well have been dead. It's been like somebody tore a hole in my chest. I just wouldn't let myself admit it."

"Yeah." His mouth tightened. "It's been the same for me."

"I need you, David. I love you. Love me."

"God, Amelia," he said, rolling her beneath him. "I already do. And I always will."

Quickly, he dragged a thumbnail along his wrist, opening a shallow cut. He lowered it to her mouth.

As she gently began to suck, his fangs sank into her throat with a quick sting. She moaned in relief, hearing his rumble of pleasure.

Then light and heat burst into her mind, and she felt his mind touch hers – strength and will and fire, backed by a purity of spirit she knew.

And most of all, she felt his love.

Her own rose in a tide of sweet joy. They came together and fused in a wash of warm light.

Home for Christmas.

Angela Knight

Angela Knight has worked as a comic book writer, a newspaper reporter, and a novelist. Her stories have won several awards, including ten weeks on the *USA Today* Best Seller list.

Angela is multi-published, as both an author and a cover artist, and enjoys success under several names, but that success would be hollow without the love and support of her friends and family. It's no surprise Angela Knight considers herself a profoundly lucky woman.

Now Playing: A Christmas Pageant
Sahara Kelly

Chapter One

The door clanged shut behind them with a solid thunk as they closed themselves off to the rest of the world in his hotel room. Snow hissed against the windows, muffling any sounds from outside. Not that there were many, since this early snowstorm pretty much paralyzed traffic and citizens alike.

It explained why he'd stopped for the night and ended up in her section of the "Boots and Pussy" strip club, but it didn't explain why she'd accepted his invitation to come here with him after her shift. *That*, she couldn't quite explain. Not even to herself.

Perhaps it had been his smile. Warm, filled with humor and charm, intensified by the deep creases at the corners of each eye. As if he'd squinted at the sun for several years, or laughed a lifetime… either could have been true.

His hazel eyes, maybe… gold in some lights, green in others, always alert, and watching. Observing life and those living it, yet without criticism or complaint – just observing.

Sure, his body was fine, if the broad shoulders beneath the leather jacket were anything to go by, and the short, *short* haircut screamed military or ex-military. His habit of calling her "Ma'am" when he ordered his beers gave him away too. Not many guys called a woman in a thong, panty hose and a micro tiny bra top "Ma'am." But *he* did, and it delighted her.

When the snowstorm blossomed into its full white intensity and he'd asked about a room for the night, Garvey happily called the motel next door. She suspected he had them on speed dial on the phone behind the bar, and probably got a nice little bonus, but what the hell. That was bartender business.

And she'd been glad of it, since she needed a room too. The hour and a half drive back to her apartment would be sheer hell on a night like this, and she wasn't absolutely sure her little car could manage it. It was one of the reasons she only worked weekends at the club, since her absence during the week might be noticed.

On the weekends, however... there was nobody to care. No husband, no family, no cat, no goldfish, not even a cactus.

She sighed, and then froze as his body brushed her spine and his lips touched her neck.

"Why are you here?" His hands kneaded her shoulders as he asked the question softly.

"I don't know." She stared blindly out of the window into the white void beyond. "I've never done anything like this before."

"I guessed that." His hands eased her jacket from her shoulders and bared her skimpy costume.

"How could you tell?" She glanced down at herself. "Let's face it. I'm dressed like a cheap hooker..." She laughed awkwardly.

"I never judge what's outside. Only what's inside. Life taught me that." The heat of his chest seared her spine and she realized he'd removed his shirt a scant moment before she saw his reflection in the window, standing tall behind her.

"And how do you know what's on the inside?" She turned toward him, letting the sequins on her costume drag across the hairs on his chest. Daringly, she raised her gaze to his, staring right into those lovely hazel eyes. "What do you see in *me*?"

His smile was slow and sensual. "Me."

His lips met hers in a fiery clash that could've melted the snow falling so thickly outside their room.

Joanna surrendered and kissed him back with every bit of passion she'd buried inside for too many years.

For Staff Sergeant Martin Todd, this particular moment with this particular woman was... unique. She was a stranger, yet fit into his arms like she'd been there forever. Her lips, her skin, her hair... all felt natural and comfortable to him, as if he'd come home at last.

After the year of physical therapy and the three years behind the desk in Washington, he was frustrated, angry and ready to quit. To leave the service and his past behind – but for what he didn't know. Until now.

Until a snowstorm stranded him in a seedy strip joint, and handed over the woman of his dreams.

She'd smiled at him over a tray full of beers and two of the best looking breasts in the place. They were her own too, he'd bet a month's salary on that fact. And he'd been completely entranced, watching her curvy ass as she deftly served drinks to the few other patrons. She'd joked with the stripper working the pole, taken a couple of phone calls when the bartender had been busy, and surreptitiously stretched her feet when she thought no one was looking. Her black hair tumbled every which way, but she'd ignored it, much as she'd ignored the couple of come-ons she'd gotten from customers. Just another nuisance.

The military hadn't trained Marty to be whimsical, but he was struck with the notion that she had a sort of glow around her, making her unique... different from the other girls.

And he'd known she'd noticed him.

Every now and again she'd flash a sideways glance in his direction – nothing too direct, but like she was checking him out, perhaps. Sizing him up, making a decision – whatever it was, Marty knew he wanted it to be in his favor. And he poured every ounce of charm he had into his smile.

It had worked.

Isolated by the snowstorm, they were alone together in his room, skin to skin, mouth to mouth and now – tongue to tongue.

She tasted of chocolate and strawberries, something sweet and wholesome, at odds with the miniscule cocktail waitress costume barely hiding her curves. Her heat filled his hands and her body pressed wantonly against his as their tongues dueled. In and out, and in once more, a parody of the act to follow, but a precursor of the pleasures they would share.

Marty's cock hardened rapidly, straining at the front of his jeans in its hunger to reach the treasures beneath the tight shorts only inches away.

"Joey..."

Her nametag said "Joey." She didn't really look like a Joey, but he didn't want to pry. Not yet. The time would come when she would reveal her secrets, both physical and spiritual. He would know all there was to know about this woman before the night was over.

But right now, kissing was the order of the day.

He stepped backwards, resting up against the door and pulled her with him. She leaned into his body, keeping her mouth glued to his.

He swiveled, reversing their positions. Now she was imprisoned between him and the door. Marty slowly raised their interlaced hands, trapping her arms above her head.

Her breasts thrust against him and he sighed against her tongue as his hips forced a place between her thighs and he ground his cock against her pussy.

She moaned back, fidgeting until she got his length where she wanted it. Marty swore the heat of her cunt burned through his jeans and branded his cock. She was on fire, and he desperately wanted to play fireman and whip out his hose.

Of course, that would involve letting go of her wrists, and probably stopping the kissing. Neither of which he was inclined to do. After all, they were in no hurry. He pushed even harder, loving the way her body molded to his, responsive and soft, opening to him, parting for him, welcoming him.

He tore his mouth from hers to say her name once more... for no other reason than he liked the sound of it. "Joey."

"Yes, Martin, oh God – *yes*." Her teeth grazed his neck as she spoke and her tongue followed, tasting him.

He moved his head giving her access to all the places she seemed desperate to nibble, leaning hard against her, loving the way her breasts swelled between them.

He thought for a moment, then pulled her wrists together, holding them secure with one hand. With the other he unfastened her bra.

"Aaaah. Better."

Her breasts still swelled, but now there was nothing to stop the taut nipples from grazing his skin, or the hardness of his chest from crushing them as he claimed her mouth once more. And his free hand could travel into the small space behind her, pushing her against him – right *there*.

He groaned with pleasure.

And so did she.

Joanna Woodbury was beside herself, inside out, upside down and frantic. Quite out of character for a woman whose reputation as levelheaded and calm was legendary. But this man and his feverish kisses shook her world out of its customary order and into something new, something exciting and thrilling that she wanted to explore.

With him.

He peeled his lips from hers and traced a line down her jaw to her neck. Joanna arched her spine, lifting her chin and inviting his touch. When his mouth reached her breasts, she sucked in a breath and held it for long moments... until the heated moisture of his tongue finally found her nipple.

She exhaled on a sigh of delight. "Ohhh... so gooood..."

His lips tugged on the bud of swollen flesh, pulling it to its limits, sending an exquisite bolt of sensation through her body to her clit. Joanna sobbed with pleasure, her thighs dampening as her juices flooded the small scrap of silk between her legs.

"Turn around." Martin's voice was rough. He stepped back a little from her body. "Please. Turn around."

Slowly, Joanna did as she was bid. "Why?" Her hands were pressed against the wall above her head, and now the cold surface teased her nipples.

"Because I want to touch your ass." Firm hands delved past the flimsy fabric of her thong and tugged away the hosiery that was attached. With a ripping sound Joanna's butt was laid bare.

"Sorry. I'll buy you another one."

She bit her lip. He didn't sound sorry at all. In fact, she distinctly heard a quiet "oh yeaaaahhh," when his palms cupped her buttocks and squeezed.

"You have no idea how crazy this ass has driven me..." Martin smoothed and kneaded – pulled, and Joanna gulped.

"All night... every time you walked past, I wondered how it would be to feel your skin... to hold these in my hands..." He pressed her cheeks together, then eased them apart, sending ripples of tension through her groin. "To touch you like this..."

Rough denim abraded her buttocks.

"Martin." Joanna swallowed past a large lump of desire that threatened to choke her.

"Yes?" He kept smoothing and caressing her buttocks.

"You have too many clothes on." She sucked in air. "Touch me with... with *you*."

His hands froze for a moment. Then she heard him take a ragged breath. "Yes, Ma'am."

There was a rustle and a grunt and then – then something hot and hard and velvety smooth crushed itself into her spine.

And Joanna's world burst into flames.

Chapter Two

"Colin..."

"Mmm?" Colin Fenton blinked sleepily into his pillow as his lover, the elegantly blonde Maude Henshaw rubbed her body over his back.

"Colin..."

He sighed. She wanted something. And it wasn't sex, since they'd just indulged in yet another round of eye-rolling, mouthwateringly hot, rip-up-the-sheets lovemaking. Colin grinned as he felt her breasts slide over onto his spine. For some reason, Maude liked to lie on his back after they made love.

He had no objections. She was a warm, sensual blanket, and several times they'd fallen asleep just like that – Maude stretched out full length on top of him.

He liked it, and only slithered out from beneath her if she started to drool.

"Honeeeey..." She licked his neck. "I was wondering..."

Here it comes.

"What, babe?" How bad could it be?

"Well, it's about the Christmas pageant." Maude dropped a little kiss on his shoulder and snuggled against him.

"What about it?" Colin mustered his thoughts. He knew Maude was directing the annual holiday play. In fact, he'd already been "volunteered" to assist. His price was reasonable, he thought – all the sex he wanted when he wanted it. Maude had grinned and given him an advance on his first paycheck.

"Well, I sort of agreed to help out the elementary school, as well."

"Huh?"

"The elementary school. Mr. Cobb, the principal, was at the theater the other day and he said how nice it would be if the school could have its play at the theater instead of in their gym, and I sort of said something like... uh... okay."

Colin closed his eyes. "You realize this is gonna cost you, don't you?"

He felt her smile against his skin. "I hope so."

He smiled too. "Look, I have an idea. Why don't we get my buddy to help out?"

"Hmm..." Maude paused. "You mean the army buddy? The one who's coming to visit?"

Colin nodded. "Yep. Marty. I was wondering what I could do with him to keep him busy while he's here, and this might work out just fine. He can handle the school thing while you and I do the pageant."

Maude slipped off Colin's back and tucked herself into his side. "If he's interested, it might work. You think he's up to it?"

Colin laughed. "Sweetheart, Marty's a Marine. He was wounded a while ago, and has been pushing papers behind a desk for several years now. If anyone can keep a bunch of school kids in line, it's Marty."

Maude was silent for a while as she thought over Colin's suggestion. "I suppose it wouldn't hurt to ask him, although he might not be interested in something as small as a school play."

Colin rolled over and tucked his arms around Maude, pushing a lock of her hair out of his mouth. "Marty'll do it if we ask. And I have a feeling it would be good for him. He needs something to keep him busy and out of trouble."

"He's in trouble?"

"Nah, not really. He's... I dunno... last time we spoke, he sounded sort of bored with life. Tired, maybe. Even talked about leaving the service."

"Perhaps that's why he's coming here for the holidays."

"Could be. We went to school here together, but he hasn't been back for years. If anywhere is home to him, this is it. No family left, mind you, just a few old buddies..."

"Like you..." Maude nudged him.

"Like me." He laughed. "Perhaps he's running away or running home. Who knows? But whatever the case may be, this school thing could work out well. Keep him busy, give me time to work on the pageant and..." His fingers stroked over Maude's thigh. "... also give me time to collect on a certain debt."

Maude's fingers did some of her own stroking. "Sounds like a plan to me."

* * *

Unaware that his old school friend was scheduling his vacation time, Marty Todd was blissfully sliding his cock along the crack of Joey's splendid ass. Round, white, firm where it should be firm and soft where it should be soft, it was an ass to cherish, relish and appreciate. Marty did all three.

"Oh God, woman... you have the most beautiful ass, you know that?" His hands gripped her hips and angled her slightly, positioning her body where he could see and feel exactly what he wanted to see and feel.

She sighed, pushing back against him, letting her actions speak for her. A snowplow lumbered past the motel, shining bright headlights through the window illuminating Joey for a brief moment.

Marty's cock jumped at the sight of her body stretched out in front of him, her hands splayed against the wall and her spine flexing as he moved. This was so... incredible. So fucking hot!

He clenched his teeth and reached over to grab the condom he'd thoughtfully pulled from his pants before he'd dropped them someplace. He knew he wouldn't last long once he got inside her, and he was going to be inside her real soon. *Real* soon.

Sheathing himself, he slipped a hand down beneath her belly and teased the tiny thatch of black curls, slippery now with her juices and ready to reveal that hard button of flesh thrusting from beneath its hood. He flicked it gently and grinned as she gasped and shuddered. "Fuck, *Martin*..."

Oh yeah. He was. He would. Any minute now...

Her pussy was boiling hot, slick lips parting as he nudged the head of his cock into her secret places. She moved her legs apart even more, encouraging him, welcoming him, urging him onward.

She was a lure he was helpless to resist. With a smothered moan of delight, he sank himself to the hilt in her body, feeling the silk and curves of her cunt caress his hardness as he thrust deeply, burying his length completely, and pressing his crotch into her buttocks.

She cried out while his fingers played with her clit, writhing now around his cock, and pressed herself hard against him, following him as he attempted to withdraw.

"Ssshhh... let me..." He held her still and plunged back inside again.

"Marty... oh *God*... Marty... *please*..."

Martin felt her tremble, and her body tensed within his grasp. She was on the edge.

Suddenly, it wasn't enough.

He dragged himself free, grabbed her around the waist and turned her, lifting her high against him. He wanted to watch her face, see her eyes as she came.

"Watch me, Joey. Open your eyes..."

He positioned her against him once more, face to face this time, and with a massive thrust, sank home, squashing her hard between his chest and the wall. Her breasts crushed between them, her breath gasping from her lungs, she stared at him, dark eyes unblinking as he pounded himself into her.

"Now, Joey... come with me. Come *now*..."

"Yessss..."

Soft as a whisper, her answer fell from her lips as her body began to spasm around his. Martin groaned aloud when her cunt clamped down on his cock, hard and fast. Her eyes never left his, although they were shadowed and vague while the orgasm took her.

Her mouth fell open and she panted in time with her shudders, sending Marty over the edge into a vortex of his own. He exploded. His cock erupted hot and fiery jets of semen, spurred on by rock hard balls that seemed completely unable to empty themselves sufficiently into this woman. He wanted to fill her forever. To never stop pumping himself into her cunt and to spend whatever was left of his life joined like this – to *her*. To Joey.

Eventually, their bodies relaxed and the savage rattling spasms gave way to a breathless easing of muscles.

Marty half-carried, half-dragged Joey to the bed, tossed the cover aside and tumbled them both into a heap. With regret, his cock fell away, and he quickly slipped to the small bathroom to dispose of the condom.

He returned to find her sprawled boneless across the sheets, dewed with sweat and grinning at him. "God, you're good."

"Same goes, babe. Same goes." He gathered her close and cuddled her into his chest, grinning himself as she shifted into a more comfortable position.

Now. Now he could find out about her, about her life… why she was working in a seedy dive, never responding to anyone apparently, except *him*.

He was full of questions, needed answers and shivered as a blast of winter wind hissed snow up against the windows.

Gently, he drew the covers over them. "So, Joey… tell me…"

The woman in his arms was sound asleep.

Chapter Three

"Whaddya mean she was *gone*? Gone how? Gone where?" Colin frowned at his friend over their beers.

"Just that, dude. I woke up – she was gone. The bed was empty. No sign of her." Marty stared angrily at his drink. "I can't figure out if I was played for a dope or what."

"She rip you off?"

Marty's head jerked up. "No way. She's not like *that*."

Colin raised an eyebrow. "Look, bud, she fucks your brains out, then disappears. She works in a strip club. What are we supposed to think? She's a saint or something?"

Marty sighed. "I know. Stupid, isn't it? It's just..." He toyed with the drips of condensation clouding the bottle on the table in front of him. "She was... special. Different. I don't know how else to explain it. I went to the club this morning, but it was shut. Nobody seemed to know anything. The guy at the motel hadn't seen her, and had no idea who she was. It's like she didn't even exist."

Colin shrugged. "Hey, man. I'm sorry. But I don't know any Joey, and neither does Maude."

"Speaking of the lady, where is she?"

Colin's face warmed. "Over at the theater. We'll stop by when we're done here. You sure you don't mind helping out with this whole Christmas play thing?"

Marty's lips curled. "I have a choice?"

"Uh, knowing Maude, no."

"To think I should live to see the day old Colin is pussy-whipped." Marty snickered.

Colin opened his mouth to protest, then shut it again. "You know something? If it's the right pussy, it ain't half bad."

The two men raised their bottles and clinked them together in a silent toast to pussy everywhere.

But it was a bittersweet toast on Marty's part. He'd found the pussy he wanted and damned if he hadn't gone and lost it right afterwards. How the hell Joey crept from their room, wearing God-only-knew what, to vanish into thin air, he had no idea. He must be seriously out of practice in his surveillance techniques, since in the field he'd have awoken at the slightest sound.

It was still bothering him as he followed Colin across the street and into the theater where rehearsals were underway.

A chorus of young voices was raised in song. Sort of.

Something that could probably pass for a vague rendition of "Frosty the Snowman" echoed around the auditorium, enthusiastically and loudly, if rather off-key.

A woman was seated to one side of the stage, her back to the audience while she played the piano for the children.

As the song staggered to an end, she lifted her hands from the keys and stood. "Nicely done, kids. Sarah, don't sway in time to the music, because you're bumping into Carla and she's losing her place."

A head drooped in the back row.

"Charlie, try to stay in time with everybody else, okay, honey? You're about half a beat behind, and muddling the chorus a little. But otherwise, you all did very nicely for a first run-through."

Her voice was calm and soothing, and Marty chuckled as the three rows of youngsters fidgeted.

"Oh, and Scottie, don't do that, dear."

Marty's eyes roamed around looking for Scottie. A short lad in the front row squirmed. Aha. *That* must be Scottie.

"Now, shall we try it once more?"

The woman moved back to the piano, but before she could sit down again, Colin strode forward. "Hang on a second –"

Heads turned and Marty blinked to find himself the object of scrutiny by some fifteen to twenty pairs of curious young eyes.

"I've brought reinforcements."

"Colin... great." Maude slipped out from her hiding place behind the curtains. "You finally dragged yourself away from your... er..." She threw a glance at the stage. "*Coffee.*"

The children grinned. Marty had no doubt they knew quite well which establishment was located conveniently across from the theater.

"Marty, come up here and meet the class." Maude held out her hand. "Children, this is Staff Sergeant Martin Todd, and he's going to help your teacher with your performance."

"Cooool." The murmurs came thick and fast.

"You a real soldier?"

"Where's your uniform?"

"You got a gun?" That *had* to be Scottie.

"Just a moment." Maude's hand went up with authority and silence fell. "Marty, before I introduce you to each of these performers, you should meet their teacher."

She turned to the woman at the piano. "Joanna, here's the help I promised you. I'd like you to meet Marty Todd. Marty, this is the children's music teacher, Mrs. Joanna Woodbury."

Marty glanced over, noting the neat bun of hair, the prim white blouse and the long gray skirt. He nodded. "Ma'am."

And froze.

And looked again.

She was staring at him, her face as white as her blouse. Her mouth had fallen open and her eyes were wide.

The children were hushed, aware that something unusual was taking place.

"Oh my God..." She whispered the words.

"*Joey?*"

He was at her side two seconds before she fainted.

"Oooh... look. He's *picked up* Mrs. Woodbury."

"Eeeuw. He's *kissing* her."

"No he's *not.* That's mouf-to-mouf insissipation."

The sound of muttered comments brought Joanna back to consciousness, and she blinked at Marty's face inches from hers. She was in his arms, being held like a baby.

It was rather nice.

"Hey, Mister Sergeant... you gotta open her shirt and thump her chest."

She felt Marty's start of surprise as he too was recalled to his surroundings by an impertinent suggestion.

"Children, please..." Maude's worried voice jerked Joanna to a sense of her surroundings and she began to squirm.

"Don't move." It was a rough order, but an order nonetheless. In spite of herself, she stilled. Marty's tones were gentle, but clearly he was used to command. His head turned away from her to the stage. "Your teacher simply fainted. And after hearing that song, I can't say I'm surprised."

Joanna watched him address her class. "You can all sing. And sing well. Now go practice together for a bit, while... while *Mrs. Woodbury* rests up for the next run-through. And there *will* be one." His gaze narrowed. "And Scottie. *Quit* it."

Joanna felt a wholly inappropriate giggle bubble up in her throat. It was the worst possible time, and the worst possible place, but if anyone could stop Scottie from – well, doing *that* –

"Now, *Mrs. Woodbury*, is there someplace private you can *rest*?"

Not mistaking his implications, Joanna sighed. "Put me down. I'm fine, honestly. There's an office behind the stage."

"Of course, come on..." Maude led them past the curtains. "Mr. Fenton will start you off, children. Go through Frosty once more, okay?"

Joanna saw Colin stare at the piano, the kids and Maude. And blink.

Then the heat of Marty's arms burned through her clothes – into her skin, and the reality of her situation smacked her upside the head with a nasty whack. He had refused to relinquish her to her own two feet.

He'd got his arms and hands on her, and clearly he was damned if he was going to let go.

She was in trouble now, no mistake about it.

Chapter Four

Marty stared at her. *Mrs.* Woodbury. The title stuck in his throat. She was fucking *married*. But still, even knowing that, it had been hard to let her slip from his arms and into the chair by the desk.

Maude had pointedly closed the office door tight behind them, leaving them alone together. Again.

"So." He cleared his throat. It was the best he could do. Nothing in his training had prepared him for a situation like *this*.

Joanna – he had to get used to thinking of her as Joanna now – funny thing how easy it was. She seemed a Joanna much better than she had a Joey. It fit her. Much like the smooth gray skirt and white blouse. Although that kid hadn't had such a bad idea. His fingers twitched with the urge to unbutton that long row of pearly things down the front and reach in to plunder the treasures he knew lay beneath.

He bit back an oath. "What the fuck is going on?"

She straightened. "You don't need to swear at me."

"Yes I *do*." He all but bellowed at her. "You give me the best sex I ever had then sneak out like... like some kind of thief in the night. Without even telling me your real *name*."

"Ssssh..." Joanna blushed. "Keep your voice down, for heaven's sake. Somebody will hear you." She glanced up at him under her eyelashes. "The best sex of your *life*? Really?"

He fought a battle with himself, and honesty won. "Yes. Really. And now..." Marty's hands ran through his hair in confusion. "Now I find out you're *married*?"

She sighed. "I'm a widow, Marty. My husband died two months after our marriage. He was in the Army." She bit her lip. "It was quite a while ago. Since then, I've taught school. I had no kids of my own, and loved music... the two go together."

Marty couldn't help a sigh of relief from hissing through his nostrils as he stared at her, trying to reconcile this – this *teacher* – with the scantily clad woman who'd turned to liquid fire beneath him.

"So." He was repeating himself and he bloody well knew it. *Fuck it.* "You're a widow. A teacher. And a frickin' cocktail waitress in a strip joint. Not to mention the hottest fuck I've ever had in my entire life. Just who the hell *are* you?"

For Joanna, it was a decisive moment. The man who'd possessed her soul was standing in front of her, demanding an answer to a question she wasn't sure she had even asked herself.

Without realizing it, she followed Marty's thoughts. Honesty was her only option. She stood slowly, moved to him and gently laid both hands on his chest.

"I'm just a woman trying to make a life for myself. I love teaching, but it has its drawbacks. I got the job as a waitress to bring in a little extra money, and yes… to walk on the wild side a little. To be an adult now and again. To see different things, different people."

She paused and stared into his eyes, willing him to understand. "And I'm a woman who met a man one night. A man that offered everything with just a smile, and followed through with the rest of him. I've never done anything like what I did with you last night, Marty, I *swear* it."

His hands crept up to cover hers and hold them in place. "I believe you." His hazel gaze burned down on her face. "I think I knew all along there was something different about you. Perhaps…" He stroked the hair away from her face where it had fallen loose from her bun. "Perhaps that's what I found so attractive."

Joanna swallowed. "Nobody knows about my weekend job. I had to keep it secret, for obvious reasons." She grimaced. "Can you imagine what they'd say if they knew their children's music teacher was moonlighting in a strip club?"

He grinned. "They'd probably fill the place in droves to see if you were stripping."

She chuckled. "Thank you for that at least."

His hands returned to hers and tightened. "I mean it. Joanna, the time we spent together… I can't explain it, but it was…"

He lowered his lips to hers and stopped a mere breath away.

She watched his face as it neared hers. "Yeah. It was."

With no embarrassment or hesitation, Mrs. Woodbury closed the space between them and kissed Staff Sergeant Martin Todd with a great deal of enthusiasm.

* * *

The little house on a quiet side street was dark but for the twinkling lights of the Christmas tree in the front window. They reflected merrily on the snow outside and gave no indication of what was happening beneath the tree branches, well out of sight of passersby.

"That was quite the most splendid pageant ever," Joanna gasped as her underwear was efficiently removed by a strong pair of teeth.

"Yeah. I thought so. Just needed a bit of organization and encouragement, that's all." The owner of the teeth transferred his attentions to the inside of her thigh, making her shiver with pleasure.

"I'm sure Maude was pleased." Joanna desperately tried to hold back the rising tide of desire threatening to swamp her.

"Fuck Maude. And fuck Colin too. Love 'em both, but right now…" Marty licked his way up to the vee of her thighs and the sensitive places that beckoned.

"Yeah, right now… fuck *me*, Marty."

He swiped her pussy lips with a smooth, hot tongue. "Why, Mrs. Woodbury. Such language. And I do believe you're wet for me." He tested his theory by thoroughly exploring every nook and cranny, making Joanna gasp out loud.

"Jesus, Marty." She squirmed away from his too-tantalizing tongue, doing some tasting of her own. She found his cock and grasped it firmly. "And you, Staff Sergeant, appear to be carrying quite a concealed weapon here."

"Cocked and loaded, babe. Just for you."

"Oh good. This'll get you an A."

"Wait till you see how well I've done my homework." Marty found her clit with his fingers and played with it, driving Joanna to the very brink of her orgasm.

"Mmmm..." She sighed and let her thighs part wide, offering him everything. It was always like this. No more secrets between them. Just exquisite pleasures shared, sensations explored and finally...

"Oh yeah, babe..." Marty grasped his cock and positioned it at the entrance to her cunt. "Want me now?" He teasingly rubbed her clit with the head, letting their juices mingle.

"Always."

And she meant it too. The past week with Marty had been as close to heaven as Joanna could imagine achieving without actually dying and getting there.

"I'm here." His voice was a promise and he slid home, burying his cock inside her. He stopped, watching her face as he filled her. "And I'll always be *here*, Jo."

She blinked back tears. He loved to call her Jo. Said it was *his* name for her, nobody else's. God, how she loved him.

"I don't ever want you to be anywhere else." She lifted her hips, mutely appealing for him to move.

So he did. Driving them both up and over the edge into places they were coming to accept as theirs alone.

Much later, cuddled under a blanket, Joanna ran idle fingers over his chest. "I meant it, Marty. I can't imagine ever wanting anyone else. Here's my Christmas gift to you." She raised herself on one elbow and looked down at his dear face. "I don't know how, or why, but you have my heart."

He stared back at her, his emotions in his eyes. "I love you, Jo. I have no clue how we'll work it out, but you're mine. For this Christmas, and every one to come."

She grinned. "Maybe you can teach school."

He grinned back. "Sure. Every elementary school should have a drill sergeant on staff."

"You did get Scottie to quit doing *that*..."

He snorted. "It's a guy thing. A word in the right place, and he straightened right out."

She raised an eyebrow. "I thought that was the problem in the first place."

He merely looked inscrutable. "Like I said. It was a guy thing."

"Riiiight." Her hand slipped under the blankets. "It looks like I might have found another guy thing that needs straightening out…"

Staff Sergeant Todd groaned with pleasure as Mrs. Woodbury proceeded to "straighten" him out. Just like she'd straightened out the rest of his life and set him on a course that headed for happiness. And great sex too.

Yeah. It was a guy thing.

Santa Claus would approve.

Sahara Kelly

Born and raised in England, not far from Jane Austen's home, Romance just naturally became part of Sahara's reading habits, even after her arrival in the States. After having her first Regency published by Zebra, life intruded upon her writing career, insisting that she become a wife and mother. Once her family became pretty much self-sufficient, Sahara returned to her writing – and discovered Women's Erotic Fiction. She never looked back.

With a variety of stories covering just about every genre, from Historical to Comedy to Time Travel, Sahara's found her niche. She enjoys being able to plunge into her fantasy worlds with vigor. Sahara firmly believes that *everyone* should have fantasies.

Sahara loves to hear from readers. You can contact her through her website at www.SaharaKelly.com.

Jingle Balls
Judy Mays

Chapter One

"Fuck, Richard, I'm puking my guts out here."

"And this is my problem, why?"

Large beads of sweat rolled down Ed's face. "Damn it, I need your help."

Richard shook his head, grimacing when his brother stuck his head back in the toilet and puked some more. Ed *was* suffering, poor guy. Still, there had to be someone else who could fill in for him tonight.

A soft clucking sound came from down the hall.

Richard rolled his eyes and moved back out of the way as their mother bustled into the bathroom. She always thought she could cure anything.

"Here, dear, drink this. You'll feel better."

Moaning, Ed wiped his mouth with a warm washcloth and stared at his mother. "Anything I drink comes right back up, Mom. If you don't mind, I'd like to stop throwing up."

She smoothed his dark hair back off his sweating forehead. "It's ginger ale, dear. If anything will help calm your stomach, this will."

Richard snorted. Last time he'd been sick, she'd showed up at his apartment and poured cod liver oil down his throat while he was still asleep. He'd puked his guts up for two hours. But Ed got ginger ale. He crossed his arms across his chest. She always did like Ed better. He was her baby, after all.

The sound of bells jangling drifted up the staircase as the front door opened followed by their father's booming voice. "I'm home, darlin'. Where's my little sex kitten?"

Her hands flying to her mouth as she blushed scarlet, their mother hustled to the bathroom door. "John! The boys are home! We're all up here in the bathroom."

Richard cocked an eyebrow at his brother. "Sex kitten?" he mouthed silently.

Ed groaned and leaned over the toilet again.

"What the hell are you all doing in the bathroom, Abby?" John bellowed as his broad form filled the doorway.

Standing on her tiptoes, she kissed his cheek. "Eddie's sick, poor dear. He'll be spending the night so I can keep an eye on him."

Richard grimaced as his father peered over his mother's head and frowned at Ed. Then he switched his glare to Richard. "You boys can't take care of yourselves when you're sick? Why, when I was your age..."

"We know, we know," Ed moaned from the floor, "you puked out your guts in the morning, went to work, and finished puking your guts out after you got home that night."

"Now, that's enough," Abby said after another quick kiss, this one on her husband's lips. "Ed's staying here tonight in his old room, and Richard will fill in as Santa Claus for him at the Prior's store."

"Bullshit!" Richard growled as he snapped to attention. "I'm not dressing in a stupid red suit so a bunch of snotty, spoiled kids can whine to me about all the crap they want for Christmas."

"Richard Allen Cassidy!" Abby snapped as she whirled and stomped over to him.

Richard stepped back. Shit. She'd used his full name. That meant she was really mad. His mother barely came up to the middle of his chest, but she was still the scariest woman he knew.

When her finger jabbed into the middle of his chest, he stepped back again only to have his ass bump against the sink.

"Richard Allen Cassidy," she repeated. "You *will* fill in for your brother tonight. What's more, you will be pleasant to each and every child who sits on your lap. And if I hear of anything to the contrary, you will rue the day you were born."

He raked his fingers through his hair. "Damn it, Mom."

Another jab in the chest. "And who said you could use language like that to your mother?"

Behind her back, his father grinned at him. "Best do what she says, son. You know she'll get her way. She always does."

Gritting his teeth, Richard reviewed every obscenity he knew – silently. Santa Claus. He was gonna have to be fuckin' Santa Claus. "Fine. I'll do it tonight, but that's it – and I'm not working any overtime. Where's the freaking costume?"

His father's grin widened. "Downstairs in the closet. Come on, I'll make you a sandwich. Gotta keep up your strength to face all those kids."

Cursing under his breath, Richard followed his father downstairs.

Groaning, Ed put the toilet lid down and leaned his head against it. "I hope you're happy, Mother."

Smiling slightly, Abby patted her younger son on the shoulder. "You did very well, Ed. You could win an Oscar for the performance you put on."

Ed choked. "Acting? Who's acting? What the hell did you put in my food?"

"That's my secret." Another pat on the shoulder. "Don't curse, dear. It's not polite. You had to really be sick you know. Richard would have known if you were faking."

Moaning, Ed pushed himself to his feet, bracing his hand on the sink when he swayed and almost lost his balance. "It would have been easier to get shit-faced drunk until I puked. Richard better appreciate what I've done for him."

Abby chuckled. "He will, dear, in ten or twenty years. I wouldn't tell him before that."

Ed gulped the ginger ale. "Are you sure this blind date crap is going to work?"

A smile lit up Abby's face. "Of course it will. Your Uncle Nick promised it would. I've met Jessica. She's a wonderful girl, perfect for Richard."

Ed gulped more ginger ale. "I don't know, Mom. You know how Richard is about blind dates. Fixing him up with Uncle

Nick's sister-in-law might not be such a good idea. Hell, we haven't even seen Uncle Nick since we were kids."

Abby patted her son on the shoulder. "Everything will be fine, dear. My brother may be a bit eccentric what with living in the wilds of Canada and not wanting to visit civilization very often, but he married a wonderful woman. And her sister is just as nice. Jessica's the outdoorsy type – just like Richard. They'll get along wonderfully."

After another gulp of ginger ale, Ed shook his head. "Just promise me you'll never try to play match-maker for me."

Chuckling, Abby turned, sauntered out of the bathroom, and hurried down the steps where she caught Richard at the front door. "Smile, dear, tonight won't be so bad. You might even enjoy yourself." Standing on tiptoes, she kissed his cheek then opened the front door, hustling him out.

Red suit tucked under his arm, Richard cursed all the way down the street until he got to his truck. There, he tossed the offending garments onto the passenger seat, stomped around the front, wrenched open the door, and slid into the driver's seat. How in the world did he let himself get talked into this one? If he hadn't seen Ed puking himself, he'd suspect his mother set up some scheme to hook him up with some girl. But Ed *was* sick. The entire bathroom stank.

Snapping his seatbelt into place, he stared out the windshield. Playing Santa Claus. Him. Richard Cassidy. Probably the only guy in the entire US of A to have not one but two serious relationships broken up by Santa Claus. Well, some fucking assholes dressed like Santa Claus. Bad enough that Carla had broken up with him with the "jolly old elf" standing right next to her, but Alison – what a bitch. Richard had walked into their apartment to find her boinking St. Nick three years to the day that Carla had dumped him.

Now, Richard hated Christmas. Even more, he hated Santa Claus. Except for the great meal his mom always cooked, the holiday sucked.

Sighing, he pulled out into the sparse traffic on his parents' street. His life could be worse. His mother could have decided to start playing match-maker again for him. Even worse, she could have found out that for the last five months he was the lead male stripper at Studs and Suds, the hottest club for women in the area.

* * *

"Nicholas!"

Sighing, the nattily dressed man with the neatly trimmed white beard tiptoeing toward the door set his boots on the floor and straightened. "Do you want something, my love?"

Hands fisted on her hips, his wife glared at him from the kitchen door. "Do I want something? Where do you think you're going?"

He smiled weakly. "Why, I'm just meeting the boys at the Moosehead for a pint or two."

Penelope stamped her foot. "The Moosehead? A pint or two? Who do you think you're fooling? You know very well that Jessica is coming to dinner."

Closing his eyes, Nicholas groaned silently. He knew damn well she was coming to dinner. How could he possibly forget his dear sister-in-law, Jessica? The woman who insisted on wearing an old bearskin coat and riding around in a dogsled like it was a Porsche. Blast and damn! And he'd been roped into the crazy plan she and his sister Abby had cooked up to get Jessica and Abby's son Richard together. Shit! He had so hoped he'd be able to sneak out before Penelope knew he was gone. Opening his eyes, he smiled at his wife. "I'm sorry, dear. It slipped my mind."

Penelope's expression was unconvinced. "Humph! I'll just bet it did. Now go on down to the cellar and get a nice bottle of wine."

"Red or white," he asked with another sigh. He was *not* getting one of the really good bottles.

She snorted. "Red, of course. We're having a nice beef roast."

Stamping into his boots, Nicholas headed for the door to the cellar.

A loud knock reverberated through the house.

Penelope wiped her hands on her apron. "She's early again. I must see to my roast. Get the door, dear." Turning, she bustled back into the kitchen.

Nicholas glanced at the fluffy white cat curled on the padded bench sitting in the hallway. "She's here, Sebastian. I suggest you go on upstairs if you want to keep your dignity intact."

The cat's ears flipped forward. His nose wrinkled. After a quick hiss, he fluffed out every hair on his body, jumped from the bench, and galloped up the stairway.

Nicholas shuffled to the door. "Lucky cat." Grasping the knob, he pulled the door open and stepped back.

A series of woofs, yelps, and barks, accompanied by jingling bells, erupted into the house to be followed by eight large, furry bodies.

Nicholas stood stoically as seven of the eight cold noses were shoved into his crotch one at a time. Then, all eight voices whuffed as each nose sniffed the spot where Sebastian had been lying. Anticipatory whines trickled out of eight throats as eight pairs of eyes stared longingly up the stairway. However, all eight dogs remembered how dangerous Penelope could be with a broom. All eight decided that discretion was the better part of valor.

A huge bundle of dark fur followed the dogs into the house.

Nicholas sneezed. "Why do you have to ride in a dogsled? Why can't you be normal and use a four-wheel drive or a snowmobile like everyone else? And must you wear that old bearskin!"

The fur fell to the floor to reveal a head of unruly honey-blond hair and a lush body.

Once her outerwear was shed, Jessica turned to her brother-in-law. "Nice to see you, too, Nick. Dogsled, huh? Isn't that a rather stupid question to come from a man who rides around in a sleigh pulled by eight tiny reindeer?"

Chapter Two

"What is all this racket out here?" Penelope called over the barking dogs. "Vicky! Into the study this instant or you all go back outside."

All eight dogs stopped barking. Seven tails whipped between hind legs and seven heads sank. The lone female, the white Malamute with one blue eye and one brown eye, woofed once then led the way down the hall and into the study. A fine, hot fire would be burning there, and Penelope would make sure they all had a taste of the dinner scraps.

"Well. That takes care of that," Penelope said as she turned toward the man and woman standing in the hallway. "Nicholas, didn't you get that wine yet? Well, hurry along. Dinner is almost ready. Jessica, how wonderful to see you again. Come with me to the kitchen. I have pies to get out of the oven."

Chuckling softly, Jessica hugged her sister and winked at her brother-in-law as he sighed heavily and disappeared in the general direction of the cellar. What a shock it would be if the world found out Santa Claus was henpecked. Of course, it might be more of a shock to find out he really existed.

"It's about time you came for a visit. I haven't seen you in a month of Sundays," Penelope continued as Jessica followed her into the kitchen.

Just inside the door, Jessica stopped and inhaled. Mixed with the delicious odor of roasting beef were the scents of cinnamon, ginger, and apples. "Penny, your kitchen smells just like Mom's used to."

Cheeks rosy with color, her sister turned to face her. "Jess, I think that's one of the nicest things you've ever said to me."

Smiling, Jessica shrugged. "It's the truth. So, you guys all ready for Christmas? It's only a couple of weeks away, you know."

Penelope set the pie on a pie rack and bent over to pull another from the oven. "Since when hasn't Nicholas been ready for Christmas? Honestly, Jessica. Why must you devil him so much?"

Jessica broke off a piece of pie crust and nibbled it. "Because he's so perfect, Penny. I mean, you married Santa Claus, for goodness sakes, just about the greatest guy in the world. And you've never had one negative word to say about him. Jeez, do you have any idea how intimidating that is? No wonder I can't find a decent man."

Penelope looked back over her shoulder. "Humph. You can't find a man because you're too particular. Not only that, you insist on wearing that God-awful coat to hide your figure."

The timer on the other oven dinged. Jessica grabbed a pair of potholders, opened the door, and pulled out the roast pan. "It's cold out, Penny. You want me to freeze?"

Penelope set the final pie down and lifted the lid off the roast pan. The mouth-watering odors of well-done beef and savory spices filled the air. "Freeze indeed. If you had a motor vehicle like normal people instead of traveling by dogsled, you wouldn't need that smelly coat."

"*Normal* people! Your husband rides in a sleigh pulled by 'eight tiny reindeer' and you say *I'm* not normal?" Jessica began fishing potatoes, carrots, onions, and parsnips out of the roast pan. "Besides, I like my dogsled. It gets me where I want to go. And what would I do with my dogs? No reason to let them lie around all day and get fat."

Grabbing the serving dish from Jessica's hands, Penelope set it on the table. "I don't know how you talked Nick into using his powder on them. Get the roast out of the pan. I want to make the gravy."

Jessica chuckled. "He was so head-over-heels in love with you, he'd have used that magic powder on whoever or whatever stood in front of him."

"Put the roast on the table and slice the bread." Jessica was pushed away from the front of the stove by her sister. "Now you're stuck with a pack of immortal dogs."

"Considering I'm immortal too, it's not such a bad thing. At least my pets don't die on me," Jessica said with a chuckle. "You wouldn't want me to be lonely, now would you?"

"Ha!" Penelope exclaimed as she stirred the gravy. "Find yourself a good man, feed him that powder Nicholas gave you, and you won't be lonely."

Brandishing the bread knife, Jessica grinned. "Find a good man, huh. You can't say I haven't tried. But, shit, Penny. An eternity with one man. Gotta be real careful about this. Not everyone is as lucky as you are. I mean, how many men are like Santa Claus?"

Penelope shook her long-handled spoon at her sister. "Most women don't take three hundred years to find a man."

"And some women couldn't find one in three hundred years no matter how hard they tried."

"Well, there's always Hiram," Nicholas stated as he walked into the kitchen carrying a dusty bottle. "He'd marry you in a minute, Jessica."

Snorting, Jessica set the sliced bread on the table. "Oh great, another party heard from. Nick, I am not going to marry Hiram."

Shaking his head, Nicholas wiped the dust off the bottle, fished the corkscrew out of a drawer, and opened the bottle. "Best let this breathe a few minutes." Turning back to Jessica, he grinned devilishly. "There's something to be said for a man of Hiram's stature. Pussy high, so to speak."

"Nicholas!" Penelope exclaimed as Jessica doubled up with laughter. "Mind your manners."

After Jessica's laughter settled to hiccups, she grabbed a glass of water and gulped it down. "Sorry, Nick, I'd like a man who can reach my lips while he's standing – the ones on my face."

"Jessica! You're just as bad as Nicholas! Now sit down and eat your dinner. The both of you. And mind your manners. No more such talk at my table."

"Ah, hell, Penny," Nicholas growled as he wrapped his arms around her and planted a big kiss on her mouth. "The kids are both away at college. Who's going to hear us? It's not like Jess is a blushing virgin."

Jessica grabbed the wine bottle and poured three glasses. Lifting hers, she toasted her sister and brother-in-law. "Yeah, Penny. Besides, you're the one who always brags about being the lucky woman who gets to screw Santa Claus."

* * *

Pushing his chair back, Nicholas loosened his belt and sighed. Penny was a wonderful cook. One of the reasons he married her. Smiling across the table he winked. "Shall I fetch another bottle of wine then, my dear?"

Setting her glass on the coffee table, Jessica stood. "I recognize that look," she said with a wide grin. "It's my cue to leave so you guys can make hot passionate love here on the kitchen table."

"Indeed?" Penelope answered, one eyebrow rising. "The kitchen table you say? Not with all these dirty dishes about."

Nicolas grinned. "We could just push them out of the way."

"No, dear, we will not," Penelope answered with a wink and a grin for her husband. "Jess and I have to get going."

Jessica stared at her sister. "Get going? Where?"

Rising, Penelope smoothed the long, black wool skirt she was wearing. "We're going clubbing. We haven't had a girls' night out on the town together in ages."

Jessica fisted her hands on her hips. "And whose brilliant idea was this?" She glared at her brother-in-law.

He held up his hands, palms forward. "Don't be looking at me with fire in your eyes. It's not my idea."

Jessica slid her glance back to her sister. What was Penny up to now?

Her sister was smiling innocently. "Oh, come on, Jess. Like you said, Christmas is only a few weeks away, and I'll be too busy to spend any time with you. Is it so terrible that I want to spend time with my only sister? Now, come on. Barry's going to drive us, so we don't have to worry about having a couple of glasses of wine."

Closing her eyes, Jessica sighed. Penny was right. They didn't spend much time together. It would be fun to go out with her. Opening her eyes, she nodded. "Okay, let me get my coat."

Penelope crossed her arms over her chest. "You will not wear that coat tonight. One of mine will fit."

For a moment, Jessica considered rebelling. If she couldn't wear her coat, she wasn't going anywhere. But then, when she took another look at her sister's face, Penny had her "don't mess with me" look on. No way would she give in.

Jessica felt her lips twitch. Penny did have a point. The coat did smell pretty gamey.

"Okay, I'll wear one of yours. Hope you don't plan on going anywhere too fancy." Jessica looked down at her sweater and jeans. "I'm not dressed as nicely as you."

Smiling, Penelope locked arms with her sister. "No. Nowhere special. Just a place called Studs and Suds."

Chapter Three

"And I want a new Xbox and lots of new video games – the ones with lots of blood in them – and a trampoline and one of those motorized scooters and a new red mountain bike and a pony and..."

"Don't you think that's enough?"

The little boy on his lap narrowed his eyes and glared at him. "What kind of stupid Santa Claus are you? You're supposed to say you'll get me everything I want."

"Danny! That's no way to talk to Santa," said the fidgety, gray-haired woman waiting for him.

"I don't care, Grandma. He's not the real Santa anyway. Everybody knows there really isn't any Santa. Daddy and you buy all my presents."

Brat. Richard closed his eyes and shifted his butt. The chair had a cushion, but it had been three hours since his break, and his ass was numb.

The boy slid off his lap. "I wanna go back to the mall," he whined. "This Santa Claus sucks."

"Are you finished yet, Danny? Did you tell Santa everything you wanted?" asked the smartly dressed woman who joined them.

That voice! Sucking in a breath, Richard opened his eyes and pushed himself back against his chair. Alison. What the hell was she doing here? He glanced at the boy. No way was he hers. She'd been practically engaged to him only three years ago.

Danny stuck out his tongue at her. "What do you care? You ain't my real mother."

After a stiff smile for Alison, Danny's grandmother grabbed his hand. "Come along, dear. Let's get some ice cream."

"I want a chocolate sundae and a Mountain Dew to drink."

Richard watched them walk away. *Just what that kid needs, more sugar and more caffeine.*

Alison sighed. "It's so hard being a step-parent." She glanced around. No one else was anywhere near them. Smiling, she stepped as close as she could. "Mind if I tell you what I want for Christmas, Santa?" Her smile was blatantly inviting. Her coat was open and her sweater was low cut.

Richard gawked. Alison was coming on to him – well, to Santa. And she had no idea who he really was, or did she? Did she regret losing him? He glanced at the huge diamond on her finger and shook his head mentally. Nope, probably not. Time to enlighten her.

When he leaned forward, she licked her lips. Her hand strayed to her breast.

"You sure have a lot of balls, coming on to *me*, Alison."

She stared, then her eyes widened. "Richard? Richard Cassidy? *You're* playing Santa?" For a moment, she seemed nonplussed. However, she quickly gathered her composure and smiled at him. She hooked her finger in the neckline of her sweater and pulled it down to display more cleavage. "If you would have put on that suit sooner, maybe I wouldn't have left you. What more could a good little girl want than to fuck Santa Claus?"

Richard grimaced. Thank God that he hadn't worn this suit sooner and she had dumped him. Then the picture of Alison sliding up and down on a cock surrounded by a red suit flashed into his mind. "Did you even know that guy's real name?"

She shrugged. "It didn't matter. At this time of the year, only Santa matters. Now, since I've been a good girl, can I sit on your lap?" She looked around. "It's almost closing time, and you always were the adventurous sort. How about a little nookie right here?" She brushed her knuckles against the nipples pushing against her tight sweater.

Richard placed his hand in the middle of her chest and pushed her back. "With you? No way is my cock getting anywhere near you. Who knows what kind of diseases I'd catch."

Dumbfounded, Alison stared. Then she lifted her hand.

Richard caught her wrist before she slapped his cheek. "Now, now, Alison. You don't want to be a bad girl or Santa won't bring you any presents for Christmas."

Wrenching her arm free, she hissed. "You were a schmuck when I lived with you and you still are. And you sucked in bed. There were times I could have done my nails while you were grunting away on top of me." Spinning on her expensive, spiked heels, she flounced away.

Muttering under his breath, Richard sank back into his chair and glanced at the clock on the opposite wall. Fifteen minutes. Fifteen more minutes and he was done. Good thing, too. His show at the club would start in just over two hours. Then he was going to go to O'Reilly's and have a couple of good stiff drinks. Then, if he got lucky, he might even find some female companionship for the evening – one who could care less about Santa Claus.

"Santa?"

Jerking his attention back to the present, Richard looked down at the small girl standing in front of him. "Yes?"

The little girl squeezed her hands together and looked over her shoulder. When she looked back, she smiled hesitantly and whispered, "I don't have to sit on your lap to tell you what I want, do I?"

Forcing a smile onto his face, Richard shook his head. "No. You can tell me from there if you want."

Her smile became less tentative. "My name is Lisa White and I live at 42 North Maple Street."

Richard leaned forward. "Forty-two North Maple Street. Got it."

She glanced over her shoulder again then looked back at Richard. "I only want one thing, Santa, please? Just a kitten. That's all. I already have a doll who I love lots and lots, but I'd like a kitten. Mommy says that kittens are nice, and they only eat a little so I can have one if Santa brings it. But she said that kittens are hard to find at this time of the year because they're mostly born in the spring. But you can find me a kitten, can't you, Santa?"

Richard stared at the little girl. For the first time that evening, a child hadn't asked for more than he or she could possibly ever play with. A kitten. Just a kitten. God, he hoped her mother found one.

"Well..."

"Lisa," scolded the small woman who scurried up to them. "I told you not to bother Santa. It's not safe for him to carry baby kittens in his sleigh."

The little girl looked at him, her eyes wide and pleading. "You know how to take care of kittens, don't you, Santa?"

"Ah..."

Her harried mother grabbed her hand. "I'm sorry. I told Lisa kittens were hard to find at this time of the year. We even went to the SPCA, and the workers there told her the same thing."

"Ah..."

Leaning forward, Lisa patted his hand. "I have faith in you, Santa. I know you can find me a kitten. I don't even care what color it is or if it's a boy or a girl."

"Ah..."

A gentle tug had the child stepping away. "Come on, Lisa. We have to get home. Daddy is waiting for us."

Smiling, Lisa waved to Richard. "Bye, Santa. Thank you for listening to me."

As they disappeared between two aisles of board games, Richard slouched in his chair. A little girl wouldn't get her kitten, and she'd blame him! Fuck. He hated Christmas.

Chapter Four

"Are you fucking crazy?"

Tanya straightened to her full five foot eleven inch height. "I – beg – your – pardon." Every word was low and clearly enunciated.

Richard shifted his weight to the other foot but didn't lower his eyes. Tanya might be the bitchiest bitch he'd ever met, but she didn't intimidate him. "I am *not* dressing like Santa Claus. Santa doesn't strip for a bunch of drooling women."

She smiled slightly – not too much – her carefully applied makeup might crack. Lifting her hand, she stroked his arm. "But, darling, you already have the costume. All you need to add is this." She dangled a red and green pouch from her fingers of her other hand. Bells jangled when she shook it. "The customers will love it."

Shaking his head, Richard stepped back. How the hell had she known he'd brought that Santa suit into the club with him? Why hadn't he left it in his car? "No. No way. This is my last night. I'm Zorro, and that's that."

Her chuckle was downright malicious. "Read your contract again, sweet cheeks, although you went through it carefully enough before you signed it. You have to personify whichever character I choose, so tonight you're Santa." She tossed the G-string to him. Bells jangling merrily, it bounced off his chest and fell to the floor. "Now quit whining and get ready. Oh, your background music will be 'Jingle Bells.' I'm sure you'll be able to adapt."

"Damn it, Tanya."

Her expression became downright frosty. "Don't you 'damn it' me, Richard. Tonight might be your last night working here, but you signed the contract of your own free will, so stop the fucking bitching and go get ready. You're on right before Jeff."

Because she was right about the contract, Richard swallowed the obscenities he wanted to hurl after Tanya as she turned and wiggled her ass down the hallway to her office. So, she *was* still pissed about the day he'd turned down her sexual advances. And now he was on *before* Jeff, huh? He'd lost the headliner spot. Fine with him. Sooner he performed his set, the sooner he could get out of here.

Fuck, but he was glad he was finished after tonight. Some men might fantasize about dozens of women panting over them, groping them, sticking hands and fingers in places he'd rather not think about, but he could live without it. This last paycheck – not to mention the money the women threw at him and tucked into his G-string – would finish paying off the loan he'd taken out to cover his father's medical bills. So what if he'd lied to his entire family and told them the money came from his savings account. They didn't need to know he stripped for it. And the constant groping, poking, and prodding was worth the look of relief that had appeared on his mother's face when she knew they wouldn't have to sell their home of thirty years.

Sighing, he bent and picked up the colorful G-string. The bells jingled.

"Cute bells."

Richard glanced over his shoulder into Jeff's smirking face.

The other man held out something white. "Tanya wants you to wear this wig and beard, too."

When Richard didn't answer, Jeff shifted his weight to his other foot. "Look, I'm just delivering a message."

Richard grabbed the wig and beard from Jeff's hand. "A word of advice. Just because you're fucking Tanya, don't think you mean anything to her. The only thing she's interested in is money."

"Speaking from experience," the other man sneered.

For the first time that night, a true smile appeared on Richard's face. "Nope. I'm not. Sex with Tanya? No, thanks. I'd rather get in bed with a hungry polar bear. My chances of survival would be better."

Spinning on his heel, Richard strode into his dressing room and pulled the door closed behind him. Damn, but that felt good.

Then he saw the red suit drooping off the side of a chair. He looked down at the beard, wig, and G-string he was carrying. He tossed them onto the chair.

The bells jingled happily again.

Fuck. Santa Claus. Twice in one day. How much worse could it get?

* * *

"Now isn't this fun?" Penelope crowed. Mocha skin glistening beneath the lights, the man on the stage fell to his knees before them. She leaned over and stuck another dollar bill down the front of the G-string. "My oh my. Have you ever seen such muscular thighs?"

He grinned at her and shimmied closer.

Oil glistened on his taut body.

The tantalizing scents of expensive cologne, coconut oil, and male sweat tickled Jessica's nose. She dropped her gaze to the pirate's thighs – at least she thought he was supposed to be a pirate. He had a gold hoop earring in one ear and a black patch over his left eye. He'd come out on stage carrying a curved sword and wearing a black vest and white pants. Neither had stayed on his body very long. Now all he wore was a black G-string that barely covered his family jewels. As a matter of fact, if he gyrated the wrong way one more time, his left ball would probably pop out.

Jessica sighed and shook her head. All around her, women were screaming and waving dollar bills in the air, their concentration centered on the man shimmying on the stage in front of them. Okay, so he did have a good body. She snorted. Okay, great body.

Leaping to his feet, he gyrated his hips above them, spun around, and pranced across the stage.

Jessica watched him go. And he had a damn fine ass.

Chapter Five

Tanya stood backstage and watched as Andre finished his pirate set, craning her neck as he strutted to the other side of the stage. Damn, but he had nice ass. Why hadn't she noticed before? Just the right size to grab onto as he pumped into her. Or… smack a riding crop across. She glanced up at his face when he turned and gyrated back across the stage. Was he into kinky stuff?

She stepped back as his music reached a crescendo. After one last twirl in the center of the stage, Andre planted his fists on his hips and stomped to a halt, his legs spread, his boot clad feet planted firmly.

As he bowed, Tanya blinked, leaned over, then looked more closely between his legs as he bowed a second time.

His left ball was hanging out of his G-string.

She licked her lips.

After his third bow, he spun away from the audience and headed toward her.

Tanya patted his slick, muscular ass cheek as he passed her. "Nice job."

His white grin flashed. "Thanks, boss."

She watched his ass muscles flex as he walked away. Oh, yes, that was an ass she'd love to spank.

She was yanked out of her fantasies by the merry rollicking music of Jingle Bells.

> *Dashing through the snow*
> *In a one horse open sleigh.*
> *O'er the fields we go,*
> *Laughing all the way…*
> *Jingle bells, jingle bells,*
> *Jingle all the way…*

Lips pinched together, Tanya lit a cigarette and watched as Santa Claus strutted out onto the stage, the bells sewn onto the red suit he wore jingling and jangling in time to the music.

Sucking in as much smoke as she could, she savored the flavor for a moment and then exhaled. Fucking tall, sexy, handsome, I'm-too-good-for-you Richard Cassidy was her one failure. He was the only stripper in her club she hadn't been able to lure into her bed, not even the night she'd cornered him in his dressing room while she was wearing nothing but a black leather corset, a silk G-string, and her thigh high boots with four-inch heels.

He'd taken one look at her, jerked on his jeans and shoes, and stomped out of the club bare-chested. In thirty degree weather!

Santa pranced across the stage, his coat hanging off one broad shoulder.

Shuddering, Tanya blew a smoke ring. He was the only one of her performers who absolutely refused to shave his chest and oil his body before a performance. She shuddered again. Damn, but her nipples hurt. She was too used to the guys who worked in her club being longer on brawn than brains. Richard Cassidy was something else entirely. When he'd first applied for the job explaining he needed money fast, and he'd work six months, but that was it, Tanya had been sure he was just like all the others. The bright lights, the eager women – not to mention the money – would be too much to give up. What a miscalculation!

She inhaled more cigarette smoke. Bastard. But she'd get even. Now that Richard had earned the money he needed, he thought he was too good for her, too good for her club. Six months ago, she'd let his dark eyes, rugged good looks, and hard body distract her. While he'd gone over the contract with a fine-toothed comb, questioning every vague clause, demanding clarification in writing, she'd been fantasizing how he would look chained spread-eagled against the wall wearing nothing but a tight, black jock strap. She'd practically creamed her panties right then and there.

Miscalculating a man's motivation was not a mistake Tanya had ever made before, and one she'd never make again.

Eyes narrowed, she watched Richard turn and saunter to the center of the stage. His coat slid off his shoulders, down his back, and puddled on the floor. He flexed his biceps then his abs. The dark hair on his chest contrasted sharply with the white beard he wore.

Dropping her cigarette, Tanya stepped on it, twisting her foot left then right. Then she turned and headed back to her office. Richard had a release form to sign before he left. And he was in such a hurry to get out of here that he probably wouldn't look at it very closely. She'd have him spread-eagled against her wall, totally at her mercy, if it was the last thing she did.

* * *

"My, oh my, oh my, Jess. Just look at him!"

Sighing, Jess pulled her attention away from the risqué prints hanging on the walls to the man posing on the stage. She glanced at him then back toward the print that initially had her attention then jerked her gaze back to the man on the stage.

Santa Claus?

He had to be kidding.

At her side, Penny sighed. "Nick doesn't have a chest like that. I can't wait to see his… er… other parts."

Jessica rested her arms on the edge of the stage – Penny had managed to wiggle her way to the front of the crowd with her sister in tow. Jessica still hadn't figured out how, but the crowd of women had parted before them like a hot knife going through butter – and watched as Santa Claus dropped his pants.

"Oh, my, my, my!" Penny muttered, her hands clasped over her chest. "He's wearing bells on his cock. Do you think I could get one of those for Nicholas?"

Jessica ignored her sister and devoted her full attention to Santa. Damn, he was hot, hotter than any man she'd seen in – well – about a century.

With one last shimmy, he kicked his pants off the stage into the shadows behind the curtain. As the chorus of "Jingle Bells" played for what had to be the twentieth time, he began to dip and gyrate. Jessica's mouth dropped open as he jumped, spun in a circle, and landed solidly on slightly outspread feet. One thrust of his hips had the bells on his G-string jangling wildly.

Penelope nudged her. "Close your mouth, Jess. You're starting to drool."

Snapping her mouth closed, Jessica leaned closer. Damn, she couldn't remember the last time she'd seen a man this hot!

Broad shoulders, a wide chest with a sprinkling of dark curls that tapered into a slim line down over his well-defined abdomen and flat stomach to disappear into the red and green G-string. His thighs were lean yet well muscled – and long.

Her gaze continued its journey down his long legs. Tight black boots with bells jangling from the cuffs hugged his calf muscles.

"Have you ever seen such long legs?" Penny yelled into her ear. With the way the other women were screaming, Jessica wouldn't have heard her otherwise.

Jessica concentrated on the red and green pouch between Santa's thighs. Was it really that big or had he stuffed it?

She looked up into his face. Dark eyes concentrated on the wall behind her.

That piqued Jessica's curiosity. All the other dancers had made eye contact with the audience, winking and teasing. Santa, here, even though his performance was hot and sexy, slid close to the salivating women in his audience only now and then, presenting one hip or the other. The green of dollar bills they stuffed there contrasted nicely with the red strings gripping his hips. No money fluttered from the red and green pouch between his thighs, however. He was very deft at sliding away from eager hands.

Jessica leaned back as he shimmied nearer and smiled. She was going to get a dollar into that pouch if it was the last thing she did.

Chapter Six

Jingle bells, jingle bells
Jingle all the way.
Oh what fun it is to ride
In a one horse open sleigh.

If I never hear this song again, it will be too soon. Richard deftly glided away from a woman who had tried to cup his jingling pouch. He whirled, took a step in the opposite direction, and faltered, covering his gaffe quickly with a dip and hip thrust. Holy fuck, that white-haired woman holding out a dollar and screaming how sexy he was, was Mrs. Fleeger, his mother's next-door neighbor. What the hell was she doing here?

Whirling again, Richard strutted away from the audience shaking his butt as he did so. Lifting his arms above his head, he shimmied and his bells jingled. As he lowered his hands, he double-checked to make sure his wig and beard were firmly in place. He also pulled his Santa hat further down over his forehead. Hell, if Mrs. Fleeger recognized him... What the hell was she doing here anyway? She had to be at least seventy-five.

Spinning around, he leaped toward the opposite side of the stage. Fuck, wasn't this damn song ever going to end?

Jessica swallowed once, then once more. When Santa had turned around and she'd gotten a look at his ass, the finest ass she'd ever seen, she'd decided then and there she had to meet him. No, not just meet him, sleep with him, bed him, do a little mattress dancing with him, whatever anybody wanted to call it. Lust. She was in lust, and at her age, she knew better than to fight it, even if it only meant one night in the sack together – which would probably be the case. No way would she meet Mr. Right in a male strip club. These guys were too wrapped up in themselves to be good happily-ever-after material. That didn't mean she couldn't have a rollicking good time in bed with one of them for a night or two.

After shaking his ass – once to the left and once to the right – he clenched his cheek muscles, one at a time, one after the other, time after time. Holy shit. She didn't know a guy could do that with his ass.

Sucking in her breath, Jessica swallowed. Her nipples were pinpoints of delicate pain and moisture seeped between her thighs. She grasped the edge of the stage so tightly, her knuckles whitened.

> *Bells on bobtails ring,*
> *Making spirits bright.*
> *Oh what fun to ride and sing*
> *A sleighing song tonight.*

Richard sighed with relief. There it was, the slight change in tempo. One more run through of the song, then a final flourish to just the melody, and he'd be finished here for good.

Leaping into the air, he spun around and pranced to the front of the stage, a smile on his face for the first time during his performance. He looked down at the crowd. *Goodbye, ladies. It was nice taking your money, but I'm not going to miss you.*

A classy, well-dressed blonde winked at him and jerked her head to her left.

His gaze traveled in the direction she'd indicated and locked on the woman at her side.

He stumbled, caught himself, and stepped closer. Who was *she*? Standing there with her arms crossed under her breasts – breasts with nipples straining against the soft wool of her pink sweater. Standing there with a come-hither look on her face.

Come-hither look? Christ, Cassidy. You're losing your mind.

Still, she was good-looking, not drop dead gorgeous, but good-looking. Her mouth was too wide, her chin too prominent, the look in her eyes too obstinate. But they were beautiful eyes, a deep, chocolate brown with long dark lashes.

He centered his gaze on the top of her head. Never had he seen hair color exactly like hers, thick yellow hair with rich golden and honey brown highlights.

Damn, he'd like to bury his hands in all that hair while he buried his cock between her thighs. A quick fantasy flashed into his mind. She was naked beneath him, her legs wrapped around his waist.

Falling to his knees in front of her, he pumped his hips.

Jessica smiled. *Got you now, gorgeous.*

As Santa spread his thighs and thrust his hips forward to jingle his bells, she reached out and grabbed his pouch.

"Nice – bells – Santa." Then she stuffed the money she was holding down the front of his G-string, making sure she patted him as she did so. She grinned up into his face. "Yep, you got some nice bells, there, Santa. The North Pole feels pretty good too."

The pouch bells jangled when it snapped back into place.

He leaned closer. His voice was low, intimate. "Sweetheart, you have no idea just how good the North Pole can feel. But if you'd like to find out, meet me in my dressing room."

Jumping to his feet, he whirled away and disappeared behind the curtain as the last strains of "Jingle Bells" drifted away.

Shrugging into a robe, Richard pulled the hat, beard, and wig off, shoved them into the robe's pocket, and stepped away from the curtain at the edge of the stage. After watching Zorro's routine for a few minutes, the sexy blonde was talking to her companion, pointing toward the doorway that led backstage. He pumped his fist in the air. Yes! She was coming. The evening was definitely looking up.

"A blonde with about a ton of honey-colored hair will be asking for me, Don. Send her back to my dressing room."

The stage manager grinned at him. "Sure thing, Rich. Saw her."

Chuckling, Richard clapped the other man on the shoulder. Things were definitely looking up. "Thanks, and it was nice working with you. If you ever get over to O'Reilly's, tell them to give you a beer on me."

* * *

When the lights went down again, and Zorro leaped into the spotlight in the middle of the stage, Jessica watched for a few minutes. His performance wasn't nearly as arousing as Santa's, in her opinion. Most of his routine consisted of thrusting his hips toward the women in the audience or turning around and bending over, inviting them to grab his cock and ass. She sniffed. No class what-so-ever. The Santa Claus was definitely far more interesting.

Legs spread, Zorro slid across the stage, came to a halt before her, and pumped his hips.

She curled her lip. Enough was enough. There was only one man here who interested her now.

Jessica grabbed her sister's wrist. "Come on. We're gonna go meet Santa Claus."

Smiling, Penelope allowed herself to be pulled along. Things were proceeding exactly as planned. She tapped her watch three times.

* * *

When his wrist started to vibrate, Nicholas pulled his concentration from the British soccer game he was watching, and looked at his watch. Sighing, he clicked the remote and the television turned black. Best pay attention to the signals from his watch, or Penelope would never let him forget it. Scratching his belly – it was expanding as it always did in December – he rose and headed for the study. Time to hitch up Jessica's dogs and send them home.

His watch vibrated again. Stopping in the hall, he read the instructions scrolling across the tiny screen. Adjusting one of the ten knobs circling the face of his watch, he checked the time then sent a message back to Penelope. There. It was done. He just hoped his wife hadn't gone too far with her meddling.

At the top of the stairs, Sebastian meowed.

Nicholas smiled. "Not to worry, my friend. The dogs are leaving – now."

Still smiling, he shuffled down the hall and opened the study door. "Come along, Vicky," he said as he patted the dog's head. "Penelope needs you to go home now."

Chapter Seven

"Richard. Richard!"

Muttering curses under his breath – Tanya was not the woman he wanted to talk to at this moment – Richard halted in mid stride and turned to face her. "Look, I already told you, I will not sign an extension to my contact."

Shaking her head and grumbling something about thickheaded men, Tanya held out a pen and single sheet of paper. "I know, I know. I've given up. Honest. This is your release form."

He cocked an eyebrow. "Release form?"

"It says your Zorro costume has been returned undamaged."

"Jeff's wearing it now. Looked okay to me."

Flicking the ashes from her cigarette, Tanya shoved the paper toward him. "Just sign it, Richard. Then you can get the hell out of here which is what you've wanted since the first time you walked in."

A warm, husky voice drifted over Tanya's cigarette smoke. "Excuse me? I'm looking for Santa Claus."

Richard smiled. His sexy blonde was here.

Grabbing the paper and pen from Tanya, Richard started to scribble his signature.

"Didn't your mother tell you to read the fine print before you sign something, Richard, dear?" her companion said.

His daydream of burying his hands in the sexy blonde's hair as he kissed the breath out of her dissolved. Looking up, he blinked – twice. "What? Who are you? How do you know my name?"

The classy blonde nodded toward Tanya. "She just called you Richard. Now, before you sign that, read the fine print."

Hissing, Tanya spun around. "Get out. No one is allowed backstage."

Gazing over Tanya's shoulder, Richard stared at the two women behind her, concentrating first on his sexy blonde. She was standing with her arms crossed under her breasts – and very nice breasts they were – her nipples staring at him. She was grinning at the other woman with her. Damn, but she was even prettier when she smiled.

Her companion spoke again. "Really, Tanya, dear, you need to control your temper. And stop being so underhanded and devious. Honestly, you haven't changed since you were a child."

Richard switched his attention to the classy blonde. The resemblance between them was obvious now. Sisters. They were sisters.

Tanya stomped her foot. "Get out or I'll call the bouncers. Here, Richard, sign this and you can get out of here."

The blonde shook her head. "I wouldn't do that if I were you, dear."

Richard frowned. What was that woman talking about? Glancing down at the sheet of paper, he perused it. It was a standard release form. Wait. What was that at the bottom of the page? Squinting, he read the fine print.

"You bitch."

"Now, Richard, you can't blame me for wanting to keep my best dancer, can you?" Tanya said as she dropped her cigarette and backed away holding her hands in front of her body.

"You bitch," he repeated as he stepped forward.

The classy blonde laid her hand on his arm. "Let her be, Richard. Believe me, she's already suffering. Unlike you, she's all alone. I'm Penelope, by the way. This is my sister Jessica."

Ripping another cigarette from the case she always carried, Tanya lit it and inhaled. Blue smoke surrounded them as she exhaled. "Who the hell do you think you are?" Stomping her foot, she yelled, "Damn it, Don. Where are the bouncers? I want these two skanks out of here now."

That got more than a grin from his blonde – Jessica, that was her name. Pretty name for a pretty woman.

Jessica was sliding her sleeve up over her arm. "Skanks! Why you bitch. I'll shove that stinking cigarette down your throat." Clenching her hands into fists, she stepped toward Tanya.

"Jessica, no!"

Penelope moved to intercept her sister, but Richard was faster. Wrapping his arms around her waist, he pulled her back against his chest. Oh yeah! What an armful!

"Let me go!"

The sharp elbow in his ribs caused Richard to readjust his hold. Wrapping one arm around Jessica's waist, he tried to grab his arm with his other hand to lock her against his chest. Instead, he grabbed a firm breast – a real breast. No silicone in this baby. This was the real thing overflowing in his hand. He squeezed it.

Her heel connected with his shin. "Let me go!"

At Richard's side, Penelope blew her bangs off her forehead and sighed. Some day, maybe in another hundred years or so, Jessica would finally learn to act like a lady. "Richard, why don't you take Jessica to your dressing room. I'll deal with Tanya."

As Richard hurried away with his squirming burden, Penelope reached into her skirt pocket, pulled out a small ball, and tossed it after him. As it arched above his head, she wiggled her fingers. The ball popped and a fine, white powder settled on both Richard and Jessica, became translucent, and disappeared.

Almost immediately after, Richard slipped into his dressing room.

The door slammed shut behind him.

A satisfied smile on her lips, Penelope turned back to Tanya. "Now, then, young lady. You and I are going to have a talk." Grabbing the other woman's arm, Penelope propelled her toward her office.

Once inside, Tanya stopped short. Penelope shoved her from behind, and she stumbled to a small settee, her eyes never leaving the two men standing next to her desk. Neither was more than four feet tall.

Penelope sauntered over to the desk, wheeled Tanya's chair out from behind it, and sat down. "Glad to see you got here on time, Hiram, Frank. Were you able to find what I asked for?"

The little man in the red coat smiled and nodded. "Yep. Found the perfect match in San Diego." Turning, he grabbed a pet carrier sitting on the floor behind him, lifted it to the desk, and opened the door.

A scraggly, wire-haired dog with a torn ear and half a tail scampered out. Leaping across the floor to Tanya, the animal sat down in front of her and barked.

She jerked her legs up onto the settee. "What the hell is that?"

Penelope chuckled. "It's a dog. I thought that much was obvious."

Snapping her gaping mouth shut, Tanya jerked her stare from the dog to Penelope. "Are you nuts? It's... it's..."

"Ugly, you think? Nonsense. He just needs a bit of cleaning up."

"I don't want him."

"Too bad. You're responsible for him now. If you don't take care of him, he'll be hauled back into a shelter and euthanized."

Swallowing, Tanya stared at the dog. "But why?"

"Because, my dear, you need something to love you, and he will, no matter what," Penelope said with a chuckle as she rose to her feet. "No matter how bad you feel or how lonely you think you are, he will always be there."

Tanya stopped staring at the dog and lifted her gaze to Penelope. "Who are you?"

"Just a messenger, dear. Just a messenger. Now, if you'll excuse me, there's a little girl who asked Santa for a kitten. She'll be getting it a little early, but that's okay." After a quick stroke to the wiggling dog, Penelope swept out of the door followed by Hiram, who carried the empty carrier, and Frank, whose carrier held a small multi-colored kitten.

Chapter Eight

Richard tightened his hold on Jessica, spun around, and strode down the hall to his dressing room to the sound of jingling bells – and sneezes – from both of them. A quick blink of his eyes, though, had his sight cleared.

The woman in his arms wasn't as lucky. She sneezed twice more, which made it easier for him to carry her. She couldn't struggle while she was sneezing.

Two more steps and he reached his door. He shouldered it open – luckily it wasn't latched – and ducked inside. Once there, he kicked the door shut, turned to the left, and dropped the squirming woman in his arms onto the small couch pushed against the wall – after another quick squeeze to her breast.

Bouncing on her ass once, she came up cursing. "You son of a bitch! What do you think you're doing? Let me out of here."

Richard leaned back against the door. Damn but she was sexy sucking in those big gulps of air which made her breasts bob up and down. He shook his head. "Nope. I don't think your sister wants you out there. Something tells me Tanya doesn't stand a chance against you, and she's the type to sue the pants off somebody who breaks one of her fingernails."

Glaring at him, she raked his body with her gaze. "You always display your wares so blatantly?"

Richard looked down at his gaping robe, which must have come loose when he held her squirming body against his.

Looking back up, he grinned. Was it getting hotter in here? "Only for you, sweetheart." He wiggled his hips and the bells on his G-string jangled. "Wanna add a few more dollars to the ones you shoved into my crotch?" Merry jingling filled the room as he gyrated his hips again.

Fists clenched at her sides, Jessica glared at him. "Shut up and let me out of here. My sister needs me."

The silly smile never leaving his face, he cocked an eyebrow at her. "Somehow I think Tanya will probably need more help than your sister." He wiggled his eyebrows. "How about a private show? Thought you wanted to see the North Pole."

A long exasperated sigh escaped Jessica's throat, and she wiped a few beads of perspiration from her forehead. Yes, she did want to see the North Pole – and touch and taste and ride it too. But not before she made sure Penny was okay. But first, she had to get six feet of a sexy, almost naked Santa out of her way.

A bead of sweat slid down the side of her face. When did it get so hot in here?

Jessica let her gaze drift down his naked chest – hmmm, nice pecs – to his flat stomach and the thin line of dark hair disappearing into the pouch of his G-string. That pouch was definitely starting to look fuller than it had been. And it had been pretty full to start with.

She licked her lips.

She felt her nipples pebble, and warmth began to seep between her legs. Damn, but this guy was making her horny.

The Santa hat dangling from his robe pocket caught her eye. Sauntering toward him, she allowed a sexy smile – at least she hoped it was sexy – to appear on her lips. "The North Pole, huh. I must admit, I am intrigued."

A smile curved his lips, and a quick downward glance confirmed that the North Pole was getting bigger.

Stopping just short of plastering her body against his, Jessica flattened her hands against his chest. Ummm. Just as hard and firm as it looked. She swallowed. Did he taste as good as he looked?

Jessica slid her hands across his chest. What was it she wanted to do? Oh yeah, Penny. Something about Penny.

He settled his hands on her hips and she shivered.

The hell with Penny. She could take care of herself.

"So," Jessica said, as she ran her hands up his chest then down his side to the straps of his G-string, "just how big is the North Pole?" She pulled the Santa hat out of his pocket.

"Judge for yourself," he said as he cupped her ass cheeks with his big hands and pulled her tight against his hips.

A small gasp escaped Jessica and she shivered. Hot damn, but this was one nice-sized North Pole. Lifting the hat, she placed it on his head, lifting her other hand to help settle it correctly on his head. "Well then, Santa, time to jingle those bells one more time."

No sooner had she settled the hat on his head, he spun around, pushed her against the door, and attacked her mouth with his.

Jessica counterattacked by stabbing her tongue into his mouth, then sucking his tongue into hers.

Their teeth clicked and clashed.

Groaning, he opened his mouth wider, his tongue dancing with hers. His cock pushed against her belly. Jessica moaned. Never had she wanted, no needed to have a man bury his cock into her so badly.

Somehow, she wiggled her hand between them, something she didn't think was possible considering how closely their bodies were plastered together, and grabbed his cock. Circling the head, she caressed it then slid her hand down its long, rock-hard length.

Moisture pooling between her thighs, she shuddered with the anticipation of his cock buried in her.

"Fuck," he moaned into her mouth. "You're gonna make me come too soon."

"Off. Get this damn thing off," she demanded against his mouth as she jerked the G-string to the side and his cock sprang free. "Oh, gods, yes." She fell to her knees, immediately sucking his cock into her mouth.

"Oh fuck," he groaned, spreading his legs and tilting his head back.

He thrust his hips forward, and she sucked him in. His cock slid into her throat.

As Jessica slid her tongue around him, she freed his balls and rolled them in her hands.

For a few seconds, his entire body stiffened. Then, grabbing her shoulders, he pulled his cock out of her mouth, slipped his hands under her arms, and lifted her back to her feet. "Clothes. Off. Now."

He didn't wait for her to strip. Shoving her sweater up over her breasts, he popped the clasp on the front of her bra, bent over, nipped a taut nipple, then sucked it into his mouth.

When his teeth closed on her already tender nipple, Jessica pounded her fist against the door, and the loud thud echoed around the room. Oh, gods, when had she ever wanted a man so much!

She tore at the buttons on her jeans, popping a few in the process. Shoving the jeans down over her hips, she grabbed his cock again.

When he buried his hand between her thighs, she arched into it, and his fingers slipped inside of her. She ground down against them.

"Fuck, you're wet."

Nuzzling the ball of the Santa hat out of her way, Jessica nipped his earlobe. "I want you, inside me, now!"

She spread her legs wider, cursing with frustration when the jeans tangled around her ankles wouldn't let her lift her leg to wrap around his hips. There were drawbacks to wearing boots.

Her tangled jeans weren't a hindrance to Richard. Cupping her ass, he lifted her against the door, and using his knee to spread her thighs as wide as he could, he dropped her onto his steel-hard cock.

Wrapping her arms around his neck, Jessica sobbed into his mouth as she stretched to accommodate his thick cock. She shuddered when he lifted her and impaled her again.

"Yes, oh yes. Harder. Harder."

He pounded into her.

Her ass thudded against the door.

"Fuck, you feel great. Twist your hips. That's it. Faster."

Jessica nipped his shoulder. "Deeper. Harder."

His fingers slid down the crack in her ass.

Pressure built.

Jessica sobbed. "Now. Oh, now!"

Richard swiveled his hips and thrust into her. His burning balls were tight against his body, and his cock was ready to explode.

She was squirming and bouncing against him, her tight, wet muscles grasping his cock far more tightly than any other woman's ever had.

He couldn't hold back. When she screamed, "Now," he surged upward one last time.

Darkness roiled around them and the lights went out.

Chapter Nine

Jessica woke up freezing. Well, her ass was freezing since her jeans and panties were down around her ankles. The front of her was nice and warm. Opening her eyes, she found herself staring into the face of the male stripper who'd been dressed as Santa, the man who had just rocked her world with the greatest sex she'd ever had. What was his name? Ricky? No Richard. That was it.

Her thighs were plastered against his.

His cock was still rock hard between her legs.

A cold wind slapped her ass.

Lifting her head, she looked around.

Snow. Lots of snow.

What the hell? Where were they? What the hell was going on?

Jessica shook her head. She remembered going backstage to meet this guy and running into his manager, a real bitch if there ever was one. Then all of a sudden, she was wrapped in this guy's arms, kicking and squirming – and sneezing.

Sneezing? Angry heat surged into her face. Damn her sister and her love potions! When she got her hands on Penny, she was going to shove one of those frickin "love balls" down her sister's throat – when Nick wasn't around.

She looked around again. What little light there was was rapidly disappearing. And judging by those dark, gray clouds on the horizon, more snow would be on the way. If they didn't want to freeze to death, they had to get out of here.

Sucking in a deep breath she shoved herself off Richard and pulled her pants up, fastening them as best she could since there were only two buttons left. Refastening her bra, she pulled her sweater down over her goosebump-covered body.

Crossing her arms over her chest, she rubbed her arms and prodded Richard with her toe thankful that she was wearing boots instead of shoes. At least her feet wouldn't get wet. "Hey, Santa, ah, Richard. Wake up. We gotta get going."

He didn't move.

Frowning, Jessica bent down, grabbed his shoulder, and shook him. The shoulder of his robe was damp. "Shit. The back of his robe is soaking wet – snow melted from his body heat, I'll bet. If we don't find some shelter real quick, he's gonna freeze to death."

Another shake and he groaned.

"Come on, Richard. Get up. You gotta move."

After a louder groan, his eyes fluttered open. Lifting his hand, he flattened his palm against his head. "What hit me?"

Reaching down, Jessica grabbed his wrist and jerked it. "Come on, sexy. If you don't get up now, you'll freeze to death."

Comprehension appeared in his eyes at the exact moment he shivered. Leaping to his feet, he quickly closed the front of his robe only to yelp an expletive when the icy cold back stretched across his skin. He shrugged it off, only to yelp and pull it on again when a blast of icy wind whirled around his body.

A wild look in his eyes, he spun in a circle, finally stopping to stare into her face. "What the hell is going on?"

Arms crossed over her chest, Jessica hugged herself. At least she had dry clothes. Richard only had that wet robe, a jingle-belled G-string, thin black boots with more bells, and his Santa hat. Not much to keep a big man warm.

"Damn it! Where the fuck are we?"

Jessica shivered. He definitely wasn't going to like the answer. "North Pole."

Richard gasped as another blast of freezing wind plastered his wet robe against his back. North Pole. What kind of joke was this? "Look, lady, I wanted to get into your pants as much as you wanted to get into mine, but this has gone far enough. Call off this joke. Now!"

Rubbing her arms, she shivered and stared at him. "I wish it were that easy. This is no joke, and this is not the place to explain anything. Come on. We gotta start walking before we freeze to death." Turning, she struggled through the knee deep snow toward...

Richard looked around. Toward what? He couldn't see anything but snow and gray sky. How the hell did she know which way to go?

Another blast of wind and another shiver. His teeth began to chatter. Fuck. He was going to freeze to death. At least walking was better than waiting to die. He surged after her, doing his best to ignore the clammy robe clinging to his back and the numbness that was already deadening his fingers and toes.

"Where are we going?"

"West."

"How do you know?"

She looked back over her shoulder. "Because I live here."

"Here? In the middle of nowhere?" He shivered and slapped his hands against his arms. Fuck but it was cold. He could feel his balls and cock contracting, trying to bury themselves back in his body. And – he was getting tired, way too tired.

Jessica trudged along in front of him, a shiver rolling from her shoulders to her ass every few steps. If he weren't so damn cold, he'd really appreciate the way it shimmied.

Her voice drifted back to him. "I like it here. Nobody bothers me." She held up her hand. "Do you hear that?"

He stopped and sucked cold air into his heaving lungs. "What?"

"Shhhh. Listen."

At first, Richard only heard the wind howling. Then, though, another sound reached his ears. Bells. Jingle bells. Closing his eyes, he shook his head. This was it then. He was dying – freezing to death somewhere in the middle of nowhere, and God only knew how he'd gotten here in the first place.

The bells got louder and he opened his eyes.

Jessica was jumping up and down, the tiny part of his brain not thinking exclusively about survival enjoying the way her breasts bounced.

"Here! Over here! Dashiell, Danny, Prankster, and Vicky. Compass, Cueball, Donny, and Blister."

Richard shook his head. He had to be hearing things. She was calling Santa's reindeer.

Then he began to laugh. That explained it. This was a crazy nightmare. He wasn't really dying. In another few minutes he'd wake up with one hell of a hangover. Yep, he'd had too much to drink last night and was paying for it with a goofy nightmare.

Jessica continued to jump up and down.

Richard cocked his head to the side and watched her breasts. May as well enjoy the one good part of this nightmare.

But the jangling of bells grew louder and interrupted his musings. Pulling his gaze from Jessica's bouncing breasts, he stared at the dark shape that grew larger as it approached. Wind gusted toward them, carrying the sound not only of jingling bells but also of barking dogs.

A dogsled? Richard forced his freezing cheeks into a grin. They were saved.

Soon he could make out the individual dogs – mostly gray and black mixes except for the leader. That one was completely white and almost invisible against the snow.

Jessica fell to her knees and wrapped her arms around the white dog's neck. "Vicky, I have never been so happy to see you. Good girl."

Pushing herself back to her feet, she stumbled to the side of the sled and pulled out something big, dark, and, thanks to a gust of wind tumbling in Richard's direction, smelly.

"Richard," she called after she'd disappeared into it, "get over here. There are plenty of blankets on the sled. We have to get warm, and Vicky will have us home in no time."

After a few seconds, he stumbled toward the sound of her voice. So what if Jessica had just turned into a smelly bear. That seemed to be a logical state of affairs for this particular nightmare.

"Shit, Richard," the bear said, "you're freezing. Get that wet robe off and get into the sled."

He stood grinning at her. It wasn't that cold anymore; and damn, but that bear had a sexy voice.

Muttering blasphemies, she grabbed him, jerked his robe off, and pushed him down on the blankets piled in the sled.

Richard grinned at her. What did she want with his wet robe?

She cursed again. Shrugging out of her coat, she slid into the sled next to him, sucking in a shocked breath as she came in contact with his icy skin. Richard tried to move over. Pulling her bearskin coat over them, she tucked it in around them.

He yawned. When had he ever felt so tired? Must have been the great sex. Smiling, he closed his eyes. A short nap was just what he needed.

"Vicky," she called. "Take us home. Now! Mush!"

All eight dogs barked and surged forward.

"Don't worry," she said as she pulled the coat up over their faces to shut out the icy wind. "Vicky and the other dogs will get us home all right. She's been traveling this same trail for three hundred years."

Eyes closed, Richard smiled and nodded. Three hundred years. Nice to know they wouldn't get lost.

Chapter Ten

"Come on, big boy, we're home."

Jessica shook the sleeping man's shoulder. Halfway home, he'd finally stopped shivering and gone to sleep. Not a good thing considering how cold he still was, but he had warmed up a bit, and his breathing had remained steady.

"Wake up, Richard. You're too big for me to carry."

"Fucking Santa," he mumbled. "I hate Santa."

"Need some help, Jessica?"

A sigh of relief escaped Jessica as she turned around. Good old Nick. He always sent a couple of his employees over with a Christmas tree. Thank goodness they'd chosen to come with it today.

"I sure could, Jack. Could you dump this guy in the hot tub for me? It's the quickest way I know to thaw him out."

Grinning from pointy ear to pointy ear, the short man grabbed Richard by the wrist and yanked him out of the sled. "What kind of moron roams around the Arctic in the middle of winter mostly naked?"

She didn't answer. The last thing she needed was for Jack to find out Penny had bonked them with a couple of love balls. All elves were hopeless gossips, and Jack was one of the worst.

"Who else is here?"

"Evan," he answered as he draped Richard over his shoulders and headed into the house.

Jessica sighed with relief again. Her dogs liked Evan. He could get them unhitched and fed and the sled put away while she took care of her guest. She didn't want Richard to lose a couple of fingers or toes to frostbite.

She nodded as Evan walked out of the house. "Hey, Jess, Jack said you were home. Hell of a package you brought with you.

Once he's thawed out, I'm sure Greta would be glad to take him off your hands."

Grabbing her bearskin, Jessica smiled. Greta would take anything with a cock dangling between his legs off anybody's hands. "I'll keep that in mind. First, though, I gotta make sure frostbite hasn't set in. Losing a few digits wouldn't do Greta any good now, would it?"

Jessica chuckled as Evan roared with laughter and led the dogs around the corner of the house. Then, her bearskin wrapped around her, she stumbled up the steps onto her front porch and shuffled into the house. Gods, but she was tired. First dog sledding to Penny's, then that wild ride to Seattle. Then some wild sex.

She smiled.

Wild, hot sex. Wild, hot, uninhibited sex with a wild, hot, uninhibited guy.

But that magic moonbeam ride afterwards! Shit. Wait until she got her hands on Penny – dropping the two of them in the middle of the Arctic barely dressed. What had her sister been thinking?

Dropping her bearskin on the living room floor, Jessica yawned, stretched, and headed into the kitchen. Once there, she inhaled and smiled. Spiced cider was heating on the stove. Lord but that was going to taste good.

Jack stomped into the kitchen followed closely by Evan. "Your gentleman friend woke up real fast as soon as his ass hit the hot water. I dumped some brandy down his throat, and now he's out there cursing a blue streak. Evan fed the dogs, so we're outta here. Tree's up, but you have to decorate it yourself this year. Nick got a back order for more wooden blocks, of all things. Whole crew is working overtime."

Smiling, Jessica nodded. "Thanks, guys. I appreciate your help. Oh, thanks for the cider. I need it."

Chuckling, Evan jerked his chin toward the back door. "So does he. Pins and needles were just starting in his fingers and toes.

I learned a few new curse words. Didn't think there were any more for me to learn. Thank him for me."

Laughing, both men trotted through the living room and out the front door. The roar of a snowmobile soon filled the night, only to eventually disappear as they headed for home.

After another yawn, Jessica poured two mugs of cider, dropped a cinnamon stick in each, and headed out the back door.

* * *

Gritting his teeth against the sharp pain in his fingers and toes, Richard pulled his sopping G-string off, dropped it over the side of the hot tub – it landed with a soggy jangle – and examined his surroundings. He sat in a cedar hot tub on a nice-sized deck behind a log cabin. A line of pine trees about 100 feet away circled the yard behind him, and he could just make out the roof of a shed to the left of the cabin. Above his head, the heavy gray clouds had blown away without dropping more snow. Bright stars shone, and a full moon sailed across the sky. And all around the cabin was snow – more snow than he could remember seeing in his entire life.

Blinking, he wiped his face with his hands. This was no nightmare. What the hell had happened to him? He remembered watching his brother puke his guts out. That hadn't been a dream.

Then playing fucking Santa at Prior's store had been too miserable for it not to have happened. First Alison coming on to him then that little girl who wanted a kitten! Not even his imagination was fertile enough to come up with both of those in one nightmare – not even after a night drinking cheap wine.

Sliding deeper into the hot water, Richard leaned his head back against the edge of the tub. The club. He'd been there, right? Closing his eyes, he searched his memory. A picture of Tanya puffing on her cigarette appeared in his mind – so did the smell. Yep, he'd been there. Did his last show. And then the bitch had tried to trick him into signing an extension to his contract. Thank goodness for Penelope.

He frowned. Penelope? Penelope who? And her sister Jessica.

Eyes still closed, Richard smiled. Oh man. Jessica. That was the one part of the evening that he was absolutely sure had happened. Hell, what a ride. She been wet and wild – wilder than any other woman he'd ever known. First, she practically swallowed him whole. Then when he'd been ready to explode, he'd pulled her up, ripped her clothes away, shoved her against the door, and slid his cock into her hot tight pussy.

He'd slid his cock into her.

Richard frowned.

He'd slid his cock into her.

When the hell did he put a condom on?

Surging up, he snapped his eyes open. What the fuck had he done?

At that moment, the door slammed open, and his hostess emerged from inside the house carrying two steaming mugs. The tantalizing scent of sweet apples, spicy cinnamon, and nutmeg wafted through the clear, crisp air to his nose.

She smiled at him. "Thawing out okay?"

He scowled at her. "We didn't use a condom."

The smile never left her face. "No we didn't."

He pushed himself to his feet then sat down just as quickly. The water in the tub was nice and hot but the temperature outside of it was below freezing. "We had sex – unprotected sex. No condom. I'm sorry. I got carried away. I never forget condoms." Richard knew he was babbling, but the nipples pushing against the soft, pink wool of her sweater were distracting him. And she didn't even look cold!

"Aren't you cold? It's freezing out here."

She blinked. "What? Cold? Hell, but your train of thought shifts faster than an elf's. I am cold. I'm just used to it. And you don't have to worry. I'm taking birth control."

Relief washing over him, Richard leaned back and closed his eyes. Birth control. She was on the pill. All his muscles relaxed as he slid back down under the water until only his head was visible. Well, that was a relief. Then he frowned again. "Elf?" He cocked an eyebrow. "What the hell are you talking about?"

Sniffing inelegantly, she lifted the mugs, walked to the side of the tub, and handed him one. "Here, drink this. How do your fingers and toes feel?"

He took the mug from her and cupped it in his hands. "My fingers and toes are fine. Would you mind answering a question for me? Where the hell am I?"

Chapter Eleven

Jessica stared at Richard as she sipped her cider. Too bad Jack hadn't added a couple of shots of whiskey. She had a feeling Richard would need something stronger to drink than cider by the time she finished explaining where he was.

"North Pole?"

He snorted. "Try again."

She shrugged and smiled. "Okay, northern Canada. No one can live at the real North Pole. Too damn cold."

At the same moment, a chorus of barks and howls erupted from around the side of the house. The sound was followed by the dogs – eight of them, big ones – with lots of fur leaping up onto the deck. One of them stuck his nose in Richard's face and planted a sloppy kiss on his nose before he could pull away. The others went straight to Jessica.

Smiling, Jessica patted heads and backs. "You guys all have supper? Ready for bed?"

Richard stared at them. Eight dogs. Did she let them all in the house? "What are their names?"

Grinning, she answered, "Dashiell, Danny, Prankster, Vicky, Compass, Cueball, Donny, and Blister."

He blinked. "Why did you name them that?"

"To aggravate my brother-in-law."

"Brother-in-law?"

She nodded. "Nicholas. Most people know him as St. Nicholas. Kids call him Santa Claus."

He dropped his mug over the side of the tub.

Cider and spices rolled across the cedar deck. "Do you really expect me to believe you're Santa Claus's sister?"

"Sister-in-law. You remember Penny, my sister. She's married to him."

His face got red really fast. "What kind of bullshit are you trying to feed me? Quit fucking around and give me some answers, Jessica. What is your last name anyway?"

"Fenstermacher."

"What?"

"My last name is Fenstermacher. And you *are* in Northern Canada."

"And I suppose I got here in a sleigh pulled by reindeer?"

She shook her head. "No, only Nick uses them and only once a year. Magic first. Then dogsled. My dogsled."

Closing his eyes, he covered them with his forearm. "I'm fucking stranded in the middle of fucking nowhere with a fucking crazy woman."

After letting the dogs into the house where they'd fall asleep in front of the fireplace, Jessica swallowed the last of her cider and smiled. Then she began to laugh.

Dropping his arm, he stared at her. "What's so damn funny?"

After a final giggle, Jessica gulped in some air and said, "I'm just trying to see things from your perspective."

"I'm not laughing."

Cocking her head to the side, Jessica nodded. "No, you're not. But except for that goofy hat, you're naked in my hot tub. And, if I remember correctly, you are one fine specimen of maleness." With those words, she toed off her boots and socks, pulled her sweater over her head, unsnapped her bra, undid the only two buttons left on her jeans, shimmied out of them and her panties, then stepped into the hot tub.

Richard snapped his mouth closed. Maybe he really was having a nightmare. His gaze fell to her full breasts and the tight pink nipples that bobbed in and out of the water.

He shifted and spread his legs as his cock swelled. Nightmare? Nope, not a nightmare. This was one hell of a wet dream.

Before he could reach for her, she was in his arms, her lips on his, her tongue caressing his. Moaning, he sucked it deeper into his mouth and cupped her breast.

She shifted and tried to settle herself onto his cock.

He pulled her mouth from his. "Oh no. Not so fast. Not this time. I want to take my time."

A delicious chuckle welled up out of her throat. "By all means, Richard, take your time. I don't have anything better to do except sleep, and that can wait."

"Good!" Sliding his hands down her torso, he lifted her high enough out of the water so that her breasts were level with his face. Leaning forward, he sucked her right nipple into his mouth.

"Oh yes," she said as she wrapped her arms around his head and arched her back, pushing her nipple further into his mouth.

He switched to the other nipple.

"Are you cold?" he mumbled against her breast.

"Oh gods, no. I'm hot. So hot."

"Good." He sucked as much of her breast into his mouth as he could.

Bending her head, she nipped his ear. "You make me so hot, hotter than any man ever has. Fuck me, Richard. Fuck me hard."

Lifting his head from her breasts, he stared into her eyes. "Be glad to." Locking his mouth on hers, he dropped her onto his lap and buried his cock between her legs.

Planting her feet on the floor of the tub, she lifted herself off of him then impaled herself again.

They both groaned.

He kissed her between her breasts. "You're so sweet and wet."

She moaned. "Oh, gods, your cock feels so good! Deeper. Bury it deeper."

"Be glad to, sweetheart." Thrusting his hips up, Richard buried himself even more deeply. "Damn but you're hot." He slid his cock out. "Turn around. I'm going to ride you until you scream."

Shuddering, she did as he asked, resting her arms on the other side of the hot tub.

Richard probed between her thighs, first with his fingers then with his cock. After positioning her hips to his liking, he surged into her.

She clutched the edge of the tub as he withdrew and thrust into her again. "Yes, yes. Harder, harder."

Richard complied, water splashed around them, slopping over the side of the tub. Cold air surrounded his upper body. Warm water surrounded him from the waist down. And Jessica's slick, wet pussy surrounded his cock.

Gripping her hips, he thrust again then swiveled his hips – once to the left, once to the right.

She moaned as more water sloshed out of the tub.

Her internal muscles clasped and sucked at his cock as he pulled back. They relaxed as he pushed forward. He ground his hips against her ass. His balls tightened.

She spread her legs farther apart.

His cock jerked inside of her.

"That's it, sweetheart, tighten that pussy. Hold me tight."

"I'm going to suck your cock dry," she groaned through gritted teeth.

Leaning over, he slipped a hand between her legs and pinched her clit.

She bucked against him. "Oh, gods. Yes. More."

Richard thrust into her again, pinched her clit again.

"I'm going to come."

"Come, baby. Come for me."

"Oh, oh, oh. Yesssssss!"

As her internal muscles rippled and shuddered, Richard thrust into her one final time and exploded.

Some minutes later, Richard slid his cock from her body and collapsed onto a bench. Pulling Jessica with him, he wrapped his arms around her and settled her onto his lap.

She rested her head against his shoulder and smiled into his face. "So, what would you think about living forever?"

Chapter Twelve

Half an hour later, Richard sat before a roaring fire wrapped in his now dry robe and a soft, multi-colored wool throw with a mug of hot coffee cupped in his hands, staring at Jessica. She was snuggled beneath a gold and black afghan in an overstuffed armchair on the other side of the braided rug – smiling at him.

Assorted yips, whines, and snores escaped from the eight sled dogs sleeping all around them.

Propping his elbows on his thighs, he leaned forward. "Let me get this straight. Your sister Penelope married St. Nicholas three hundred odd years ago. Since she didn't want to live through the centuries without any of her family, she convinced Nicholas to use his 'magic dust' on you."

Still smiling, Jessica nodded.

He glanced at the sleeping white dog at her feet. Her feet twitching, Vicky whined as she chased a rabbit in her sleep. "And you insisted on keeping your dog team."

After another sip of coffee, she nodded again.

Richard leaned back. He was in the Twilight Zone. There was no other reasonable explanation. Because, if he wasn't in the Twilight Zone, then what Jessica was telling him was true. And that wasn't possible, was it? Santa Claus didn't really exist, did he? People didn't live for three hundred years, did they?

Her chocolate brown eyes twinkled. "Richard?"

Before he could answer, the door was shoved open. The sound of jingling bells rolled into the room followed by a man wearing a red coat.

All eight dogs woke, leaped to their feet, and began barking their welcomes.

Penelope was a few steps behind, a large red and green shopping bag looped over her wrist. "Richard. How nice to see you again. I'd like you to meet my husband, Nicholas," she shouted over the general mayhem.

Before he could answer, Jessica was out of her chair stomping toward her sister, her braless breasts bouncing beneath her gray sweatshirt. "Dashiell, Danny, Prankster! Compass, Cueball, Danny, Blister! Vicky, take them all out for your evening run."

With a woof, the white dog complied. The other seven followed her.

Richard glanced back at Penelope and her companion.

Nicholas's eyes were glued to Jessica's chest.

A burst of anger rolled in Richard's stomach. Those were his breasts.

"Damn it, Penny. We could have frozen to death!" Hands fisted on her hips, Jessica glared into her sister's face. "And you!" she exclaimed, switching her attention to Nicholas. "What were you thinking to transport us into the middle of nowhere without proper clothing?"

Lips twitching and eyes twinkling, he answered, "I didn't think you'd be half naked."

"That's enough," Penelope said as she slipped an arm beneath Jessica's. "What's done is done, all's well that ends well, I always say."

Jessica snorted. "You never say that."

Bells jingling, Nicholas shrugged out of his coat. He turned to hang it on the coat rack but stopped short and wrinkled his nose when he saw Jessica's bearskin coat hanging there. "Jesus, Mary, and Joseph, Jessica. Do you have to hang that coat in your house? It's a wonder the whole place doesn't smell like a hibernating bear's den."

Tossing her hair back over her shoulder, Jessica sniffed. "It's my house. I can bring in a hibernating bear if I want to."

Nicholas dropped his coat over the back of the sofa. "Well, don't ask me to help you get him back out again."

Still sitting in his chair, Richard listened to the banter between Jessica and her sister but continued to stare at the bearded man. Fuck, but he looked exactly like Santa Claus was supposed to look, even if he was wearing blue jeans. But then lots of guys looked like Santa Claus. Still, there was something else familiar about him.

Setting his coffee mug on the table next to his chair, Richard leaned forward, studying Nicholas's face. He'd seen it somewhere before – and not on a Christmas card.

A picture appeared in his mind, a picture sitting among all the other family pictures his mother had on the mantel.

His mouth dropped open. He snapped it closed, swallowed, and said, "Uncle Nick?"

Nicholas chuckled. "I was wondering if you'd recognize me."

Jessica looked from one to the other. "You two know each other?"

Richard continued to stare at the older man, so Nicholas answered, "The one and only time Richard saw me was when he was eight years old and his brother was six. His mother is my sister." Then he chuckled. "Well, not really. His mother's I don't know how many greats grandmother was my sister. Did you ever meet Anya?"

Jessica shook her head.

Nicholas shrugged. "She was a good ten years older than I, married, and living in Germany when I met Penelope. However, I have kept track of her descendants. It's a closely guarded secret, but one girl in every generation knows the truth – that she's a relative of St. Nicholas. They explain me to their families as their much older, eccentric, antisocial brother Nick who lives in the wilds of Canada."

Shaking his head, Richard continued to stare at his "Uncle" Nick. Eccentric didn't even begin to describe him.

Richard leaned forward again. "How did you get here?"

Nicholas grinned at him. "Snowmobile. Snow's too deep for the four-wheel drive."

Relaxing his tense muscles, Richard leaned back.

"And I only use the deer on Christmas Eve," Nicholas continued.

Richard slumped in his chair. "I'm going fucking crazy."

Chuckling, Penelope leaned over from where she was now sitting on the sofa and patted his knee. "No you aren't, dear. I know all this is hard to believe, but how else can you explain sitting here right now?"

Directing a baleful glare her way, he answered, "Twilight Zone."

Her merry laugh bouncing around the room, she clapped her hands together. "You have the most droll sense of humor." Lifting the shopping bag, Penelope set it in his lap. "Here, I thought you might like some of your clothing."

After looking in the bag, Richard locked his gaze on Penelope. These weren't the clothes he'd worn to the club. "Where did you get these?"

"Your mother, of course."

"My mother?"

She smiled. "Well, how else would I get them?"

"This is fucking insane," Richard growled as he wrenched himself to his feet. "I'm stranded in the middle of nowhere with two women and a lunatic who thinks he's Santa Claus."

Rising from her chair, Jessica said, "That's enough. Thanks for bringing Richard his clothes, Penny. Nick, it was very thoughtful of you. But it's time for you to leave."

Stomach churning, Richard stared at the three of them. They were all nuts, him included. Still, he had a bone to pick. "I hate Santa Claus."

Chapter Thirteen

That brought all three of them up short.

"I hate Santa Claus," Richard repeated.

"Why?" all three chorused.

"Because he's fucked up my life."

Nicholas puffed out his chest, a very indignant look on his face. "I have not 'fucked up' your life! You got almost every toy you wanted when you were a boy."

Richard shook his head. Maybe he was nuts, but he finally had a Santa in front of him, he was sitting in a cabin somewhere in northern Canada without a clue as to how he'd gotten here, and he was going to tell him exactly what he thought. Rising to his feet, he stepped in front of Nick and poked a finger against his chest. "Because every time I got serious about a woman, she ended up fucking some asshole Santa and leaving me for him. So what do you have to say to that, you jolly old elf?"

Sticking his chin out, Nicholas stepped into Richard's finger. "Wasn't me, you young whippersnapper. Penelope'd have my balls in a vise grip if I fooled around. Not that I want to. Not a woman anywhere can compare with her."

Well shit. Jessica stared from one man to the other. Just what she needed in her living room, raging testosterone. Her gaze rested on Richard. Damn, but he was the finest man she'd ever met, and considering her age, that was saying something. But was the baggage from his past worth dealing with? The last thing she wanted or needed was a man dwelling on the lost loves of his past, especially since the real Santa Claus was her brother-in-law. Animosity could really screw up a family picnic.

Jessica shifted to her other foot. Besides, she didn't even know if Richard was interested in hanging around for the next millennium. Hell, she wasn't even sure if she wanted him hanging around that long. Yes, they'd had fantastic sex, but sex wasn't everything.

Her lips twitched. Okay, sex was a lot; but, shit, she would like to have a man around who could carry on a decent conversation.

"Time for you to make up your mind, Jessica."

Blinking, she turned to her sister. "What?"

Penelope nodded in the general direction of the growling men. "Is he worth the trouble? Men are rather like children, you know. They have to be guided. It's a lot of work, but certainly has its rewards."

Sighing, Jessica shrugged. "I don't know, Penny. Hell, I've known him less than twenty-four hours. I can't make a life-changing decision only based on great sex."

Chuckling, Penelope patted her shoulder. "Never settle for anything else. Convince him to stay a few days. Get to know each other. If he's the right one, you'll know. So will he. Now, I better get Nicholas home before they come to blows. Santa has never delivered toys with a black eye, and he's not going to start now. Just let me know if Richard wants to go home. We'll have him there in a jiffy."

With those words, she stepped between the two men, grabbed Nicholas's coat from the back of the sofa, and tossed it to him, the bells sewn onto it jingling. "Time to go home, Nicholas. Only a few weeks left until Christmas, and there's still a lot to do."

Far more quickly than seemed possible, Penelope had them both bundled up and out the door. The loud roar of the snowmobile's engine faded quickly into the distance.

Richard stared at the closed door then down at the gaily colored shopping bag he still held in his hand. He shook it. When the bells fastened to the handle jingled, he cringed. "If I ever hear another fucking bell, it will be too soon."

Jessica's voice was dry. "Really?"

Dropping the bag on the floor, he turned to look at her. "Yeah. What's it to you?"

A devilish smile on her face, she held up his G-string and shook it. The bells jangled. "I was rather hoping you'd model this again for me some day."

He cocked an eyebrow. "Oh?"

She nodded. "Want to hang around a few days and get to know me, so to speak?"

A smile tugging the corners of his mouth, Richard stared at Jessica. Hang around a few more days? He'd already gotten to "know" Jessica very well, but...

A full smile stretched his lips... there was a lot more about her he'd like to get to know. "Are you ticklish behind your knees?"

She chuckled. "I don't know. No one ever bothered to find out."

Letting the wool throw slide off his shoulders, he stepped toward her. "And after I find out just where you're ticklish, then what?"

Tossing her long hair back over her shoulder, she slid her hands under his robe, scissoring his nipples between her fingers. "Oh, well, I could find out how many places you're ticklish."

Bending down, he brushed his lips against hers. "Then what?"

She stepped closer. "Do you like to fish?"

Placing his hands on her hips, he slid his hands under her sweatshirt up the soft skin of her back. "Yes," he answered before he nibbled the exact spot her neck and shoulder met.

Sighing, she tilted her head, giving him better access. "How about cooking? Can you?"

He slid his hands down her back, under the waistband of her sweatpants – no panties – and gently massaged her ass. "Nope," he breathed against her neck. "But I'm a hell of a Bar-B-Quer."

"Hmmmm. That's great. Do you care if there's a little dust around the house?" She tugged the robe loose and slid it off his shoulders.

It puddled at his feet.

She stepped closer.

His erection nudged her belly.

"What dust?" he asked as he pulled her shirt over her head.

Both pebbled nipples got a quick suckle and kiss.

Jessica arched her back into his mouth. "Dogs!" she gasped. "Do you like dogs?"

He slipped his fingers under the waistband of her sweats again and slid them down. "Dogs? Man's best friend."

"Oh good. I have eight of them, you know." She shivered in his arms as he lifted her and set her on the back of the sofa.

"Yeah, I know. Dashiell, Danny, Prankster, Vicky, Compass, Cueball, Donny, and Blister," he answered as he lifted her legs and placed one on each side of his hips.

She locked her legs around his waist. Breathlessly, she answered, "They're good dogs."

He dipped his fingers between her legs. "They saved my life." He slid two fingers into her.

She arched. "Yes, they did. And mine too."

As he twisted his fingers, she gasped, "Richard!" and dug her blunt nails into his shoulders.

He covered her mouth with his and sucked her tongue into his mouth. Pulling his hand from her body, he probed with his cock – once, twice, then slid into her.

She shuddered both inside and out.

As she arched her back, he lifted his mouth from hers and slid his hands around her sides to cup her ass. As he thrust, he pulled her closer.

Hot, moist heat surrounded his straining cock.

Did he want to stay around and get to know Jessica?

Hell yes.

Judy Mays

Judy Mays spends her days teaching English to tenth graders in a small town in Central Pennsylvania. Outside of work, she's a wife and mother. After her children, pets are a very important part of Judy's life, and she's had many over the years. Currently, Zoe the cat and Boomer the Lab mix help keep things hopping around the house. Judy loves nature in all its myriad forms and can often be found outside in her garden or hiking through the woods.

Judy dreams of hot passionate love on sultry summer nights, festive fall evenings, winsome winter mornings, and sparkling spring days – spent with werewolves, vampires, witches, aliens, and shape shifters. Judy loves writing "spicy" romance. She assures us her wonderful husband of seventeen years provides plenty of motivation.

Judy would love to hear from you. You may contact her directly at writermays@yahoo.com, visit her website at JudyMays.com or join her reader's group at groups.yahoo.com/group/judymays.

Sealed With a Kiss
Marteeka Karland

Chapter One

Valentine's Day. It was Marie Donaldson's favorite holiday and only two days away. Unfortunately, she was two galaxies and *billions* of light years away from anyone who celebrated it.

But that wasn't the worst of it. Oh, no. Not by a long shot.

She was stuck on a piece of shit, two man supply runner headed toward the asshole of the universe. It had seemed like a good idea at the time. The ship was fast, the money even faster... and her captain the tastiest piece of eye chocolate a girl could ever feast her eyes on. And the best kisser she'd ever had the pleasure of locking lips with.

But what had started out as a promising voyage had quickly turned into the most frustrating job of her life.

* * *

One Month Earlier:

Captain Daxon Sha'gar's vivid violet gaze roamed Marie's body hungrily. Her light gray work unitard must surely give him an eyeful, for it hugged every curve of her body, including the painfully hard nipples she knew were not hidden beneath the built-in bra.

God! The man was gorgeous! Her breathing quickened as she took in his angular features. She hadn't been this excited for a man in her whole life, and she'd only seen him for a few seconds.

He quizzed her for almost three hours on technical and operational issues in the quiet back room of a local pub. The inquisition wasn't abnormal; after all, she was hoping to be his computer and mechanical engineer. The *length* was another matter entirely.

She became restless after an hour, edgy after two. When he began repeating himself at the beginning of the third hour, she could feel her face heating up with her anger. Still, she needed this job, so she put up with it.

After telling him for the second time that the only Oscillation Overthruster she'd ever heard of was in a Buckaroo Banzai movie, she snapped. She planted her hands on her hips, knowing it would thrust her breasts forward and would probably cause his attention to wander. Sure enough, his gaze fell from her face squarely to her heaving chest. Inwardly, she rolled her eyes. So, Captain Hot-to-Trot liked what he saw, too.

But irritation was her predominant emotion and he had to know he could only push her so far. "Look, buster. Are you going to hire me or not? I could go to any skin bar in this crummy sector and get my tits ogled and I'd at least get paid for it."

When he opened his mouth, she added, "And it wouldn't take three fucking hours, either." His smile was slight, but acknowledged her statement. She was a little shocked at him for not denying it, as most men she knew would have.

"In that case, you're hired." His expression was mild, but completely unreadable. "I'd hate for you to have to make your living showing your tits in a skin bar." He glanced at her bosom once more. "Some of the clientele in those establishments aren't content to simply *ogle*."

He rose smoothly, muscles playing under the snug, black pants molding his thick thighs. Marie was considered average in height for a human female. She wasn't sure where her new captain was from, but he made her feel positively tiny.

She probably hit him about mid-chest, if she was lucky, and the amount of muscle on this prime specimen of manhood was matched only by the amount of muscle between his legs. Those snug britches clung to one healthy, mouth-watering bulge, and Marie wanted to explore every square inch of it. Along with the rest of him.

As he rose, she followed suit and extended her hand. He simply looked at it until his bewildered eyes met hers once more.

"It's an Earth tradition to shake hands after a deal is made," she said. "It means the negotiations are over and the deal won't be changed on the word of both parties."

"Ah," he said and smiled. "On my planet, we also have a custom." He moved toward her with the grace of a feline. A feline stalking his prey. "We seal our bargains with a kiss."

Without another word, he pulled her into his arms and kissed her. It should have been simple, but there was nothing simple about it. His lips played with hers, his teeth nipped, and his tongue darted between her lips easily to duel with hers. He dominated without being overpowering; she knew she could break the kiss at any time. But the mastery of it made her want to continue wherever he wanted to lead her.

Her hands slid up Daxon's massive shoulders into his thick mass of red – almost purple – hair. She easily found and released the leather tie that held the locks in place at the nape of his neck, tangled her fingers in the silky depths, and simply held on for dear life.

His large hands squeezed her ass and pulled her against him. She responded by hooking one leg around his hip and meeting his obvious arousal with her pelvis. She had never been so lost in a kiss before. He could have taken her right there and she would have given him everything he wanted without a word of protest. She reached for her orgasm with all the strength of will she possessed... but he ended the kiss as abruptly as he'd begun it.

He peeled his body away, and Marie staggered. She probably would have fallen if he hadn't steadied her. *What* a *kiss!* She'd forgotten where they were. They were in a public bar, for crying out loud! She'd never lost herself like that before. It was a heady, intense sensation. A slow smile played across her lips as she came to her senses.

This man, she had to have!

But when she met his eyes, they were the same unemotional, expressionless, violet eyes she'd encountered when she'd first walked into the pub. How could a man who could kiss so passionately be so difficult to read?

Oh well. She'd just have to get him to lose a little of that control.

Her thoughts were interrupted when he picked up the bar tab and addressed her once again. "The *Burning Star* is docked in bay ninety-four. I leave at exactly seventeen hundred hours, Earth Standard Time. If you're one second late, I'll leave without you."

Daxon had not given her a chance to reply. He'd simply left, settling the tab as he went. Marie wasn't sure if she should be insulted or not. If the kiss was a custom on their world, she may well have offended him. Her brow furrowed in thought. This could prove to be an interesting run.

And it had.

Just not in the way she'd expected.

"The fastest ship in the sector" had proven to be full of mechanical failures and computer glitches. As soon as she fixed one problem, another would pop up. Captain Sha'gar, aka Captain Good-Kisser-But-the-Asshole-Slave-Driver-from-Hell, kept her in the mainframe room or the engine room every minute of her work cycle. The only time she emerged was to eat. At the end of the cycle, she was usually frustrated and not in the mood for company. That didn't stop her from fantasizing, though. His strong-looking, work-roughened hands were busy all through the night in her dreams.

She was so preoccupied, she never saw those "unemotional" violet eyes actually glow with lust every time they caught sight of her.

* * *

Daxon just knew this damned supply run would never end. He'd managed to keep Marie busy chasing ghosts, but it was only a matter of time before she caught on to his little game. Just a couple more days and he'd be back to civilization. Then he'd fuck her senseless.

He wanted her. Wanted her more than he'd ever wanted a woman in his entire life. Had wanted her from the moment she'd sashayed her sweet, tightly clad ass into that damned pub. He'd made up that damn kissing thing just to get a taste of her. She'd probably not appreciate that little bit of embellishment if she ever found out. He just could not afford any distractions until this run was complete. If the slightest thing went wrong with navigations, they'd end up in the middle of one of the nebulae surrounding Solum, his home world. As it was, they had to stop every resting cycle. He simply didn't trust the computer to fly them straight.

So here he was back from the ass end of the galaxy, and fast approaching his home world and civilization. Marie would probably have his balls for breakfast, but he'd try to smooth things over with her. Once he had her beneath him, screaming out her orgasm, she'd forgive him, he thought with a smirk.

She was sharp, his little Marie, and really quite adept in the engine room as well as with the computer. He'd only just managed to keep one step ahead of her, and only because he knew his ship better than anyone else.

A screech from down the corridor signified his sexy crewmember had found his latest little "glitch." If nothing went wrong, this one should keep her busy for the remainder of the trip. Thank the gods! He was running out of systems and circuits he could sabotage.

"You fucking, asinine son of a bitch! You fucking did that on *purpose!*"

Her screech sent chills down Daxon's spine. He winced. *Busted!*

Oh well. It was bound to happen. Only thing he could do now was own up to it and take his medicine. He'd probably just ensured she'd not be hanging around after they docked, and he wasn't sure what to do to rectify that situation. But he would. Somehow, he would have his little Earthling.

The cute little flaxen-haired vixen stormed into the cockpit. *Good name for it right now.* Marie's finger stabbed his chest as he rose to meet her. The top of her head didn't even reach his chin, but her presence made up for her lack in stature amply.

"You've had me chasing my tail this whole fucking run! Care to enlighten me as to why?" Her demand was presented formidably. This was a woman his mother would be proud of. He almost chuckled at the thought.

Not sure exactly how to proceed, he decided he'd simply give her the truth. "Because I need my full attention to navigate the Nebulae Maze. If we end up off course, the gases could fry this ship."

"So why not just tell me to keep my mouth shut and let you do your job? Or tell me to keep out of your way? Or any *number* of things and I wouldn't have been a bother!"

Just as he was about to respond, she added, "Creep!"

She was really good at that. Taking a breath, looking straight into her angry blue eyes, he said, "Because, if you're frustrated at this ship, you won't feel like following up on that kiss."

Marie opened her mouth to retort just as his words apparently registered. She closed her mouth and blinked. "Come again?"

He chuckled. "Marie, when we get to Solum, I'll definitely come. Again, and again, and again. And so will you."

The blush that stole across her fair cheeks was completely charming. He could almost forget about the sharp edge her tongue had.

"Go rest. Hopefully, we'll make it to Solum in two days, then we'll talk."

She sniffed, composure firmly back in place. "Well, if talking is all you intend, then don't bother. After that kiss, I thought you were a man of action." Her gaze drifted the length of his body. "I guess I was wrong."

What man could refuse *that* little taunt? He grabbed her arm as she turned to leave and pulled her lush body into his. "One of these days, that mouth is going to get you into trouble," he promised, crushing his own against hers.

He wasn't gentle this time. He wanted her to beg for it. The only flaw with his plan was he was damn near close to begging himself. And he was only kissing her!

As he opened his mouth, her tongue invaded. Damn! He was supposed to be leading this, but all he could think about was how greedy she seemed for him. She pulled his head more firmly to her and licked and nipped his lips. His head spun.

Grabbing her ass in both hands, he lifted her, pulling her against him as he ground his pelvis into hers. When she let out a little whimper, he almost shouted with joy. She was as affected as he was.

When she wrapped her legs around him, aligning her pussy perfectly with his throbbing hard cock, he almost lost what little control he possessed. Backing her against the console, he rubbed himself against her heat, still devouring her mouth. With her ankles locked around his waist and her arms around his neck, he mimicked fucking her, each stroke pushing him desperately close to release. Her pants and cries told him she was just as close as he was.

Just when he thought she'd find her orgasm, just when he knew he was about to come in his pants for the first time since he was a youngster – with absolutely no intention of complaining about it – an alarm sounded on the console somewhere underneath her ass. That was the end of that. Spinning them both away from the panel, he glanced at the readout. "Damn it!"

"What's wrong?" Her voice was husky, needy, and a little alarmed.

"We've drifted off course," he bit out, angry with himself for his lack of self-control when he knew how important control was right now. "I have to get us back on the flight path or we'll fry an engine." He needed to concentrate or they might never reach Solum. "We'll finish this later, Marie. Now leave."

Not saying anything, for once, she turned stiffly and left. He watched her cute little ass twist as she hurried down the hall. Daxon groaned. Getting her into bed was definitely a priority.

Suddenly, home seemed a great deal farther than it had been an hour ago. Gods, let the ending of this journey be as uneventful as the rest of it had been. He didn't think his poor cock could stand much of a delay.

Chapter Two

The egotistical bastard! She wasn't even sure she wanted to fuck him anymore. She would stay in her quarters until he docked, then leave. And she would, if she wasn't so curious. If his kiss was that good, how would his lovemaking be? She got shivers just thinking about it.

That settled it. She'd definitely fuck him. But that would be the end of that. She wasn't going to hang around for him to tell her she'd done it wrong, or some stupid *male* thing like that. He'd already had her scampering around his ship like an idiot. Once was enough, thank you very much.

They were due to dock on Valentine's Day. Well, looked like her favorite holiday had promise after all. Who'd've thought! Rummaging through her things, she found just what she was looking for. *Yes, this will do quite nicely.*

* * *

Daxon hadn't seen Marie since she'd discovered his little subterfuge. It was just as well. He had arrived on Solum without incident and on schedule. But absence does something to the mind. He had begun to fantasize about her continually. The one resting period he'd taken in the last two days had been spent in contemplation of what he would do to her when he got her home.

Well, that and a masturbation session or two. The woman had gotten completely under his skin in the brief time he had known her. She was intelligent, creative, and had more spunk than any woman he'd ever met.

And, by the gods, she was *beautiful*. Her skin was pale, but not unhealthy looking, like so many career space runners. Her hair was like spun gold and softer than anything he could ever imagine. She was strong, both of body and will. It was a heady combination. And very sexy.

He remembered how her body felt when she had pressed it so wantonly against his in that bar. He could almost feel her moist heat enfolding his cock. Not that she was wearing enough to prevent it. That unitard clung to every enticingly mouthwatering curve of her body, especially her breasts. They were magnificent! They were perfectly proportioned to her hips and waist and all he could think about was burying his cock between those luscious tits until he had spent himself. He wanted his scent on her.

The thought was unsettling. He prided himself on his control, though where she was concerned, it seemed he had very little – a fact she'd soon learn. The pleasure would be mutual and lengthy. When it was over, they would part.

Strange how... empty that felt.

Bah! A fuck was a fuck. He was just overly primed. Even though he had managed to keep Marie busy, he couldn't help hearing her during the rest cycle. Her quarters were next to his and the walls weren't exactly soundproof. Just before she slept each cycle, she screamed her pleasure. Several times.

She was driving him crazy. Which was probably what she wanted.

Oh well, he'd find out soon enough. She should meet him at the landing ramp in twenty minutes. If she intended to tease him, she wouldn't quit until she was well and truly fucked.

Tucking his thoughts away, he made docking preparations. His family was meeting them to help unload their cargo of medical supplies and equipment. Any supplies that made it through the nebulae were a miracle to Solum. As his thoughts drifted back to Marie, he wondered what his family would think of her.

He was in over his head. *Way over.*

Having docked and confirmed his family awaited them, he made his way to the landing ramp. No sooner did he reach the airlock than Marie appeared down the corridor. She moved toward him, gliding rather than walking, dressed from throat to toes in a crimson cloak. Her flaxen hair hung freely across her shoulders and halfway down her back. She was stunning.

He swallowed.

"Ready?" She raised an eyebrow when he didn't answer.

As he opened the airlock, Daxon's gaze came back to the ethereal beauty before him. When he didn't move, Marie simply moved ahead of him down the landing ramp.

Solum had the most beautiful sky Marie had ever seen. In the fading twilight, it was a mass of swirling purples and reds and pinks. Clouds drifted at varying levels in the atmosphere, making the busy spaceport seem to float in cotton candy.

As Marie neared the bottom of the ramp, she was met by two men and a woman. Taking a firm grip on her cloak, she fiddled with the soft material. She hadn't planned on being here with anyone but Daxon while the docking crew unloaded their cargo. While she wanted Daxon to discover her little surprise underneath, she didn't want anyone else privy to *that* little secret.

The woman spoke first. "You are Daxon's new engineer?" All three looked at Marie curiously.

"Yes. And you are?" A stab of jealousy hit Marie, and she hoped her smile didn't look as fake as it was. Tall, slender with a very curly head of waist-length blue-black hair, the woman was stunning. She looked a bit older than Daxon, but not by much.

"I'm Xandra," she said. "This is my husband, Mikkhal," she indicated the tall, muscular man, who looked only slightly older than Xandra herself, "and my son Kamar."

Marie had to admit, Xandra was incredibly beautiful, and didn't look anywhere near old enough to have an adult son. The relief she felt knowing Xandra was married was almost overwhelming, but not nearly as great as when Kamar embraced Daxon and said, "It is good to see you again, brother."

"Mother. Father." Daxon hugged both parents then laid a hand on Marie's shoulder. "I see you have met my family," he said. "Everyone, this is Marie."

"Marie, dear, how was your journey?" Xandra asked.

Marie glanced at Daxon. "Not bad, once I got the gremlins out of the machinery." At least Daxon had the good grace to blush.

Xandra said, "She is a good engineer, Daxon?"

"The best I've had the pleasure of working with since Kamar took his own ship," he agreed, grinning affectionately at his brother.

The compliment caught Marie off guard. At least she hoped it was a compliment. When Xandra smiled warmly at her, Marie let out a breath she hadn't realized she was holding.

"Hm." Kamar brushed a finger under his chin in contemplation. "Perhaps we should think about more permanent employment, if the lady is willing." He took a step toward Marie.

She felt Daxon's arm around her shoulders, and Kamar stopped his forward progress. He smiled before continuing. "Daxon hasn't made a run in over a year without complaining about the company."

Marie looked from one brother to the other. She couldn't tell if Kamar was serious or not. She had almost forgotten about Xandra and Mikkhal when the older man joined the conversation.

"Yes. A wonderful idea. If you are interested, of course, Marie."

Kamar looked at her as if gauging her reaction. "Do you think you could work with Daxon?"

Marie shrugged. "I don't know. I was planning on starting back home."

"Why not think about it while you're here? At least agree to consider our proposition."

Marie looked at Daxon. He was so handsome. And the infuriating oaf was getting under her skin. She hadn't missed the possessive gestures or heated looks he had given her and she'd be willing to bet his family hadn't missed much either. Especially his mother. There was a wealth of motherly knowledge within the depths of her brilliant emerald eyes.

Hell, why not give it a shot? What else did she have to do? If Daxon proved too much of an asshole, she'd ditch him. Still, what was the harm in waiting until she was supposed to leave to give them her decision?

"Sure. I'll think about it."

Kamar smiled, genuinely pleased. "Wonderful," he said, offering her his hand. "I understand Earth's custom is to 'shake hands' when coming to an agreement."

Marie smiled. "Yes. But we're on Solum. I think it more fitting to observe your customs."

She wasn't sure what made her do it. But she stepped closer to Kamar and slipped her arms from her cloak. Almost casually, she slid them around Kamar's neck and gently pulled him to her. When her lips met his, she sighed.

At first, Kamar didn't move. Then his arms found their way inside her cloak and snaked around her waist. He groaned as his tongue traced her lips, slipping into her mouth.

Kamar was an excellent kisser, but Marie didn't lose herself in his kiss like she had when Daxon kissed her. It was pleasurable, though.

At least it was until she was roughly pulled away from Kamar and found a furious Daxon standing between them.

"You would be advised to keep your distance, brother," Daxon snarled.

"Hey." Kamar raised his hand and backed away, smiling. "She kissed me."

Daxon grimaced. "So she did."

Xandra looked amused. Mikkhal raised a hand to his mouth and turned away.

"I have a feeling there is more here than meets the eye." Xandra raised an eyebrow. "And, Marie, dear, we do *not* complete our bargains in quite that manner."

Marie looked sharply at Daxon. "You don't?" Her question was also an accusation, and judging by the flush creeping up his neck, he realized that.

"Uh, no," Mikkhal said helpfully. "We usually clasp arms, very similar in fashion to your handshake."

Marie didn't waste a second.

She slapped Daxon full across his handsome cheek. "Asshole!"

"Marie, I can explain."

"I'll just bet you can," Marie spat.

She turned to move farther down the landing platform, but Daxon scooped her into his arms. "We'll discuss this inside," he said.

She pushed and squirmed, but ended up tangled hopelessly in her cloak. "Put me down, you ape!"

Daxon grunted when she managed to make contact with a well-placed kick, but otherwise remained silent. He carried her into the spaceport, through the crowded terminal area, Marie kicking and screaming the entire time. He noticed more than one amused look but went straight to a planet-side gate.

"Sha'gar estate," he barked, when they stepped into the shimmering gateway. "Daxon residence."

* * *

Daxon knew he was in a shitload of trouble, but he didn't care. Marie was his. She just didn't know it yet. She had quit most of her struggling after she got that damned cloak tangled around both of them. He wasn't sure he could disengage himself from her, even if he'd actually wanted to.

What the hell did she have on under that thing, anyway? She was slung over his shoulder, and he had one hand on her rump, the other around the back of her legs. If he didn't know better, he'd have sworn she only had some kind of body stocking on. The garment felt silky to the touch, but his work-roughened hands snagged every now and then on the delicate material.

And it didn't feel like she was wearing any panties.

Lust was a living thing inside him. He stumbled and almost fell to his knees. The little vixen had worn this attire for a reason. Could it be possible *she* was trying to seduce *him*? No woman would wear something like that unless she had a plan. And his Marie was definitely capable of creating one hell of a plan.

Despite the fact that he knew she was furious at him, Daxon found himself sporting the best hard-on of all time. If he had known sex was truly what she wanted, he'd have wrestled her to the ground, ripped her clothes from her delectable body, and fucked her until neither of them could move. Instead, he restrained himself. At least from the fucking part. For now.

He managed to drag her to the floor and pull that cursed cape from her slender, muscular body. She was next to naked under it, the thatch of neatly trimmed blonde hair between her legs clearly visible. The effect took his breath, and made his already painful erection even worse.

And she definitely wasn't wearing any panties.

On some level, he knew he should at least *try* to make it to his bed with Marie, but all he could think about was that damned sexy nest covering her sex. She was wearing some stretchy, mesh-like material that hugged her body as tightly as the unitard she favored for work. But this outfit stopped mid-thigh and obscured his view of her treasures only minimally.

He growled.

She jumped when his hands came up to span her tiny waist from his position between her legs. When he slid them up her rib cage, she arched into him and whimpered.

By the gods! She was as hot as he was.

Without another thought, other than getting inside her as quickly as possible, he captured the flimsy material between his fingers and ripped it easily from her body. She cried out and raised her hips in invitation as he pulled the remains of the garment from her. He then did what he had been wanting to do since he had first met her in that damned bar. He took a breast in each hand and buried his face between them.

Bliss! She smelled like fresh, clean air and her own personal fragrance of warm woman. It was nothing like he'd ever experienced before. And he wasn't even close to penetrating her.

Taking a nipple into his mouth, he drew on it until she cried out, pulling his head closer to her breasts. When he released her, it was only to fasten his greedy mouth on the other peak.

He stretched out over her body, settling into her curves. When she arched against him, pushing her pussy at him, seeking contact, he bent one leg, letting her stroke herself at her leisure. When she made contact, she ground her pelvis into his leg as she whimpered her need.

He knew she was close. Her breath was coming in quick pants, her lovely face was flushed, and a fine sheen of sweat covered her body. He pressed his knee more firmly into her pussy and she squealed, tightening her legs around his own.

She was coming apart for him!

NO! Not yet.

Daxon pulled away from her, trailing his tongue down her body to her navel.

"Daxon," she pleaded. "Why did you stop?"

"You were on the verge of a powerful climax, yes?"

"Fuck, yeah!" she gasped. "I was almost there!"

Daxon threw caution to the wind. This woman was his. It was time she learned that. "When you come, my dear Marie, it will be when I say and it will be for me alone," he growled. "Before this night is over, you will know you belong to me and no other."

Chapter Three

Marie should have been shocked by his bold words. She should have put a stop to everything because she wasn't even sure she *liked* Daxon right now. But, damn, the man knew how to drive her wild!

Before she could tell him he could go screw himself, he had his tongue wrapped around her clit and she couldn't remember why he should screw himself instead of her. Hell, she couldn't remember her own name when he sucked her just like *that*.

She knew his name, though. In fact, she was sure she screamed it several times as he brought her to the brink only to let her slowly sink away from the ultimate pleasure.

She clutched his head with her thighs in an effort to force him to let her come, but he only pushed her legs apart and continued his assault on her sex. Her whole world centered on his mouth, and teeth, and lips, and the way he used them with expert precision on her vaginal lips and clit before stabbing her opening with his tongue. She was wound so tight, she was trembling with the pressure inside her.

The pleasure built. She gasped for breath. Just as she was about to plunge over the edge into her own personal heaven, the growling, snarling man between her thighs stopped his sensual onslaught and crawled up her body, resting in the cradle of her thighs.

His cock, trapped between them and still encased in his pants, throbbed against her clit, and she whimpered at the sensation. It felt incredibly good, but not good enough. She wanted him. Inside her. Now.

"Daxon," she panted when he settled his weight atop her body, "if you don't fuck me right this second, I swear I'll kill you."

His chuckle sounded a bit strained, as he fumbled with his pants, but he still managed to tease her with little nips to her neck and chin as he freed his cock.

When he entered her, she screamed. The pleasure was incredible! He filled her, stretching her, every inward stroke rubbing her clit mercilessly.

She met each thrust eagerly, passionately. With her every movement and every sound, she urged him on, needing him to understand what she needed. He smelled of masculine musk and sweaty sex. She doubted she'd ever be able to get that smell off her skin. And she didn't ever want to.

As he plunged into her again and again, Marie locked her legs around his hips. Using every ounce of strength she possessed, she met each thrust with one of her own until they both grunted and panted their passion. Her orgasm erupted with the force of a thousand volcanoes and was just as hot. Her muscles seized as spasm after spasm washed over her.

She screamed.

Daxon had never been so out of control in his life. He had intended to take Marie slowly, savor her. Make her savor him. But once he was inside her, all his intentions seemed insignificant. All that mattered was giving her the ultimate pleasure, and then taking his own.

As soon as she shrieked her pleasure and her legs held him tightly within her, he spilled his seed deep inside her body. He'd never felt the need to hold a woman after sex before. Avoided it usually. But now he clung to this woman.

He'd known the moment he first laid eyes on Marie that the only place he needed her to want to be was right where she was now – in his arms. Only now that he had her there, he realized the reverse was also true. The only place he truly wanted to be was right where he was now.

In her arms.

Daxon managed to pull himself away from Marie's sweet body just long enough to finish removing his clothing. Then he picked her up and took her to his bed.

She shattered every ounce of self-control he possessed. Even now, he knew she needed rest, but he wanted her again. Which was exactly why he should leave. Put her in a guest room and leave before he did something really stupid.

Like fall in love with her.

He sighed as he pulled the covers around her before going to wash himself. Her hair fanned out around her like a silken cloud. Before he realized what he was doing, he stroked the golden strands gently. His finger tugged at a curl that teased the top of one breast, and his chest constricted almost painfully.

He froze.

Well, shit.

Looked like he'd already done something really stupid.

* * *

Marie had never been so confused in her life. She finally had a Valentine's Day she'd never forget, and forget was exactly what she wanted to do. As it was, she doubted she'd ever forget the way Daxon gave her exactly what she needed when he made love to her.

Made love to her.

That was the problem. Marie had expected a fuck. Yes, their mating had been wild and reckless, but it was more than a simple fuck. At least it was to her.

What if it *was* just a fuck to Daxon? He was her boss. The last thing she wanted was to find out that this, that she, meant no more to him than a one-night stand after a long time in space. Could she watch him pick up another woman at the next port? Could she work beside him every day and keep her feelings hidden?

No way in hell.

Well, shit.

Marie wasn't sure what to do, but she knew she couldn't stay where she was. Moving quickly and quietly, Marie grabbed her cape and left, hoping she could get her things from the *Burning Star* and find a transport off world without much difficulty.

* * *

She was gone.

Puzzled, Daxon stepped to the computer terminal in his living room. If she'd left through the door, she was still on his family's grounds and would be easy to find. If she used his planet-side gate, the computer would tell him her destination gate. Then it was up to him to locate her.

He wasn't surprised to find she had transferred back to the spaceport. She needed clothing. Dressing, Daxon stepped into the gate.

The brief disorientation passed quickly as he focused on his ship, looking for any sign Marie was still there. She had to be. He'd only left her for a few minutes. He doubted she'd had time to do much more than dress.

The landing ramp was down. Either she was incredibly careless with his ship, or she didn't intend to be there very long. He wasn't sure what her intention was, but apparently she wasn't sticking around.

A brief stab of hurt jolted through him before he convinced himself it was anger that she would leave without saying good-bye.

As he boarded, his chest tightened and he couldn't seem to get enough air into his lungs. What if their time together was a simple pass among the stars for her? Did he really want to work beside her, alone in the vastness of space for weeks at a time knowing she didn't want him? Could he stand to see her with other men when they stopped at a port?

Like hell!

She was his.

Except he wasn't sure it wasn't the other way around.

Maybe he was hers.

Her door opened at his approach. She was packing, but stopped when her eyes met his where he stood in the doorway. "You're leaving." It wasn't a question.

She looked away, nibbling her lower lip. "I need to go home. I never intended to be gone this long."

"I see," he said quietly. "Why not just ask me to take you?"

She shrugged, her back to him. "You have other obligations. If you were going my way, I'd have asked to tag along."

"You would rather go back to Earth than explore the known universe with me?" He hoped he'd kept the hurt from his voice, but strongly suspected he hadn't.

When Marie turned back to him, there were tears glistening in her eyes. "I – I can't stay with you, Daxon. I just can't."

He took a step toward her, looking at her intently, needing to see in her eyes what he felt in his heart. "Why not, Marie? We may not have spent a lot of quality time together, but you have to know I'd never hurt you."

"Not on purpose," she muttered and rummaged through another drawer. "I've made arrangements for a transport off world. I'm leaving in twenty minutes." She turned to him. "I have something I'd like you to have."

When she approached him, she held a small, gold heart on a thin gold chain. "Today is a special day on Earth. It's called St. Valentine's Day. Now, I don't pretend to know its origins, but it's celebrated as a lover's holiday." She looked directly at him, not trying to hide her feelings. "I guess I'm a bit of a romantic, but Valentine's Day has always been my favorite holiday. I've just never actually celebrated it with anyone special."

She held out her hand with the charm. "Keep this." She shrugged. "So you don't forget me."

He took the necklace, never taking his eyes from hers. She had feelings for him, he was sure of it. When he looked away from her to examine her gift, he saw that the heart opened. Inside was her likeness. His heart melted. This spur-of-the-moment gift was very personal.

"It was a gift from my grandmother. I've never had a picture of anyone I cared to put beside mine."

"This giving of gifts is a tradition on Valentine's Day?" he asked, unable to take his eyes from the tiny picture.

"Sort of. But usually only to your special 'Valentine'." She turned away to resume her packing and said quietly, "Only to someone you love."

Daxon's head snapped up. Did she just say what he thought she'd said? He smiled. If her feelings for him were that strong, getting Marie to stay was simply a matter of convincing her he loved her, too.

"Marie." Her name was no more than a murmur, but it was enough for her to stop her work again. He placed a gentle hand on her shoulder. "It is a lovely gift, and I'll treasure it always."

Marie smiled over her shoulder then closed her travel case.

"But I hope that I won't need your picture to remember you." He needed to touch her, to look into her eyes when he asked her to stay.

"Daxon, I can't work with you." Her eyes filled with tears again. "I just can't."

"And I can't let you leave me," he said as he raised a hand to caress her face. "You've given me this lovely, golden heart, but the only heart I want is here." He tenderly placed a hand just above her left breast. "You already have mine."

Her eyes widened. "What?" she whispered.

"You said you can have a 'special Valentine' on this day. I want you to be mine, but not just for one day. Forever."

Marie couldn't believe what she'd just heard. She'd been so afraid her heart would be broken that she had never even considered Daxon might feel the same as she did.

With a glad cry, she flung her arms around him and sighed with pleasure and relief as he enclosed her in his strong embrace.

"I don't know how you got so completely wrapped around my heart, Marie, but I need you with me." He sounded so sincere that Marie never doubted his words. He sounded just like she felt – relieved.

"If you want me, I'm not going anywhere," she said. "I only wanted to leave because I couldn't bear to think what happened didn't mean anything to you. I didn't want to care, but I do. I guess giving you that locket was symbolic of me giving you my heart."

"So you'll stay? We can, perhaps, enter a more permanent working, and personal, relationship?"

Marie smiled. "Yeah, I'd like that."

"Would you say we've come to an agreement?"

"Of course."

Daxon pushed her away to arm's length and stuck out his hand.

Marie laughed. No way she could let that pass. She grabbed his shirtfront and kissed him soundly.

Marteeka Karland

Marteeka makes her home in Kentucky with her brat husband and her darling son. (Or is that the other way around?) Family is her passion in life. For her "day job," Marteeka works as an Emergency Room Technician.

Marteeka has been writing for most of her life. Science Fiction has been her favorite topic since she saw her first episode of *Star Trek*. Now she combines sci-fi with Erotic Romance and feels she has found her place in the writing world.

Marteeka welcomes comments from her readers. You can contact her at mkarland@net-power.net.

My Valentine
Kate Douglas

The Legend

A priest by the name of Valentine served during the third century in Rome. Emperor Claudius II believed single men made better soldiers than those with wives and families, so he outlawed marriage for his crop of potential soldiers. Valentine, believing the emperor's decree to be unjust, defied Claudius and continued to perform marriages in secret for young lovers. For his bravery and his belief in love, Valentine, the priest, was put to death... but St. Valentine lives on.

Chapter One
North Dakota, 1918

Ginny took one last, nervous glance at the northern sky and slapped the old cow on the butt. She watched the scrawny beast trot out through the open gate with a sense of the inevitable. The chickens had already gone to roost in the small tangle of willows near the creek and the horse had been dead so long she didn't even give his skinny carcass, still lying somewhere in the back forty, a second thought.

As she turned to head back to the house, though, Ginny paused a moment to think long and hard on what she was about to do. Her gaze fell on the two graves near the old oak. One, still fresh, she would always think of with loathing, the other, dug a year ago, she thought of with a sweet pain that never left her heart.

Soon, my precious babe. I'll be with you soon, God willing.

The good Lord didn't look kindly on someone ending their own life, but with any luck, Ginny hoped He might make an allowance for her. And if not... well, she'd done all she could to make a go of it out here on the bitter plains of North Dakota.

She'd almost celebrated when Richard died of the influenza last week. She was free, now. Free to join her sweet baby boy, free to leave this world that had brought her nothing but misery.

Oh, Joel...

Richard hadn't wanted her to name the babe, the perfect child she'd held close to her heart and her aching breasts for such a brief time. Her husband's anger still burned in Ginny's memory. He'd blamed the woman who bore him a dead son, cursed her, then wrenched the lifeless little body out of her arms, wrapped it in a bloodstained blanket, and buried Joel in a hastily dug hole near the oak.

Ginny had named him Joel after a little friend she'd had in a time long ago, that almost fantasy time before her parents had died, before her uncle had bartered her to Richard Matson.

Traded for an almost-new shotgun and a beat-up mare. That was the extent of her worth. There'd not be much value at all, now. Now that Ginny Matson was all used up.

A gust of icy wind lifted the hem of her threadbare skirt. Stinging drops of rain cut through her thin shawl and she glanced skyward once more. The temperature would drop quickly now. By morning, this gray and brown landscape would be covered with ice, frozen solid. It might be mid-February, but temperatures plummeting below zero were typical for this Godforsaken land.

Ginny opened the door and took one last look at the barren log and sod cabin Richard had called their home. She'd done her best. She'd tried so hard, even after Joel's little body was in the ground, even when Richard had beaten her half to death. She'd tried, but it hadn't mattered.

Nothing mattered. Nothing at all.

She stepped inside, went directly to the wooden cupboard near the dry sink. Took down a beautifully carved ivory box that had once belonged to her father and withdrew a small, lacy card.

Tears filled her eyes, but she willed them away. No, this was not a day for tears. That day had been exactly one year ago, February 14, 1917, the day her precious Joel was born.

The same day he died without ever seeing the sunrise, much less the beautiful little card she'd made for him. Ginny stroked the finely woven lace surrounding a paper heart, a precious scrap of fabric she'd saved from her mother's wedding gown... all she had left of her mother's.

The only gift Ginny'd made for her son.

Carefully, she set the card on the small wooden table in the center of the one room cabin and propped it there, against the stub of a candle.

Be My Valentine. Ginny stroked the letters she'd drawn so carefully during the long, slow hours of labor, and smiled. Today, God willing, she'd see her baby boy again.

Wrapping her thin shawl around her shoulders, Ginny walked slowly outside, closed the cabin door behind her, and sat down on the front step to face the blizzard.

* * *

One minute he'd been enjoying the sweet song of angels and a bit of celestial cheer, the next he was slogging through a freezing blizzard on the back of a shivering white stallion.

Val glanced skyward and shook his head. What he'd really like to do was shake his fist at the Boss, but he figured He wouldn't take that sort of thing lightly.

Especially now. Not if what Val suspected had actually happened.

Be careful what you wish for...

He'd wished for love, for the chance to understand and experience the emotion, the passion and the physical, sensual side of love. Val never dreamed it would actually happen.

For whatever reason, his Lord had seen fit to release him from his vows. Val accepted the knowledge with a soul-deep certainty that left him feeling strangely empty. To have existed so long with a finite set of rules – now to have those rules changed without warning or preparation.

He sent a silent word of thanks skyward, careful to hide whatever misgivings he felt.

Why now? Now, when he was finally getting used to the lifestyle, the perfect weather, the sameness of days, always clear and warm, the sense of "otherworldliness" one felt when no longer attached to a temporal existence.

An icy blast hit him. Val shivered and hunched his shoulders against the wind. Couldn't get more temporal than this. Val hadn't been cold since, oh, around the third century. There was that icy dungeon just before Claudius had him put to death. Water running down the walls, cold blasts of wind through a metal grating. Not a particularly pleasant spot to spend his final days, though he didn't actually remember dying.

Waking up surrounded by angels... now that was memorable.

Angels who were a lot warmer than he was about now. Val glanced skyward and shivered again, almost missing the camaraderie, the fellowship and friendships he'd found over the millennia.

Powerful winds blew ice crystals horizontal to the ground. If it weren't so blasted cold, he might appreciate the beauty, the power of a storm like this, but whatever clothing he was wearing, though it was definitely better than a linen tunic, wasn't sufficient to keep him warm.

Val glanced down at his legs, covered in rough blue britches. The fabric was stiff, like the cloth used for sails on fishing boats. His coat was more familiar, made of some type of hide with fur around the collar. Wool gloves protected his hands, leather boots covered his feet and lower legs. A woolen scarf wrapped over and around his oddly shaped, wide-brimmed hat. It appeared to serve the double purpose of holding the hat down on his head and the blowing snow out of his collar.

Whatever the purpose, it wasn't enough to keep him warm, and from the look of the storm in the fading light of afternoon, he'd better find shelter, and fast.

He gave the horse his lead, figuring at least one of them would know which way to go. Val certainly didn't have a clue. He had no idea *when* this was, much less where. At least he had some idea of why, though the details weren't clear.

A blast of icy air practically lifted him off the saddle. He clamped his knees down tight and leaned close against the beast's neck.

A few moments later, the horse snorted and jerked to a stop. Val raised his head. A small building with a porch across the front stood directly in front of him, barely visible through the swirling snow. White drifts blocked the door, but at least the cabin would offer shelter.

Slowly, stiffly, Val crawled off the horse. Grabbing the halter, he led the animal around behind the cabin in search of shelter. He found a small lean-to, pulled the saddle off the large beast and led him into a protected stall out of the wind. From the musty odor, this had obviously been home quite recently to at least a cow or two.

Val couldn't find any grain, but he did find a few flakes of hay. It wasn't much, but should keep the horse happy for now. Val broke the ice on the water trough. The stallion snorted, as if just being out of the frigid blast of wind had raised his spirits.

Val spotted a heavy striped blanket neatly folded over a sawhorse, grabbed it, and covered the horse's back. The animal turned his head and whinnied, as if in appreciation.

Rubbing his hands together, Val walked once more into the howling blizzard and around to the front porch. The cabin appeared empty, cold and dark without fire or light, but with any luck he might find enough dry wood inside to start a fire. Then and only then would there be a chance to figure out what he'd been sent back for. Freeing a man of his vows, returning him to the mortal plane... neither was an act lightly taken.

Pondering the potential challenges facing him, Val headed up the stairs to the front door.

He almost fell over the woman's body. Buried in drifted snow, she slumped against the porch railing, as cold and still as an ice sculpture. Her hands were frozen, clasped around a thin shawl that barely covered her shoulders. Her eyes were closed, her dark hair stiff with sleet.

Heart suddenly heavy in his chest, Val carefully lifted the woman in his arms and carried her inside the tiny cabin. He couldn't tell if she still lived, saw no sign of pulse or breath, but finally he understood.

This fragile being was the reason he'd been yanked back to life.

Chapter Two

Her limbs were stiff from the cold, her skin like ice. Val undressed her carefully, yet quickly, uncovering a body as pale and still as alabaster. The bed in the corner was neatly made with a heavy quilt on top. He slipped everything from her slim body, including the rough cotton underthings.

He almost groaned with the ethereal beauty before him. His heart ached to think he might have been too late. With trembling hands, Val wrapped the woman in the quilt, laid her carefully in the center of the bed, and set about building a fire.

She made no sound. She didn't even shiver, just lay there beneath the cold blanket. He got a fire roaring in the open fireplace, stripped off his own clothing, and crawled naked into the bed beside her.

Foremost in his mind was the thought he'd never been naked with a woman before. As a celibate priest, the closest he'd come to the pleasures of the flesh was watching the joy in the eyes of the couples he'd married.

Already, merely from the sense of warming a woman with his own body's heat, was a new appreciation of the bond between man and woman. A sense of the wonder he might finally begin to understand.

Once more, his heart and soul choked with emotion, he sent his thoughts winging skyward.

Thank you.

Val pulled the woman close against his much larger frame. She felt like a skinny little block of ice in his arms, but before long she began to shiver. Her chilled bottom pressed tightly against his belly, but rather than make him cold, it appeared to have exactly the opposite effect.

He cuddled her closer, one arm holding her against him, his forearm across her chest, while he rubbed his other hand along her slim arm. Silently, prayerfully, he willed her to live.

He felt a tiny puff of air against his forearm. Saw, in the flickering light from the fire, a subtle flare to her nostrils. Her chest rose, fell, then rose again, though her eyes remained closed.

He discovered an unaccountable need to see the color of her eyes, then felt foolish the moment the thought entered his mind.

A strange peace stole over him, a sense of awe. Love had escaped him on that other plane, in that earlier time. He'd never imagined the chance to experience what he'd missed, the opportunity to know love.

Was it finally his turn, in this unfamiliar time, to discover what he'd only imagined? Sighing, snuggling closer to the warming body of the woman in his arms, Val drifted off to sleep.

* * *

He had to be Joel, the adorable little toddler who was standing in front of her. She was warm, warmer than she'd been in a long time, and the sweet little boy with blond curls and pink cheeks had to be her baby. He'd be exactly a year old today. Ginny reached out her hand, smiling her encouragement. The baby took one awkward step toward her, then another.

Almost there, almost close enough to hug, almost…

Cold. So very cold. Ginny's toes and fingers burned as if icy shards of glass pierced them. The baby disappeared, lost in a haze of excruciating pain, flashes of light. Ginny struggled. *Trapped!* Held captive with strong ropes wrapped tightly around her chest.

Ginny's breath rasped against her throat, thoughts whirled in a cyclone of pain and despair. She wanted her baby, needed Joel with a visceral pain that ripped her wide open and left her bleeding, screaming, fighting whatever held her.

"Calm down. You're all right. You're dreaming, but you're all right."

Ginny froze. Awareness flashed through her. All of her senses rebelled, unable to accept what her brain was telling her. She wasn't tied up, she was held in the arms of a strange man.

A strange, naked man.

Naked, hot as a pistol, and obviously very aroused.

The blizzard still whistled around the cabin. Now, though, coals glowed in the fireplace. Her dress and shawl were neatly folded over the wooden chair at the table.

The Valentine card, the one she'd made for Joel, was right where she'd left it, but next to the card was a dark brown cowboy hat on top of a pair of neatly folded pants. Worn boots rested on the floor beneath the table. A wool scarf hung to dry on the back of a chair.

Ginny's breath whistled in and out of her mouth but she was suffocating. Her lungs spasmed, her heart stuttered, stopped, started again. Who? How?

She'd been so close. First so horribly, painfully cold, then aware of the warmth stealing her life away. Taking her to her baby.

She'd almost held Joel in her arms.

Dipping her head, Ginny rested her forehead on the strong arm holding her and cried.

Muscular arms caught her close, turned her around so that her face was buried against a hard chest. Shifted her body, stroked her back, and held her while she cried the tears she'd kept inside for this last, long year.

Tears she'd held inside for a lifetime. Grief for the parents lost so long ago, for the babe who'd never drawn breath. Tears for the love she'd never known... all of it, pouring out of her in a maelstrom of grief and despair.

At long last, her body depleted and weak, Ginny felt the comforting stroke of his big hands softly rubbing her back, heard gentle words in a strange tongue whispered against her temple, felt the soft brush of even softer lips kissing away the tears.

Ginny's hoarse cries weakened, her breath rasped in her chest, and a strange lassitude entered her bones. She'd never expected to awaken. She'd not wanted to awaken, but somehow, this someone had come along and, without permission, stolen death away.

But why?

A long leg looped over her thigh, a large hand cupped her bottom and pulled her up tight against what could only be an erection. She'd never even seen Richard's, not that she'd wanted to. They'd always lain together in darkness, but she knew from what little experience she'd had in her marriage bed that Richard's male parts were nothing at all like this man's parts.

Ginny shifted her hips beneath the weight of the muscular leg pinning her to the bed and felt the stranger's chest expand in a deep sigh. She still hadn't looked at his face. Once she looked, once she saw him, she'd have to make sense of all this.

Deep in her soul, Ginny knew if she had any sense at all, she'd be terrified. Then his hand stroked her hip, cupped her bottom and squeezed gently, and thoughts of terror fled. She'd never been touched by a man before, not once. Not like this. Ginny rubbed her face against the man's chest. There was a soft mat of hair beneath her cheek and it tickled her nose. She fought a growing urge to plant a kiss on the warm flesh, an urge that made her bite her lip to keep from acting on it.

For a woman who'd set herself out to die, she suddenly felt very much alive. Having faced death, actually wanting death, she knew nothing could hurt her now.

Not even this. Especially this.

Not something so life-affirming, so completely comforting.

A strong hand cupped her jaw, tilted her head back. She closed her eyes, felt warm lips on hers, smelled the sweet scent of washed man, tasted a hint of coffee on the tongue that parted her lips.

"Oh." She'd never, not once, realized people could do that, but he slipped his tongue inside her mouth and it seemed like the most wonderful, natural thing in the world to purse her lips around his tongue and suckle him.

She heard him groan, felt the thrust of his hips as he pressed close against hers. Joined him with a soft moan of her own when the hot, hard head of his shaft rubbed against her belly.

This was a power unlike anything she'd known.

Ginny opened her mouth to his, pressed her tongue against his lips and tongue, then surged forward into his mouth. Their tongues danced, mating in the hot cavern of his mouth. Ginny heard him groan again and the sound rippled against her mouth.

Fluttered across her breasts.

Centered itself deep in that hidden place between her legs.

She thrust her pelvis forward, wanting... something. Needing... but what did she need? She knew what sex was, that painful act for making babies. Knew that Richard seemed to like it. He'd taken her once a week, always here in the bed where she'd been told to await him, to lie on her back with her gown pulled up to her hips.

Richard would make sure the fire was almost burned out, he'd douse the kerosene lamp, and when it was completely dark, he'd climb onto the bed and kneel between her outspread legs.

Then he'd stick that hard thing, that thing he called a cock, inside her and he'd pump back and forth, grunting like a wallowing pig.

The first time it had hurt and she'd screamed. He slapped her. Told her this was her wifely duty and she was not ever to scream.

Even though it almost always hurt, she'd not screamed again.

She hadn't even screamed when Joel was born, not after hours of agony. She hadn't screamed when Richard told her the baby was dead. Not even when he'd blamed her for the cord wrapped around her baby's fragile neck, leaving his perfect little body blue and lifeless.

She hadn't made a sound.

She hadn't screamed when Richard took the baby's body away, either. No, she'd cried later. There by the freshly turned earth where she'd built a cairn of rocks to cover the tiny grave.

Ginny hadn't covered Richard's.

No, she'd scratched out a shallow grave in the frozen ground, buried him in the snow, and walked away.

Then she'd planned her death.

Val wished he could read minds because he certainly wanted to know what was going on in hers. The woman hadn't said a word, not since she'd stopped crying. He'd never witnessed grief so powerful. The deep, wrenching sobs looked as if they might tear her apart. He'd felt her pain, felt her need as surely as he felt his own.

The woman stirred again in his arms and nuzzled the patch of hair in the middle of his chest. Val suspected they shouldn't be doing this, holding each other so close. It seemed wrong for a woman to allow a man the liberties he'd taken after she awoke, but the feel of that warm, feminine body so close to his, the knowledge he was finally free to experience his own sexuality, had sent blood rushing to his groin in a most spectacular fashion.

At the same time, the woman seemed to need the contact, the touching and kissing, the closeness of another warm body.

But did she need him?

Val touched her chin with his fingertips, tilted her head up, and forced her to look at him. Her eyes widened and for the first time he saw their color, a deep, emerald green. Her lips parted and he felt her breasts move against his chest as she took a deep breath.

Before she could speak, Val followed his instincts, lowered his head, and took the woman's mouth in a hot and powerful kiss. Lips melted, parted beneath his, tongues connected, danced and twisted, but this time, her body joined the rhythmic thrust of their sparring tongues.

He reached down between them, his fingers sliding along satiny skin and soft belly, finding the tangled growth of crisp hair at the juncture of her thighs. When he touched her there, movement ceased, her hips stilled. He kissed her even more thoroughly, using his tongue to sweep the inner recesses of her mouth, diverting her attention from the slow movement of his fingers gently exploring between her legs.

All the mysteries he'd heard of, the wonders he'd read about, here, within his grasp, seemingly anxious for his cautious examination. His middle finger bumped over a bit of raised flesh and the woman pressed her pelvis close. Val brushed it again, then once more, softly, slowly. From the woman's soft moans of pleasure, Val knew he'd found her pearl, that tiny jewel unique to the feminine gender.

He took her needy whimpers against his mouth as an invitation and slipped his finger between her damp and swollen lips. Her passage was hot and slick. Feminine muscles rippled around his intruding finger. He slipped in and out until the woman clenched her legs around his wrist, cried into his mouth, and shuddered.

Val felt her inner muscles tightening and relaxing in a hard, fast rhythm that left him breathing as if he'd run a hundred miles.

His cock ached, his balls ached even more, and whether it was the right thing or wrong, the woman wasn't telling him to stop. With a tiny, heartfelt prayer, he slipped his middle finger from her hot passage and slowly began to replace it with his cock.

Whatever she'd expected when the day began, it certainly wasn't this! Ginny shuddered and trembled in the arms of the most beautiful man she'd ever seen, his finger deep inside her woman parts, his breath sweet and soft against her ear.

She had no idea at all what had just happened, but she certainly wouldn't mind if it happened again. Her body seemed to have a mind all its own. She felt muscles tightening and releasing without her telling them to, and she was so damp and sensitive between her legs. It had always been so dry there when Richard shoved his cock inside. Right now she felt as if she'd been greased!

Ginny almost giggled, wondering what it would feel like if the man put something inside besides his finger, when he suddenly slipped his finger out of her.

A tiny whimper of frustration spilled out of her throat before she caught it. Just when his finger was beginning to feel really good again!

The man shifted his hips away, but before she could follow him, Ginny felt something big and round between her legs.

She held perfectly still while he brushed it back and forth, sweeping over that strangely sensitive part she'd never touched, never really acknowledged. Her breath caught with each smooth pass while he rubbed her with the silken head of what could only be his cock.

It was hard and slick. Ginny blushed hot and cold when she realized it was slick because of her! All that wet stuff that made it feel so good down there, all of that had to be coming from her body.

Ginny wanted to weep for what she didn't know. When a little girl lost her mother before she was ten, there were so many things that went unlearned, so many womanly secrets not passed on. Her first menses had terrified her. If it hadn't been for an understanding neighbor, she might have died of fright.

Her neighbor never told her about this, though!

Feeling bolder, Ginny rolled to her back and let her knees fall to either side. The cabin was growing brighter now with daybreak, though the raging storm made it much darker than it would normally be.

Still, she wanted to get a better look at him. That one, quick glance hadn't been nearly enough. Ginny wanted to see his face in the light of day, wanted to know more about the man who was making her feel so alive.

He followed her, coming to his knees between her legs. Even in the semi-darkness Ginny could tell he was a perfect specimen of a man, with broad shoulders and a powerful chest muscled and dusted with a coat of very thick, dark blond hair. She wanted to look down, to see what manner of cock he was preparing to put inside her, but instead, she looked up into eyes as blue as a summer sky, a square jaw, high forehead, and the most beautiful shoulder-length blond hair she'd ever seen on either a man or woman. It curled softly at the ends in a thick fall, a perfect frame to a beautiful face.

Like an angel.

His was the face of an angel and he'd come to her when she needed him most.

She reached up and touched the end of one long strand.

He circled her wrist with thumb and forefinger, turned Ginny's hand, and kissed the center of her palm.

Then, without saying a word, he reached down between them. Ginny followed the movement of his hand, saw his long fingers wrap themselves around that massive, muscular part of his body and guide it carefully toward her center.

Once more she felt the satiny tip against her softest parts, but he just held it there, touching her but not entering. She moaned and lifted her hips, feeling terribly wanton as she invited his penetration.

His big hands slowly gathered up her hips, clasping her buttocks, lifting her to meet his thrust as slowly, so very slowly, he pushed himself between her legs.

Ginny closed her eyes and waited for the pain.

Instead, she felt a growing pressure, a sense of fullness that was all about pleasure, about heat and passion. Hot and hard, he pressed against her. The feelings welling up inside Ginny were wanton and free and she knew that whatever she was doing must be a sin.

But no... not something this sweet and tender. There was no sin in an act so perfect, in the sharing and giving between lonely souls on a stormy night. This man's tenderness saved her life.

Now his loving gave hope. He pressed forward so slowly there was no time for pain, no reason to fear. Watching him, studying his face as he tilted his head skyward, his eyes tightly shut, his jaw clenched as if he searched for control, she knew she'd never seen anything more beautiful, felt any emotion more powerful.

He filled her, closing the gap between their bodies until she felt the weight of his balls resting against her butt and the pressure of his cock touching the mouth of her womb. The hair on his groin was darker blond than his chest, tangled close against her own deep red thatch of hair.

Looking down at their bodies so tightly linked, Ginny felt a hot rush of tenderness, a feeling of love so deep inside she thought she might cry with the beauty of it.

Linked with the feeling was one of anger, that Richard had taken something so beautiful and made it ugly. Ginny closed her eyes and put all memories of Richard out of her mind, then she tilted her hips up to receive the stranger's powerful thrust.

They still hadn't spoken. Val didn't know her name. She'd not asked his. Val wondered if that was common behavior in whatever time he'd come to, but he didn't think so. There was too much wonder on the woman's face. Too much passion in her soul.

That same wonder might be written on his own face, for all he knew. He'd never really known what this could be like, this physical act of love. Oh, he'd made it possible for uncounted numbers of couples to experience this most marvelous thing, but he'd never held a woman in his arms, never felt the slick, wet heat welcoming his cock inside, clasping him with muscles designed to birth a baby or make love to a man.

Val raised his eyes skyward. Once more he sent a quick but heartfelt word of thanks.

He moved his hips, sliding out of her woman's sheath in a long, slow glide that brought a look of wonder to her eyes. Heavy waves of hair lay tangled about her face, luminous, like dark, burnished copper in the morning light. Her skin, so pale the night before, had taken on a healthy glow, though she was still a fair-skinned beauty.

Val noticed a look of sadness about her eyes, a troubled line to her mouth, but he knew it had nothing to do with him and everything to do with why she'd been sitting, half frozen on the front porch in the midst of a blizzard.

Val leaned down and kissed her as he thrust his hips forward once more. *Later.* He'd learn all about her later. Right now, he wanted to learn more about this marvelous act of procreation.

Lips parted beneath his. A sigh whispered across from her mouth to his. Val smiled at her soft exhalation as he filled her once more, then very slowly withdrew. Her hands came up, fluttering about his shoulders as if she were unsure what to do with them. They settled finally on his upper arms, grasping firmly as if he were an anchor and she a boat tossed on stormy seas.

The woman tilted her head back, spilling copper waves across the pillow. Val lifted her hips, filling her faster now, thrusting harder. She seemed to welcome whatever he did, so he leaned forward and wrapped his lips around one of her perfect red nipples, the one that had been calling out to him since she'd rolled to her back.

Her cry startled him, the sharp, strangled gasp when he suckled her into his mouth. Her back arched and once more he felt her stiffen, felt the tightening of her inner muscles. This time, though, it was his cock in the silken vise, not his finger.

Dear God, to think he'd gone his life without this knowledge. How could he have neglected what his body was obviously designed for? How could God have allowed it!

His anger evaporated as quickly as it peaked. God didn't allow it. He, Valentine, had chosen the vow of celibacy of his own accord. God had freed him of that vow. God had sent him here, to this perfect woman.

Once more Val sent a word of thanks heavenward. At the same time, he stilled all motion, unwilling to spill his seed so quickly. He concentrated instead on the texture of the puckered nipple caught between his lips. Sucking hard on first one breast, then the other, he nuzzled the firm flesh in between until he found the control he'd been searching for, then once more thrust his cock inside, going hard and deep.

This time he knew there'd be no stopping. He filled her, sliding in and out, the woman's muscles clenching, grasping, trying to hold him, finally catching his sensitive cock on a particularly penetrating thrust. His lips lost contact with her breast. He arched his back and pushed forward, pounding into her, burying himself completely as he tilted his chin to the heavens and cried out.

Fire raced through his veins, an electrical storm more powerful than the blizzard still blowing outside. The woman arched against him, her mouth open in a soundless cry, her muscles clenching, holding, milking his seed.

The coil of heat and energy that had been waiting in his balls burst from the end of his cock, filling the woman, leaving him empty and strangely exhilarated.

Exhausted but fulfilled. Complete in a way he'd never experienced, never understood or even dreamed of. Val only knew, if he ever had to explain this most amazing sensation, he would have to say heaven paled beside it.

Paled beside the woman lying in his arms, her eyes wide open and watching him with a look of pure amazement.

Chapter Three

It might have been awkward, greeting the dawn beneath a man who had just shown her the true meaning of ecstasy. Even more awkward, knowing how he'd found her, near death by her own desire. But somehow, his touch, his compassion, his gentleness as he'd shown Ginny what her body was capable of, left her feeling warm, replete, and totally at ease.

He held his weight off of her, resting with his elbows at either side of her shoulders, his cock still buried deep inside her body. The tiny muscles she'd never known existed still clenched and released with a rhythmic pattern she found more than seductive.

She might have been shy. Now she felt bold. Looking into his warm smile and brilliant blue eyes, Ginny knew a depth of love, of emotion that brought tears to her own eyes.

She reached up and touched the harsh line of his cheek, ran her fingers down to his full lips and pressed lightly, as if feigning a kiss. "Thank you. How do I ever thank you?"

"No, the gratitude is mine." He leaned close and kissed her. His lips were soft, not demanding as they'd been earlier. Soft and loving, like a benediction.

"I was alone in the storm, lost and in need of shelter. I have found shelter in your arms. Warmth from your heart. Love in your bed. It is you who must be thanked."

His accent was unusual. He spoke as if this were a second language to him. She found each word, each nuance, intoxicating.

He leaned close and kissed her chin, her throat. Her lips. He spent a long, long time on her lips. When he raised his head, she was once again breathless.

"Why?" He pushed himself away from her, leaving her feeling empty and bereft. Then he twisted around and, before she realized what he'd done, was sitting with his back against the rough-hewn headboard of the bed and she was tucked against his chest, her butt resting firmly in his lap.

"Why what?" She knew, though. Knew exactly what he asked.

"Why did you sit out in the storm? Why did you want to die?" He ran one finger along her cheek and she realized there were tears in his eyes. "Why would you want to give up on life?"

She dipped her head, unwilling to look him in the eye, but he deserved an answer, no matter how painful. "One year ago today, I gave birth to a perfect baby boy. He was born with the cord around his neck and he died. It was my fault. He was perfect except for what I did, birthing him. I had no reason to live."

"Ah... to lose a child." He stroked her face, ran his finger along her throat, across her shoulder. "I cannot imagine the pain, the terrible grief, even though this accident was most certainly not your fault. But, there will be others. You will have more babies."

She shook her head. "No. No more. My husband tried to get me with child. None came. He died last week of the influenza. There was no reason to keep trying, no reason to live. That's why I waited out in the storm. I wanted to go to Joel."

"Joel is your husband?"

"No. Joel was my son. My husband, may he rest in hell, was a mean, hateful man who did his best to beat me to death before he died." She pulled away from him. "I'm sorry. I shouldn't speak ill of the dead, but..."

"No matter. He is gone. What is your name?"

She laughed. It felt so good to laugh. To think she'd had the most glorious night of her life with this man and he didn't know her name. Nor did she know his.

"My name is Ginny... Virginia Walker Matson. And yours?"

"Val. My name is Val. Short for Valentine."

He left her sitting there with her mouth hanging open and walked across the small room to the fire. The coals burned low and he added a few pieces of wood. They caught immediately, flared up, then settled into a good, steady burn.

Even in the pale light of the new day, his body gleamed, strong, healthy, so sensual he made her mouth water. She'd never known such feelings, so many desires. Too much, too soon. Would he stay? Would he leave her once the storm ended? Leave her alone with nothing but memories, alone with the grave of her lost child, the grave of the man she despised... alone with her desire for death and the peace of never after?

He turned to walk back to the bed, paused by the table, and reached for the card she'd left there. The card she'd made for Joel. Ginny's heart twisted, almost stopped when he picked it up, read her carefully printed greeting.

When he raised his head to look at her, she could have sworn his eyes sparkled with tears. "When did you write this?"

She bowed her head. Not embarrassed, just terribly bereft. "When I was in labor. It was St. Valentine's Day, the day my son was born. The day he died."

"St. Valentine's Day? What... I've not heard of that day."

"It's a day for lovers. February 14th... I'm not sure if it commemorates the saint's birthday or his death, but it's a day when lovers exchange cards and gifts." She scooted up in the bed and leaned against the headboard, watching him. He looked sweetly perplexed, a half smile on his face, his perfect body caught in a pose reminiscent of a child receiving a wonderful treat.

He turned to her then, his face no longer childlike. No, he looked like a man who had made a huge decision, a man determined to get his way. The kind of man to make a woman weep with wanting, to make her body tingle, her breasts ache, that private place between legs grow damp with joy.

How she knew this, how she understood the depth of her need, was as much a surprise to Ginny as the need itself. She didn't question it. She merely pulled the blankets aside and made room for this amazing man.

He slipped into bed beside her, pulled her into his arms, and hugged her as if she were the only thing keeping him alive. Held her in a passionate, loving embrace, so close she felt his heart pounding against her cheek, felt the rush of blood in his veins, the rush of air in and out of his lungs.

"Dear God, let me stay with this woman. I need her. Don't make me leave."

His prayer, heartfelt as it sounded, frightened her. She raised her head and cupped his cheek in her palm. "Why would you leave me? Please, I want you to stay. You give me hope. I..."

She couldn't say she loved him, could she? Even though she knew the feelings bursting in her heart must be something more than mere passion, more than the physical act that had bonded them during the night.

He kissed her. Slow, dark, and dangerous, a kiss that curled her toes and frightened her at the same time. "I don't want to leave you, but my Master..." He sighed. "My life is not always mine to control."

She knew she must look like a fool, staring at him, mouth slightly open, eyes wide with confusion, with need. "You can't..."

"I..."

He faded in front of her eyes. Wavered like a cool fog, his form going misty and bright. Ginny held her hand out to touch him, to hold him close but, like the morning's frost when the sun rises, he was gone.

She gasped, cried out, then fell... down, so far down, until she was merely a breath of air falling, twisting, floating, a bit of thistledown on the morning air.

* * *

"Valentine, what I offer you cannot be undone once chosen. You may return here, to dwell forever in Paradise. You may join the woman in what is probably one of the most inhospitable spots on this world. If you join with her, you will once more embrace mortality. You will live out your years and grow old. You will die and once more return to me, but it will be a long, possibly painful journey."

"But it will be a journey shared?" Val squinted against the glow surrounding the Master. "I'll have Ginny beside me?"

He sensed, more than heard the laughter. "Ah, yes. She will be beside you... she and your progeny."

"Children? We'll have children?"

"She is with child now, Saint Valentine. She carries your daughter."

"Send me back to her. Now."

Again, Val was almost sure he heard laughter. "Your wish is my command. Be happy, grow old with your true love. I'll miss you... Happy Valentine's Day, Val."

Suddenly, Val was back in Ginny's bed, holding her chilled body in his arms. He glanced across the room and realized the fire had gone out. He looked once more at Ginny and saw the path of dried tears on her cheeks.

"Ah, Ginny, my love. What's wrong?"

She blinked, as if coming awake after a long, hard sleep. "Val? I saw you dis..." She blinked again, shook her head slowly. "Val, where did you go?"

He thought a minute of telling her the truth then changed his mind. "Out to check on my horse," he said. Val hoped the horse was all right. He had no desire at all to leave Ginny's bed. At least not in the foreseeable future.

Val took Ginny in his arms, took her lips, her soul, her very being, into his heart. There would be no going back, no desire to return to Paradise, at least not now, when he held Paradise in his arms.

"I love you, Ginny. I know we're practically strangers but I do love you. I promise to be good to you, always to love you. Will you be my wife? Will you carry my babies? Will you be my Valentine?"

My Valentine. Ginny glanced toward the card on the table and said a gentle good-bye to Joel. Then she looked at the man holding her so close. In the past twenty-four hours she'd gone from despair to hope, from the depths of pain to a lightness of being she'd never before experienced.

All because of this man. Whatever it was about him, whoever he was or wherever he came from, she knew he was her anchor, her savior, the one she needed most. She reached up and cupped his beautiful face with her palm, smiled, and kissed him full on the lips.

"Yes. Yes, I will be your wife. I will carry your babies, should we be so blessed. I will love you, now and forever. I will, now, always and forever, be your Valentine."

Kate Douglas

Wonderfully talented, whimsically perverse, and always the consummate professional, Kate Douglas has been lucky enough to call writing her profession for over thirty years. She's produced ad copy for radio, flown over forest fires in a spotting helicopter as a photojournalist, drawn a weekly comic strip for a worldwide health agency, co-authored a cookbook and written numerous freelance articles. She's won three EPPIES, from the international authors' organization, EPIC – two for Best Contemporary Romance, and a third for Best Romantic Suspense. Kate's also won EPIC's Quasar Award for Cover Artists.

She and her husband of over thirty years live in the northern California wine country where they find more than enough subject material for their shared passion for photography, though their grandchildren are most often in front of the lens.

Visit Kate at www.katedouglas.com.

Changeling
Shelby Morgen

Chapter One

Carefully – very carefully – Arien circled the Human, staying just out of his reach. Human. Elf. Whatever he was, he was definitely male.

He thrashed about, trying to break loose.

Mine.

He was hers. All hers. She'd caught him, fair and square, clamoring about in her woods on St. Patrick's Day. Now all she had to do was *keep* him. Her wings flapped so fast she might have been mistaken for a hummingbird. Damn. That always happened when she was frightened.

Or excited.

In this case it might be a little of both. She wanted to get a bigger – er, better – look at him, but he was *just* not cooperating. Here he was, this perfectly fine specimen of male, laid out all naked before her, and he was fighting her! Didn't he know *anything*? Most males would give their wolf teeth to be caught by her.

Which was exactly why she didn't want them.

But he wasn't most males. He was big, and powerful, and if he kept flailing about like that, he might actually *hurt* her.

Well, she didn't know if he was big in Human terms. That was hard to judge when you were only five inches tall. But he was much bigger than she was, that much was for sure.

One arm thrashed about again, nearly breaking free this time. Quickly she aimed a bit of her magic at it. There. Just a little bit more Fairy dust – well, Fairy silk, to be accurate – and he was locked back in place.

Now. What to *do* with him?

No use to have caught him if she couldn't mount him. She certainly couldn't do anything with him this big. As long as he fought her, there was nothing she could do about their size ratio. Rules were rules. He had to give his consent before she could change him.

He had to kiss her.

She'd tried. But every time she got anywhere near his face he started flailing about again, despite the Fairy dust.

Well, there were no rules that said she couldn't make him wish he'd kissed her. A slightly malicious smile settled across her tiny face. She could feel it turning the corners of her mouth up in a wicked grin. *All right, big guy. If I have to be frustrated and horny because you won't cooperate, so do you.*

With no sense of remorse, Arien dug into her pot of Changeling magic.

* * *

"I don't believe in magic."

Looking back, that was probably the stupidest thing he could have said, seeing as he was in a pub in Ireland on St. Patrick's Day. But at the time, the simple statement seemed nothing more than the truth.

It all started when he sat down at the bar in the local pub to order an Irish Stout. The bartender's smile looked friendly enough as he pulled Mich's beer, but Mich could tell the man was giving him the once-over.

"You'd be the new tenant on Fairy Hill, I'm guessin'."

Mich nodded. That hadn't taken very long. "Michael. Michael Matthews." That would be the end of that discussion. Now they'd all clam up and treat him like he was some kind of evil corporate espionage guy. Or worse, try to sell him something he didn't want.

"So, what brings ya to Glencolmcille, Michael Matthews? Old family in these parts?"

Mich took a deep draught of his beer, not sure whether to be pleased or offended. The name obviously meant nothing to the bartender. "I'm not chasing ghosts, if that's what you mean. On vacation, you might say." Which was the truth, in a manner of speaking. He needed one – badly – and this was as close to a vacation as he was likely to get.

No reason he couldn't combine the two. A working vacation. What more could a man ask for? All expenses paid, two months to travel across Ireland, at his own pace, evaluating local breweries and drinking beer. This beer was a prime example. A strong, peaty taste to it, with a deep, dark tint like liquid amber. "Good brew. Local?"

"Oh, aye. From just down the road a piece."

Well. That was vague enough. "Good flavor to it."

"Aye. There's a bit o' the Fairy magic in that one, there is."

Mich laughed. "I don't believe in magic."

The room fell silent, even the constant clatter of glasses and bottles coming to a standstill. "You what?"

"Fairies. Wizards. Banshees. Leprechauns. That's all well and good for children's tales. But we're adults. We're well past the ages of Santa Claus and the Tooth Fairy. I don't believe in magic."

"And ya' rented the cabin on Fairy Hill?"

The silence broke, the room erupting in laughter. A bit unnerving actually. As if everyone else knew the secret handshake and he didn't. No one ever laughed at him. For the most part, people didn't *talk* to him, unless it was to say "Yes, sir. Can I get you anything else?" But here, at this little pub in the back end of nowhere, the rules had changed.

Fairy Hill? "Yeah, that's the name of the place. So what? Everything around here's got a Fairy name."

"Did ya no' think there might be a reason for that?"

How did one answer a question like that without getting assaulted? *Tourist Trap* popped into his head, but he held the words in check with more restraint than usual. Probably not the answer these locals were looking for. "Didn't pay much attention to the name. It was the only cottage for rent in the area."

"Aye. Well there's a reason for that, too." The bartender laughed again. A friendly laugh, from a friendly face. Something Mich was not precisely used to. "Drink up, and I'll tell ya a story."

So it was, Mich did something he almost never did, being a professional and all. He drank the rest of his mug of beer. And followed it with another.

The bartender pulled another draft of Irish Stout. "Time was, long ago, Fairies ruled this land. But they were only interested in the bits with the strongest magic, ya see. Men knew where they could build their houses and till their fields, and they stayed away from the Fairies' lands, sort of by mutual understanding. So the Fairies and the Humans lived together on the same island we call Eire, neighborly like.

" 'Tis no secret what happens when a man steps over the boundaries of Fairy. Fairies are a wee, small folk, but that doesn't mean they're harmless. Many a man's wandered into Fairy and never been seen again.

"Still, as the Human population of Eire multiplied, what with being fruitful and all that, the Fairies found their wee bits of land crowded up against, and hemmed in. The Fairies didn't often take much notice of Humans, and when they did, 'twas not often a good thing. The King's Court met, and they decided to leave Eire, for the magical island of Tir na nÓg, and have nothing more to do with Humans."

Somehow, Mich found a second mug of this local brew in his hands. Or maybe it was the third. He'd rather lost track. In any case, it was definitely a tasty draft. Well worth investigating further.

"The Queen's Court, however, disagreed. They thought without their influence, we Humans would become dangerous, threatening the balance and harmony of the lands. So they split, the King's Court leaving for Tir na nÓg, and the Queen's Court going into hiding here in Eire.

"Now the Fairies from the Queen's Court mostly did fine without the men, as women mostly do. But every so often, a Fairy Maiden gets lonely. With none of her kind about, she has naught to seek for company than a Human. Many a young man's wandered into the forest and been caught in a Fairy's web, never to be seen again. Those who come back have a different way about them."

Fairies. Riiiiight.

Apparently the locals had downed a few too many Irish Stouts. Still, it was a mighty tasty brew. Worth another, in fact. Just to be neighborly. And – just to be neighborly – Mich nodded, and smiled. Damn. Needed to do that more often. His face didn't quite remember how.

"Séamas O' Riley was one of those who wandered off. He was gone for some time, was Séamas. When he came back, he built the cottage up on Fairy Hill. By day he tilled the fields and tended his few head of cattle, like any man does. But by night he wandered the forest, lookin' for something he'd lost, but would always remember. Touched, the local women folk named him. Touched in the head w' the Fairy magic.

"Some time after Séamas built his cabin, a son appeared at his side. He'd no wife, mind you, or any other women folk who might have gifted him with such. He made no explanation of the boy. But as the boy grew, everyone could see he was a Changeling. A boy born of Fairy magic, with a touch of the Fey in his blood.

"Mostly the Changeling children wither and pass on once they're separated from the Fairy magic, but Séamas had been touched, you see, and his Changeling son grew to a man, and in time the Fairy son married, and his wife bore him a son, as is the way of things. But always those of that line had a touch of the Fairy magic. The last of the line moved to America a long, long time ago, so now the cabin sits empty, waiting. Many a man's rented that cabin and walked the forest at night, hoping to find what Séamas found. Whether he does or not, a man's not likely to say."

Three – or was it four? – mugs of this fine local brew was enough to loosen Mich up a good bit, but not enough to turn him into a fool. He swallowed the scoffing laughter that threatened and grinned broadly instead. "Well, that's a fine story. Almost makes a man want to take a walk in the woods."

The locals laughed first, so it was all right to laugh with them, though not, perhaps, for the same reasons.

So it was, Michael Matthews, acquisitions manager for Fulson Microbreweries, found himself wandering about on Fairy Hill in Ireland on a balmy moonlit St. Patrick's Day evening. A tad tipsy, Mich was, with more beer in his blood than he'd consumed all at once in many a year.

Perhaps *blundering about* might have been a better description. He seemed to have blundered directly into a patch of spider webs. He stumbled, trying to break free. More of the wispy, sticky stuff appeared, clinging to him, until he couldn't raise his legs off the ground. The harder he tried to break free, the worse things got. Now one arm stuck as well. Next the other.

Mich struggled against the bonds, but all he did was wear himself out. His left arm broke free, but whatever had him stuck it down again before he could free anything else.

Think, Mich. Think.

It was awfully hard to think with bugs flying around his face, damn it.

Bugs. That was the clue.

The bug didn't exist that could trap a man in its web. Maybe in the Congo, but not in Ireland. A dream. That's what it was. A dream brought on by too much beer and a bartender's story. Mich tried to sort out the pieces of the evening. He'd left the pub and that delicious golden brown beer and wandered up the hill to his little cottage on Fairy Hill. Decided to go for a swim in the lovely little pond in the woods. Then when he got out of the water he couldn't find his clothes. He must have fallen asleep. That was it. Yeah. If he just lay still for a few minutes, the world would settle back in place again. He let himself relax, flowing with the dream.

Chapter Two

"Wake up! Ya must kiss me."

Ummm. Some dream.

"Just kiss me. Is that so hard?"

Well, it was his dream, after all. Maybe in his dream strangers – female strangers with a wee bit of an Irish brogue – flew up to his lips and buzzed those words against his skin.

Right.

"Kiss me, damn it!"

The tiny voice sounded annoyed. That, at least, was familiar.

Mich was a cautious man by nature. He wouldn't normally have complied with such a request had it come from a woman of his acquaintance, let alone someone he didn't know and couldn't even see. It wasn't that he was opposed to kissing. But kissing led to other things, like sex, which, though he rather liked sex, led to other things.

Like alimony, and child support. Something three out of five of his business partners were now saddled with, along with new sources for kissing and sex. Along with college tuition payments that would last well past their plans for early retirement, which had now gone out the window.

Beer was easy to understand. Beer rarely needed much more than a taste or two to fully comprehend. Beer...

Had probably gotten him wherever he was now, and in whatever condition he was in, where an invisible woman with a fuzzy, aggravated voice wanted him to kiss her. So much for cautious.

"Damn, I must've used too much. Ya were no' supposed to pass out on me, just quit flailin' about like an Ogre." Something small and soft bounced off his eyelid. "Wake up! Ya must kiss me. It will no' work unless ya kiss me."

What the fuck? What wouldn't work? Who was she? *Where* was she?

" 'Twas you who came looking for me, are ya rememberin' that? Why did ya bother if ya did no' want to change? Ya wanted an interview for the local rag mayhap? Are ya going to kiss me or no'?"

Came looking for her? Damn, he didn't remember looking for anyone. He'd only had – how many beers had he had, anyway? Two? Three? at the most. So why was he lying here on the – ground? He checked. Yes. Definitely dirt, and plantlike things. Not grass. Leafy things. The ground, in any case. This could not be good.

She bounced off his eyelid again. That was it! He flung it open.

"OUCH!"

Mich turned his head to see where the voice was coming from. Then he shut his eyes again. No. Not good. When he opened them, she was still there. All five inches or so of her, nursing what was apparently an injured wing.

No, definitely not good. "Look, I'm really sorry. But you were bouncing on my eyelid. Are you okay? Please tell me you're all right."

"All right? *No,* I'm no' all right. Ya broke me wing!"

Oh, God. He *was* an Ogre... "Is there anything I can do? Help set it or something? If you'll just let me loose..."

"No! I do no' want your help. Look where that's gotten me. You *broke* me wing! Get yourself free, why don't ya? I hope ya lie there and rot."

Unbidden, the bartender's words came back. *Fairies are a wee, small folk, but that doesn't mean they're harmless. Many a man's wandered into Fairy and never been seen again.*

No. He didn't believe in magic.

Now she was crying. He often had that effect on women. "I'm really sorry. There must be something I can do to help."

"Oh, aye. Like I'm to trust *you* to help me." She spread her wings experimentally, then winced in pain, curling into a pitiful little huddle. "I canna' even fly!"

"I can't fly, but I rented a car. There must be others of your kind who could help you. I can take you to them."

"No!" she shrieked. "I'll no' be lettin' ya touch me. I do no' want ya anywhere near me. You *hurt* me!"

"I can't touch you. I'm all tied up, remember? Look at you. You're shivering. You're probably going into shock or something. At least come over here and curl up against my shoulder where you'll be warm."

She looked down at her decidedly blue skin – maybe part of that was her natural coloring? He couldn't be sure – and sniffed loudly. Another shiver wracked her small body. Yup. No doubt about it. She was cold.

Creeping closer, that angry, petulant look still on her face, she pressed herself against the curve of his shoulder. At least she'd quit crying.

"Is there someone who will miss you? Come looking for you if you don't show up by a certain time?"

Her tiny body convulsed, and the tears came back like a waterfall. "No. They'll all just be figurin' I got lucky, and found a Human who wished to mate with me."

Oh, good grief. *This* was why he was single. He had a rare talent with women. If there was a wrong thing to say, he could always find it. It wasn't as if he'd rejected her. He simply hadn't been able to see her.

"Don't cry," he pleaded. A woman's tears always made him feel big, and clumsy, and awkward, like an oaf, and now he really was an oaf. He'd broken her wing, for God's sake.

She turned around and kicked his shoulder. Hard. Well, as hard as a five inch tall whatever she was could. "Oh, aye. And what'll ya do if I cry? Break the other wing?"

"I'd feel really, really bad. I already feel pretty bad. I never wanted to hurt you. I wish there was some way I could fix this."

"Well, you can no' undo what you've already done," she sobbed, turning to huddle against the warmth of his skin. "Nothing can fix it. It's broken. *I'm* broken."

A fresh flood of tears assaulted his senses.

Kiss it and make it better.

Now where the hell had that thought come from? A half-smile quirked his lips. He hadn't heard that expression since his mother had passed on.

Kiss it and make it better.

Sometimes he thought he could still hear her, whispering advice to him. Surely she'd have had a thing or two to say about this situation.

Michael. Are you listening to me? Kiss it and make it better.

He shook his head. *Ma?*

What?

Ma, is that you?

Of course! Who else would it be? Now kiss the little woman.

Ma, you're dead.

So?

You're dead, and you're still giving me relationship advice?

Quit arguing with me, Michael.

Ma, go away. I'm naked!

What does that have to do with anything? I've seen you naked before, young man. I changed your diapers. You're all covered with spider webs anyway.

Maaa...

Michael Morgen Matthews, I am appalled by your behavior. You hurt this woman. The least you can do is apologize.

Well I was trying to do just that when you interrupted.

You're gay, aren't you.

"What? What makes you think I'm gay?"

"You're gay? Well, why did ya no say so? What were ya doin' out on Fairy Hill on St. Patrick's Day? Or did ya think we might have another sort o' Fairies to offer ya?"

"I'm not gay!"

"Honestly, Mich, I don't understand why you couldn't just be honest with me. I'm your mother. I would have understood."

"You can no' lie to your mother, Mich. They always know."

"You can hear my mother?"

"Hear her? Aye. Why would I no'?"

"Why wouldn't she be able to hear me?"

"Well, because you're dead, Ma. You seem to keep forgetting that part."

"How in the name of the Fairies can she be dead? She's standin' right here."

Mich blinked – and blinked again. His mother was, indeed, standing right there, next to the broken blue Fairy. She, too, was about five inches tall. Oh my God. This had gone from sexy dream to worst nightmare scenario *way* too fast. "Ma, tell the nice Fairy you're dead."

"Well, I'll give him that one, honey. I am dead."

"Thank you. Now, where the hell did you come up with this gay idea, Ma?"

"You're forty-two years old, you drink beer for a living, and you've never even had a steady girlfriend. Why couldn't you just tell me you're gay?"

"Ma!" Mich fought for the patience he'd called on so often during the last five years. "You left out an important point there. Michelle?"

"Michelle? Who's Michelle?"

"My wife."

"His wife."

"Your *wife*?"

"Ex-wife," they answered in unison.

The little Fairy cupped her head in her hands. "I'm getting a headache."

"Tell me about it."

"You poor dear!"

"Ma – is it all right if I call you Ma?"

"Of course," Ma agreed. "What is your name, dear?"

"I can no' tell ya my true name, but you may call me Arien."

"Arien. Such a nice name."

"Thank you. Ma, tell me, if you would, why are ya so sure Mich is gay if he was married to Michelle?"

"I forgot about Michelle."

"You forgot his wife?"

"Michelle was very forgettable."

"Ma – Ma was having some – problems. With her memory, before she died."

"That's why ya weren't dating, isn't it, Mich? After Michelle?"

"Yeah. Pretty much."

The Fairy bonds holding him down disappeared. As he sat up, his clothes reappeared in his lap. Turning away, he pulled on his shorts, then sat down cross-legged next to them on the forest floor. "Thanks."

"Ma, if you're dead, why are ya here?"

"Mich brought me here."

"Mich? Do ya always haul your dead mother about with ya?"

"Mom died last winter. I brought her ashes to scatter into the ocean here. It was a promise I made her."

"You're from Glencolmcille, Ma?"

A wistful look passed over his mother's little pixie face. "My grandmother was. She always talked about how beautiful Ireland is. I never got the chance to come while I was alive. So Mich brought me here now. He's a good boy. He's always taken care of me. Ever since his father died…"

The little blue Fairy glanced up at him, a look of understanding and sympathy on her face. "I'm thinkin' we better get ya back to the cottage on Fairy Hill now, Ma."

"Perhaps that's not such a bad idea," Ma greed. "I am a bit chilled."

Tugging on his shirt, Mich held out a hand, and both of the wee creatures stepped into his palm. He slid them side by side into his breast pocket, where their heads and shoulders just stuck out the top, and their tiny little bodies pulsed gently against the thin cotton.

Not the end to the evening he'd planned, he thought as he trudged up the hill. Not the end at all. He'd been looking forward to a vacation in Ireland with no responsibilities. Instead now he had two. But then, he was used to responsibilities.

Tomorrow he'd deal with how his mother got to be five inches tall and alive again. Or at least vocal. For tonight he wrapped her in a washcloth and tucked her into the bed in the guest room he wasn't using.

"Good night, dear."

"Good night, Ma. Sleep tight."

"Kiss it and make it better," he heard again as he gently closed the door behind him.

Right.

He settled the Fairy with the broken wing onto the pillow next to him as he undressed again and slipped into bed. Carefully, feeling like a fool, he leaned over and brushed his lips against her broken wing. "Sleep tight, little Fairy. I really am sorry about your wing. Good night."

"Good night, Mich. You're a good man."

He laughed. "That and three bucks will get you a mug of beer."

Chapter Three

Heat.

Long, smooth curves of woman flesh, molded against him.

An arm thrown carelessly around him, the hand draped against his chest as if it were accustomed to doing so. A soft cheek turned and resting against his back.

It was still dark out, the dawn still hours away. God. How long had it been since he'd woken up like this? This was better than sex. This was... intimate.

There was only one problem.

Who the hell was she?

Mich tried to shift, just a little, without disturbing her, in the hope that once he saw her face, the night might come back to him, and he'd remember who she was, and how he got here, because otherwise he had no clue. The arm was lithe, well muscled, but still soft to the touch, neither fat nor thin, but some place in the middle, as if it belonged to a woman confident enough not to starve herself to fit some measure of corporate appeal.

Shifting was probably not the best course. The body the arm was attached to shifted with him, and the hand stirred, tracing down his chest toward the cock that had suddenly remembered the joys of morning sex.

"Good morning."

The voice was thick and sultry with morning desire, tinged with an Irish accent. Oh, Lord. He was in trouble. He'd never been able to resist a deep, throaty voice, and this one just bubbled with sex. He swallowed, twice, trying to find his voice, then gave up when her hand closed around the hard, swollen throb of his cock.

"I see parts of ya are glad I'm still here."

"Ummmmm." He rocked his hips gently into a lazy thrust against her fingers. "Almost all of me."

"Almost?"

"There's this one nagging little voice that keeps telling me I need to check on my mother before she burns the house down..."

"She's gone, Mich."

"Gone?"

"Fairy dust. She's with others of her own kind, now. She'll be well taken care of."

He wasn't sure exactly how he felt about that. He'd said his goodbyes months ago, and he hadn't exactly expected her back. Especially since she was dead. Still...

Fairy dust?

Fairy dust... Fairy dust would presumably come from a Fairy. A tiny, bluish creature with a broken...

Yesterday evening came crashing down on him. But that arm, and the hand currently stroking his cock, did not belong to a tiny creature. It was harder to panic with the tips of her fingers brushing along the curves of his balls.

There was a reason he didn't pick up women in bars, beyond AIDS and other STDs. He'd done a few stupid things in his youth – what young man hadn't – and the morning after was always... complicated.

The woman who lay beside him uncurled to raise up on one elbow, her silken hair falling across his arm and chest as she looked down at him. His skin caught fire everywhere she touched him. Not to mention the fact that his dick was about to explode from the slow, steady pressure of her questing fingers.

He ought to reach for her hand. Make her stop, before he did something he'd regret – they'd both regret – later. When the complications set in. Instead he slid his hand up the length of her arm, across the curving surface of her shoulder and neck, to where he could sweep the hair back from her face.

Laughing blue eyes smiled down at him from an angel's face. Oh my God. This was his five inch tall Fairy? He was definitely going to have to eat more Keebler's stuff. He pulled her head down to kiss her, taking his time, licking her lips with tiny swipes of his tongue before he sucked her bottom lip between his teeth.

It had been so long…

The tiny tip of a tongue stole out to meet his, sending electric shocks of desire from his lips to his cock, searing everything they touched along the way.

"Oh, gods!" He felt the shudder pass through her. "It's been too long, Mich. Way too long. I have to have ya, Mich. Now. Right now. Fuck me!"

His cock nodded in approval as he – she – they – swung her astride his hips, the point of his cock hovering below her slick wet heat. "Oh, crap. I haven't got anything for protection. Quit carrying those things in my wallet when I got married. Thought I was beyond needing them."

"That's all right. Ya don't need protection with me. We don't get Human diseases, nor can we pass them along."

"What about – could you get pregnant?"

"Oh, aye. 'Twould be my fondest wish." She said it like she cherished the idea. Her clever fingers wrapped around his cock again, rubbing him against her clit, her face a straining grimace of pleasure so strong it might have been taken for pain. "*AAAAaaahhhhhhh.*"

With a strength he'd earned working his way up through the company, hefting boxes and unloading trucks and making deliveries, he captured the Fairy-woman and rolled, pinning her beneath his weight. "You want to get pregnant? What am I? A suitable sperm donor?"

Her hands unwound themselves to touch his cheeks, her smile bold and possessive. "Aye. You're a Human. A gorgeous one, at that. I'd say you've a touch of the Fairy in your blood, as well. I chose you because I thought you'd make an incredibly good lover. And yes, I want a Changeling child. But more than anything I want to feel your cock buried to the balls in my pussy."

Which was exactly what he wanted as well. But…

"We have a saying here – *Cé aige a bhfuil a fhios nach dtig deireadh an tsaoil roimh mhaidin* – who knows the end of the world won't come before morning. Sometimes you don't need all that care and planning, Michael Matthews. Fuck me."

Hooking her heels over his shoulders, he plunged his cock into the welcoming heat of her wet pussy, burying himself until the pressure of his balls trapped against her ass made him stop. The tip of his cock sat throbbing against the entrance to her womb, as if panting for breath. Dear God she was hot. Tight. It had been much too long...

Leaning forward between her legs, he swiped the tip of his tongue over an upthrust nipple, fighting not to come from the sheer joy of each almost forgotten sensation as she wriggled against him, mewing in protest. "Ohhh," she moaned, stretching to raise her hips, her vaginal muscles trying to pull him in even deeper, her hands clutching at his hips. "Mich..."

"Yes? Tell me what you want."

"Anything. Everything. Fuck me!"

Capturing her hands, he held them in his, their fingers laced as he pulled out of her, waiting until only the very tip of his cock remained trapped within her folds before he reversed direction, then rammed back in hard enough to shake the bed frame. She moaned and twisted beneath him, as if fighting for something she wanted, needed, but couldn't name, gasping for breath as she gripped him with muscles that fluttered, then clenched.

Again, and yet again, he thrust into her, pulling out slowly, so slowly, trying to put off the final rush of sensation he wanted as much as she did, wanting to make this moment make up for all the others, the opportunities missed, the years that had gotten away...

The rhythm pulled at him, demanding more, demanding faster, harder, demanding *now*. *Slow* lost in the battle to *more*, to *now*. Her body started the rhythm. Squeeze. Pulse. Or maybe it was his. Thrust. Pull. In. Out. Harder. Hotter. Faster. He caught a jiggling breast in his mouth and sucked, her scream as she shattered around him part of the rushing, pounding rhythm in his ears, like the surf on the rocks at the shore. In. Crash. Out. Suck. Wet bodies pulling and twisting and battling for release.

She screamed again as she arched up under him, her hips slamming against him, her pussy clenched like a fighter's fist around his aching shaft as he struggled to maintain their rhythm. He laughed as the pleasure that was nearly pain broke over him, his seed spilling into her in hot waves which made the precious last few thrusts fast and slick despite her clenching muscles. With each thrust their coarse hair mingled, abrading the delicate skin on his balls, pulling more from him than he'd thought he had left to give.

He let go of her breast, despite her small cry of protest, only to find the other one, sucking once before he bit, just a little harder than he'd intended to. Her delicate body jerked under him, her neck pressed back into the pillows.

As the white light of the most intense orgasm he'd had in years – maybe in forever – faded to the dull glow of a passing sunset, her legs slipped down over his arms. Their fingers unwound, but their bodies only settled more tightly together, their gasped breath coming in long, measured pulls that shared the same fading urgency.

The soft light of pre-dawn teased the edges of the curtain, dusting the thin fabric with a hint of lilies that would appear faded, later, but looked fresh as the morning now.

How much time did they have? He wanted to ask, but didn't dare, for fear he'd remind her she should be someplace else. Instead he stroked her skin, pushing the hair back from her face, comparing the ways in which the Fairy and the woman were the same. Her skin was soft as a butterfly's wing. Her hair fell like silken cords across his hand, smooth and silky and ready to bind him to her will once again.

He didn't believe in magic. Didn't believe in love at first touch. Didn't believe there was good in this world meant for him. She couldn't be real. Any moment now he'd wake up alone. Because that was the way of things. He was destined to be alone. He'd discovered that years ago as he watched the fates slowly take away everything and everyone he'd ever loved. That was the way of things.

He believed in beer.

A fine comfort that was on a cold winter's night…

It defied all logic, went against everything he knew and every sense he trusted in, but he wanted to ask her to stay, to be real, to be here when he woke up in the morning. Wanted – desperately needed – the magic that lived in Fairy wings.

Mich reached out to trace the line of her cheek with his fingertips, and she turned her face into his palm, kissing the spot where his lifeline faded into his wrist. By all that was holy, he wanted her to be real. He almost offered a prayer to a God he no longer believed in, an offer of penance for services missed and blessings he'd not taken the time to be thankful for, if only she would stay.

A nagging little voice warned him it was wrong to offer prayers he didn't expect to be answered. She was magic. The magic of St. Patrick's Day. But she was here now, and she was his, and he'd not waste another minute mourning for what he hadn't lost yet.

Studying her face in the soft light, he memorized the curve of her lips, the ridge of her brow, the line of her nose. He leaned in to kiss each part as he took down its shape. Her eyes – incredibly blue eyes, even by the pre-dawn light – fluttered open again to smile up at him.

With slow, languid strokes he caressed every inch of her skin, following his hands with his mouth, worshiping, kissing, touching, arousing. She giggled when he licked the back of her knee, laughed when he traced the outline of her navel, gasped when he slowly circled the swelling bud of her nipple, licking his way to the top and back down again in a slow, lazy pattern designed to provoke.

The first time had been all about sex – about getting naked and getting off and have-to-have-you-right-now. This was different. A journey of discovery. This was about making memories that would last a lifetime. When he left her nipples behind and moved to her thigh, she tensed, then spread her legs wide, offering him access to whatever he wanted.

What he wanted was to make her shake, and tremble, and moan with sweet, languid desire. She fulfilled that wish. She tasted of woman and musk and of him as he kissed his way up her thigh to the pussy that called to him. He'd never tasted himself before. Somehow it felt right that the first time his tongue found the taste of his own cum it should be on the lips of her pussy.

Funny. Much as she liked to complain, Michelle hadn't ever said anything about that. She'd just discreetly waited till he was "asleep" and snuck off into the bathroom to clean herself up.

Of course he'd never gotten up to find a washcloth, as he did now, and coax tepid water from the fresh awakened pipes, carefully wiping her clean, and spreading a towel over the wet spot on the sheets.

Morning would be here soon enough, and somehow he knew she would fade with the sun. He wanted to hold her forever, trapping her here in his arms. Surely if he held her, touched her, she couldn't disappear.

Another thought occurred to him. She might only be St. Patrick's Day magic, and St. Patrick's Day might only come once a year, but it came every year.

Could he wait an entire year to have sex with this beautiful creature again?

What difference did it make? He'd waited for years already. He'd found her. He'd be back. Next year they'd start earlier in the day. Long, slow, lazy kisses trailed up and down her thighs, over her hips, across her belly, creating a picture of her every curve and burning it into his mind.

Perfect. So perfect.

It was her turn this time, rising up to lower herself over his hungry cock, rocking forward to kiss him, letting a breast dangle within his reach. She cried out when he sucked the nipple as far into his mouth as he could take it, tonguing the stiff peak with soft, lingering strokes.

Sensing her urgency as it built once again, he feathered his fingers through the soft blue curls on her mons, then slipped his fingers between her folds above where he split her, spreading her open so he could watch as his cock emerged, then disappeared again with each rock of her hips. He touched her, caressing her, exposing the small hooded organ to his gaze and his single flicking fingernail.

She gasped with each flick, her vaginal walls contracting around him, as though desperately seeking release.

It pleased him to make her wait.

Harder, faster, she rose, slamming herself down now against him with each thrust, yet helpless to drive herself over the edge as he slowly, methodically built the intensity with each caress to her clit.

It was fire – the slow burn of banked embers consuming dry tinder, building once again to a roaring blaze. It was want and need and raw passion layered together until he didn't know where one stopped and the other began.

When he could stand it no longer he pulled her down over him so her breasts grazed his chest with each pass, sending her surfing over his body, riding the wave, thrusting hot and heavy into her. He lifted her hips, up and back, pelvis rising, cock trembling, the need so intense his lungs threatened to burst when he drew in the long, shuddering breaths that sustained him.

Who knows the end of the world won't come before morning...

There was no tomorrow, no more putting things off for another day. He wanted. He needed. Now.

"Now!" she cried, as if reading his mind. "Now, Mich. Now!"

Like the waves on the rocks they broke together, the surf pounding high, the sea spray a taste that washed them away, until they lay panting together on the cool sandy beach.

Slowly the room returned... a small bedroom in a quaint old-fashioned cottage on a hill in Ireland. A place where a man who'd worked his way up from a boy stacking boxes in a warehouse after school could never have imagined himself. The place itself was magical, and more than he'd any right to expect out of life.

No woman – no human woman – had ever matched him so perfectly. Therein lay the problem. She wasn't human, was she? She wasn't even real. She was magic, and he didn't believe in magic.

A man who had worked hard with his hands all his life held a small piece of magic in his arms, and closed his eyes, knowing he'd no right to ask for more. Her words kept echoing in his head. *Who knows the end of the world won't come before morning.*

"You're poetry," he whispered against her neck. "The song I wanted to write. The words I wanted to say. The picture I wanted to paint. And when morning comes again and you're not here, I know you'll have taken something from me I'll never get back. You own my soul, little one. You own my soul..."

"Find my name, Mich. Find my name and hold it close to your heart, closer than anything, and I'll come back to you."

"Find your name? How? Where do I look?"

"Find my name, Mich. Another did, long ago... it was the only other time I changed, instead of the mortal one."

The mortal one... Séamas. Séamas O' Riley, from the bartender's story. For Séamas she'd become human, as she was now, rather than spiriting him off to Fairy. If Séamas could find her name, so could he. If it could be done, he would. "I'll be back," he promised. "Once I know your name, I'll be back, little one. Then nothing will keep me from you."

"I'll be waiting, Mich." She snuggled tight against him, her Fairy tears cool against his chest, and he held her clasped as if the strength of his embrace could keep her there past the dawn...

Chapter Four

Michael Matthews ran a hand through his graying hair, waiting as calmly as he could for the barrister to finish his spiel. Six years. Six years it had taken him to pull this off. Now the minutes ticked by like hours while he waited. He was a patient man, but not that patient. St. Patrick's Day was fast slipping away.

He came back to Glencolmcille and Fairy Hill every year now on St. Patrick's Day, the one day a year she could come to him. It wasn't enough. Nowhere near enough, though it was more than the boy from the wrong side of the tracks had any right to expect. But he'd grown bolder. Learned to expect more. Every year he'd searched frantically for some clue, some hint of her name.

Nothing.

But now it would be different. Now he was here to stay.

As of today he owned Fairy Hill.

Mich smiled as he thought back on the meeting he'd had the first of the month – his last official act as acquisitions manager for Fulson Microbreweries. He'd turned over his keys and copies of all his files and reports to Fulson himself.

Fulson – the son, not the man he'd worked with for more than three decades – stared at the paperwork in bafflement. "What's this all about?"

"Simple. I quit."

"You can't quit."

"I just did."

"But – but – you can't just walk away from here, Matthews. You've never worked anywhere else. You know you can't do this job for anyone else, either. You signed a non-compete clause with us. You're not a young man anymore, Matthews. You're forty-eight years old. Who's going to hire you?"

"I know how old I am. I got to be this old working for this company. I know my way around, and I know what I've signed. I have every right to sell my stock in the company. It's my money I'm taking back. Call it an early retirement if you will. Besides, with you as the CEO, this company won't be here a year from now. Your father was a good man. I miss him. Goodbye, Fulson."

And just like that he'd walked out the door.

It felt damn good, looking back. Felt good knowing the investments he'd made had paid off, and he could do any foolish thing he wanted to.

Including buying a house on a hill in Ireland, overlooking the ocean. Including spending the rest of his days walking the woods, looking for Pixies and Fairy dust if that was what he wanted.

And he did.

He was a careful, planning sort of man, was Michael Matthews. He'd had years to think about this. Yes, to the rest of the world it might look foolish, but if he never tried, he'd never know what he might have missed. Even if they were to have just one day a year together from now until the end of his time, it was one day he wouldn't spend without her.

"Congratulations, Mr. Matthews. Your deed will arrive by post in a few weeks. You are now the owner of the parcel of land, with cottage, known as Fairy Hill in Glencolmcille. Part and parcel, all current fittings and furnishings to convey with the land. Will ya be keeping the name, Mr. Matthews? I'll need to know for the records."

"The name?"

"Buying a place is rather like a marriage. Not all follow the old practices. Some change the names, some don't."

A smile lit Mich's face, an even bigger smile than the one he'd conjured when he walked out of Fulson's. He knew how to find her rightful name. Had all along, if only he'd thought of it.

"Mr. Matthews? Don't you want –"

"I don't need anything, thanks. I've got it all."

"Mr. Matthews? Your keys?"

Mich laughed as he swept them up, almost running toward his brand new Mini. He went over it all again in his head on the drive to Glencolmcille and Fairy Hill. He couldn't be wrong.

He barely took the time to park the Mini before he ran to the woods. "Arien! Arien, I'm back," Mich shouted. "I'm here!"

Something small buzzed in his ear. Once he'd have swatted at it. Now, he cupped his hand, tilting up his lips to offer his kiss.

"Sure and it took you long enough, Michael Matthews. Have you been drinking again?"

"No. Not yet. Though I'd love to tip back a pint of Irish Stout with you at the pub someday. But not this afternoon. Right now I want you in my arms."

His Fairy, it seemed, had other plans. "Here and you've left me waiting and worrying over you for hours and now you think I'll just fall into your arms? Oh, I think not, Mich Matthews. If you want me, you'll have to catch me!"

With that she buzzed away on hummingbird wings, careful to stay in sight if just out of reach. It might have occurred to him he was being led where she wanted him to go, but he knew her by now, trusted her with all his heart. If she wanted to lead he would follow. He laughed as he reached for her, dodging trees and following her deeper into the forest than he'd ever ventured before.

So it was, he paid little attention as he blundered headlong into a patch of Fairy web. He turned, twisting in the mass, opening his mouth to protest, only to watch helplessly as she blew a handful of Fairy dust into his face. The last thing he saw as he tipped slowly to the forest floor was the pleased grin on her face.

"Clothes!" With a flick of her wand, Arien made his clothing disappear. There. Much better. Another flick of her wand spread his arms far to either side, binding his wrists with Fairy web. One more and she'd straightened his legs, spreading them slightly and anchoring them tight to the ground.

Make her wait, would he? Oh, he would pay.

She wouldn't tell him how the fear had coursed through her all morning, how the dread had finally claimed her. This time he wouldn't come back. He was mortal, after all. She'd known one day she would lose him. But not today. Not this soon. Not yet.

Then she'd heard his voice, his blessed, lovely voice, and she'd known he was all right. The relief flooded in first, and then the anger, and now the resolve. He would pay for every drop of fear that had leaked from her body.

"Awake!" She knew him now, knew just how much Fairy dust to use, knew just the right tone to bring him back. His eyes popped open at her command.

"Arien? What…"

"Shhhh." She marched across his chest to stand on his shoulder, her wings fluttering helplessly. By the gods, just the scent of him still got her excited. She shivered in delightful anticipation. "Kiss me."

His first kiss was still as shy and awkward as it has been that very first time, as if she were too fragile for his big, clumsy, human lips. She loved that about him. That and so much more.

The change came swiftly now, bringing with it the rush of delightful anticipation, flooding her pussy with the warm rush of juices meant to welcome him into her tight, lonely passage.

But not yet. First he must pay. And this she would enjoy very, very much.

"Ya know 'twas wrong to tease me so, making me wait half the day for your coming."

His eyes sparkled with anticipation. "I am sorry. Forgive me, Arien."

"Ya don't look sorry. I think I need to punish you, so you'll no' make such a mistake again."

His mouth pursed into a thin, straight line of a frown, but his cock jumped to full attention. "Punish me? How?"

"I could walk away and leave ya here to wait for the Fairy webs to fade. Ya might find your way out of the forest by morning."

"You wouldn't."

"And why wouldn't I? Have you no' heard the Fairy Forest is a dangerous place, Michael Matthews? Many a man's been known to disappear in these woods."

"You wouldn't, because I can see from here how your pussy weeps for me. You've captured me, Fairy, fair and square. I'm your prisoner. Does that turn you on? Do you like having so much power over me?"

She giggled. "Aye. I think I do."

"You captured me years ago, Fairy. I've always been yours – you may do whatever you want with me." His voice dropped to a low, seductive tone, melting her heart. "I love you, Fairy."

A fierce, possessive jolt stole through her, the way it did every time he said those words. "And I love you, Human. But that will no' spare you your punishment."

"And how will you punish me?"

"I shall leave you just as you are, while I do as I please with ya."

His cock bobbed again, the veins standing out prominently, and a small drop of glistening pre-cum leaked from the tip. "Ummm. I'm *soooo* helpless. Do what you will with me, *Mistress*."

She laughed again, knowing he was enjoying her game. With a flick of her wrist she summoned a tiny bottle of Fairy oil. Unfortunately, the spell didn't compensate for her decidedly larger form. The tiny bottle was smaller than her fingernail. Still, it would contain several drops of oil... She warmed the small bottle between her palms, breathing hot air over its miniature surface.

She wouldn't need much. He raised his head to watch as she tipped the tiny bottle. The first drop fell, almost in slow motion, to land exactly where she wanted it, the warm oil splashing off his left nipple to leave the dark skin wet and shiny. The second drop she let roll down his right nipple, then below, slowly dripping toward the light covering of hair just below her target. The third, and last, landed in his navel, filling the tiny cavity like a little lake, the tide lapping at the shore as he shuddered.

The subtle smell of warmed cinnamon filled the air. He closed his eyes, the veins on his arms and neck popping as he fought *not* to fight her. Standing with a foot on either side of his waist, she bent, until her nipple touched his, guided by her touch, spreading the oil in a circle around the tight, glistening bud.

A harsh, needy groan stole from between his tight pressed lips as she repeated the nipple to nipple contact on the other side, this time marking him with an X. The friction of his nipple against hers felt so good she palmed both breasts, rubbing them back and forth over both sides at once.

"Fuck. Are you trying to kill me?"

"I do no' think you can die from this, mortal."

His cock jumped against her ass as she lowered herself to press her pussy against his lower chest. Sliding down, she rose slightly, then pressed close again, trapping his thick, burning cock between their bodies.

Oh, yeah. Right there.

She rocked back and forth, rubbing the ridge of his cockhead over the sensitive nub of her clit. That would do for a while. Especially since it made him moan and twitch beneath her, his hips raising greedily, trying to force his cock into her.

She wanted him. Oh, how she wanted him. Almost as much as she wanted to make him wait.

Lower. A little lower.

Now his balls rested against her heated folds, and the third drop came back into view. She bent down to lick the oil from the skin where it had spread around his navel. Once, then again, then spearing the tip of her tongue into the cleft.

"Oh fuck. Jesus fucking Christ. You are trying to kill me, aren't you?"

He needed a ring, like many Fairies wore, for her to play with. But since he didn't have one, she stretched up to lick his nipples.

He tossed so violently under her she feared the Fairy web might break, but it held. She licked, licked again, then sucked the hard bud into her mouth. He writhed under her, twisting and turning, trying either to get away or to force the small brown nub farther into her mouth. She wasn't sure he knew which he wanted.

The blatant signs of his arousal and excitement were more than she could take. Moisture flooded her pussy, along with a screaming ache only he could fill. Spreading her thighs wide, she opened herself up to him, sliding down over the smooth, slick heat of his engorged cock.

Yes. Oh, yes. That was what she'd wanted. Needed. Waited an entire year for.

She rode him, but he was in control now, setting the rhythm, pounding up into her hot and wild, driving her over the edge almost instantly, then taking her back time and again.

She fought to maintain her hold on him, sucking first one, then the other nipple, and finally whatever piece of skin she could find, needing the feel of him, the taste, the closeness only this man could give her.

Too soon it was over, her cry of both pleasure and loss splitting the afternoon air of the forest as she shattered around him for the final time, taking him with her. Spurt after spurt of hot, searing seed pumped into her, filling her, drenching them, feeding the fire in her that wanted more, more, always more.

As if by magic the Fairy webs fell away, loosing arms that tangled around her, pulling her closer, while his cock trembled within her, pulsing with aftershocks.

"By the gods I've missed you," she cried, burying her face against his chest to hide her tears. "I'm a coward, Mich. I have no' your strength. I die each time ya leave me, and I do no' live again 'til you're back in my arms."

"I won't leave you again, Arien. On that you have my word."

"What? Do no' tease me so, Mich."

"I know your true name, Fairy. I've come here to claim my prize."

No. He couldn't. It was impossible. A trick of the elders, to prevent the mating of mortal and Fairy. No mortal since Séamas O' Riley had known her true name. Surely he couldn't...

He rose, setting her on her feet before him, then dropped to one knee in front of her. "Say you'll marry me and be mine, and take the rightful name of Mrs. Michael Matthews."

That wouldn't work, would it? No. Too simple. All she had to do was choose... could it be so simple?

"Marry me, Fairy. Take my name. Stay with me. I will love you to the end of my days, and beyond. When you scatter my ashes over these cliffs, I will return to you in Fairy, as my mother has. I will come home, to be by your side for all eternity."

Too perfect...

She fell to her knees beside him, kissing whatever she could reach as the tears fell from her eyes. "Yes. Yes, it has to work. I'll take the true name of Mrs. Michael Matthews, as is the way of your people."

"Does that mean you'll marry me?"

"Oh, aye, Michael Matthews. That I will. But we must do it today, before the magic breaks. Do ya think we can find a priest who'll agree to perform the ceremony on such short notice?"

"That we will. There's a priest waiting for us in the church in Glencolmcille."

"And how did ya manage that?"

"Cell phone. I've learned to live by your advice. I don't put anything off till tomorrow any more. *Who knows the end of the world won't come before morning.* If it does, I won't care, as long as you're by my side. I love you, Arien."

"As I love you, Michael Matthews. As I love you."

Shelby Morgen

Shelby Morgen loves writing off-beat tales that defy as many rules as possible. She likes chocolate with her peanut butter, Suspense with her Romance, and kink with her sex. She's always had a hard time keeping Science Fiction and Fantasy from mixing with her kink. Fortunately for Shelby, electronic publishing has opened many new doors for cross-genre authors and artists.

Shelby shares her belief in electronic publishing with her long time friend and partner, her husband Bill.

For more about Shelby's world please visit www.ShelbyMorgen.com.

Elven Enchantment
Willa Okati

Chapter One

Days like this were enough to make a girl wish she batted for the other team.

Men! Ciara ignored the noise of the bar to pick at the label on her bottle of imported beer, shredding the edges with her short-clipped nails. No polish; just a thin coat of gloss. Most men weren't worth the spit to shine your shoes with. At least, not the men she'd had the misfortune to date.

Most recently, Paul.

She growled under her breath and tore off a strip of label. Men like Paul could drive a woman to drink. That – that moron, Paul. Sweet as honey when they first met, but with a Madonna/whore complex to end all Madonna/whore complexes. He'd told her she had no imagination in bed, even that she was frigid, but she found out later that he'd been going straight from her to Hooker's Row every time they slept together.

Just today, she'd thrown the pictures the private detective had taken into Paul's face and told him to go fuck himself. Then she changed her number and headed to O'Dougal's, the best – okay, the only – Irish bar in her area.

It was St. Patrick's Day, and when better to pay the place a visit? She *liked* O'Dougal's, although it would never win any awards for class. All dark woods and dim light, with folk singers and occasionally a Celtic band. Things went on in that bar that wouldn't see the light of day in any other bar – God, the hookups she'd watched – but they always had a booth available for someone who needed it, and the best beer in bottles or on tap that she could want.

She took a sip and muffled a slight burp behind her hand. So she'd wanted a bottle tonight. Not as classy as a glass with a head of foam, but hey, what did she have to worry about with class? No one else here cared. She could sit in her corner booth in the near-dark, drink herself silly, and call a cab to take her home to her lonely bed. And that's just what she planned to do.

The Irish band tonight was on a break, quaffing down ale at the bar. The way they were going, she'd be surprised if they had the cognitive ability to go on halfway in tune. A rowdy little college-age gang, they had a nice enough hand with the fiddle and the *bodhran*. They were all too young for her, though, even if she had been looking.

Other people in the bar worth noticing? Well, there was a woman with long, curly blond hair, hanging on a nicely dressed man's arm. She was tottering on stiletto heels and wore more makeup than a trowel could shovel on, but he didn't seem to care. Ciara made a small disgusted noise. Probably like one of those ladies Paul had seemed to go after so much.

Two women sat at a table, eagerly discussing something. Looked like young businesswomen out for a night on the town. They'd flipped over the paper placemat and were scribbling frantic notes on it. Ciara watched them with interest. At least they seemed like they were having fun.

She was a people-watcher. Always had been. It served her well in her job as a secretary at the law firm. She could tell the good clients from the bad ones. Her bosses relied on her intuition.

Too bad that same savvy sucked when it came to dating.

She took another swig, finishing the bottle. Right on cue – another reason she liked O'Dougal's – the bartender waved at her and sent a perky little thing over with a second icy brew. Ciara passed her a five. After thought, she gave her a fifty – what the hell? – and said, "Keep 'em coming. When I can't count how many bottles are on the table, call me a cab."

"Man troubles, sweetie?" the barmaid said sympathetically. "Work got you down?"

Ciara sniffed into her sweet, sweet beer. "That rotten loser," she said miserably. "Why I ever trusted him…"

"Man troubles." The barmaid poked a pencil behind her ear and pocketed the fifty. She jerked her thumb back at the bar. "Not that I'd be interested while I was in your situation, but you should check out the floor show."

"I've been listening to the band."

The barmaid giggled. "Not the band." She pointed again. "*Them.*"

Ciara followed her finger to a dark corner of the bar. Her mouth fell open a little. Two men, each one a hunk of the highest order, wrapped around each other like white on rice. Mouth to mouth, they kissed as if they'd eat each other alive starting from the lips and moving on down. Hands roved over backs and down to gorgeous, tight asses in leather pants.

"Whoa," she said faintly.

"Ain't that the truth?" The barmaid grinned. "Men get hot thinking about two women. So women get hot thinking about two men."

She wasn't wrong. Ciara could feel her nipples starting to pucker as she stared at the men. One light, long and lean, wearing eyeliner and a shirt halfway unbuttoned, showing off a ripped chest. The other taller and stockier, dark, with big hands that looked like they knew what they were doing. From the way Blondie humped against him, Ciara guessed that they did. Both men wore their hair long, sweeping their shoulders and blending together in a curtain of blond and black.

A shudder of excitement washed through her.

The barmaid grinned at her. "I just knew that would catch your eye."

More than my eye. Ciara wriggled a little, trying to ease the sudden pulsing between her legs. God, but they looked hot together.

"You enjoy the pretty action, hon. I'll keep the beer flowing."

"Yeah," Ciara said absently. "You do that."

Okay, so she might have to revise her opinion on all men being good for nothing. At least these two were pretty. Too bad they looked like they were only into each other. Her pussy was starting to ache from wanting a taste of Blondie – and hell, a sample of Mr. Dark and Delicious, for that matter.

"And Paul called me frigid," she muttered into her beer. "Look at me. Getting off on the gay action. That's me, all right. One wild and crazy girl."

Who talked to herself. Wasn't that the first sign of madness? Or being drunk? She hadn't eaten anything all day, so the beer might be hitting her harder than usual. But it tasted so good, washing down her throat in cool bursts of flavor.

She rounded her lips around the neck of the bottle, still staring at the two men. She couldn't look away. Tilting it back, she took a wonderful, icy sip. Mmm. There was something else she'd rather have her lips on, and she knew it.

Stupid Paul. The one time she'd tried to go down on him, he'd pushed her away. Said he didn't want that from her. And to be frank, she hadn't made an issue out of it. Oral sex, not so much her thing. Besides, he was a little – she snickered, able to admit it now – on the small side. *Overcompensating much?*

But she knew her way around a man's cock. College life had taught her how to please a man. You just had to put your lips together... and blow.

She laughed again. Maybe a little too loudly. At the bar, Blondie and Dark startled apart from their passionate embrace and turned to glance at her. She colored deeply, flicking her eyes down – but not before she saw Blondie give her a leer and a wink. Saw Mr. Dark's lips curve into a smile.

"I'm not just kinky, I'm a pervert," she muttered to herself, tearing off a fresh strip of label. The table was getting messy. "But hell, why not? Enjoy it while you can."

"That's always been my philosophy."

It was Ciara's turn to jump. Sliding in across from her, confident as if he had every right in the world to be there, a short and ugly man wearing a horrible green bowler hat gave her a grin. He had his own glass of beer, and used it to gesture at the men. "Nice scenery, huh?"

Ciara gathered her dignity. "Look, I don't know who the hell you are, but I so don't feel like company. If you don't get out this second, and I mean *now*, I'm calling the bouncer over."

He held up both hands. "Easy, easy! All I'm sayin' is, you're not the only one gettin' into the floor show."

Despite herself, Ciara glanced up through her lashes. Still standing at the bar, Blondie and Dark were at it again, Blondie lavishing kisses down Dark's neck. Dark had his head thrown back, and his fingers threaded through Blondie's hair, as if he were in ecstasy. Their groins rubbed together, gyrating in a slow dance.

Fuck, but it was sexy.

Ciara wriggled again. Then she gave herself a good mental slap. No staring at the pretty men. Focus on the toad. He was still sitting across from her, grinning. "Knew you liked it," he said smugly.

"Listen, you," Ciara said, angry over having to deal with yet another man who didn't seem to understand plain English. "Get out of my booth. Or I'm not kidding, I'll have you out of here on your ass."

"So defensive. Got all those walls built up inside, don't you? Can't let them down." The man took a swig of ale. "Now, take those two. While you're not watching them, they're watching you."

"They're what, now?" Ciara's head shot up. Sure enough, Blondie and Dark had stopped their heavy petting and were gazing at her. Hands wound together, hips joined as if fused, but giving her heavy-lidded looks that promised sex better than chocolate and a whole lot more.

"I happen to know them. They're into each other, but they like a little pussywillow, too, you know what I mean?"

Ciara tore her gaze away from the men, which wasn't as easy as it sounded. "Listen, you –"

He cut through her anger with an offer that went straight to her… well, it wasn't her heart. "Take it easy, I keep telling you! You want a piece of that? Want to be the filling in that sandwich? All you've got to do is ask."

Ciara eyed him suspiciously. "And who are you to say so?"

"Me? I'm a leprechaun. And okay, no rainbow, but it's been a gray St. Patrick's Day for you and I figured you could use a pot of gold." The man winked at her. "It's all yours, if you wanna take it."

Ciara looked down at her beer. "I – I –"

She glanced up. Her lips parted. The man was gone. Vanished, like he'd never even been there. "What the hell?" She craned her neck and stared around, but no one in sight even vaguely resembled him.

She gave a shiver. Okay, that was definitely odd. But... what if he'd been telling the truth? Half-shy, she looked up at the men.

Blondie was staring at her, his lips quirked in a smile. He ran his hand down Mr. Dark's chest, tweaking one nipple through his shirt, and grinned at her. Mr. Dark didn't lower himself to a smile, but gave her a look that smoldered. God, he could set her on fire with those eyes.

As if he already hadn't. Her panties were growing damp. "Kinky," she said to herself. "I can do kinky. Stupid Paul. He'll never know what he missed out on."

Taking a last, final draught of her beer, she gathered all the courage she could scrape together and slid out of her booth. Walking over to the men at the bar seemed to take ages, but then she was there, facing them down. "I saw you staring," she said, her voice low. "See anything you like?"

"A great deal," Blondie said. "An unhappy lady, in need of a little affection."

"Take that hair down," Mr. Dark said in a voice like silk and sex. "I want to see it spilling over those pretty breasts of yours."

She colored and drew back, abashed by his bold words despite her determination to go for the kink. "No, no," he chided. "Here, let me do it." He reached out for her with those long, strong hands and gently undid the pins holding her hair in its knot. Unbound, it scattered across her shoulders and down her chest in a riot of flame-colored locks.

Mr. Dark gave a soft, satisfied noise. "There. Isn't that better?"

Ciara turned a little darker. Damned Irish complexion.

"Such green eyes," Blondie murmured. "Like jewels, they are. Little hearts of the ocean."

"She's a pretty thing," Mr. Dark murmured, reaching out to run a hand through Ciara's hair. "You've been watching us, little one. Enjoy the show?"

Kinky. Remember the kink. Ciara straightened her spine. "Yeah," she said brazenly, "I have been. You guys are hot together."

Blondie laughed. "Can't be denying that. But a woman like you, now... that's the sort of woman who needs a little action herself."

Ciara faced him down, green eyes meeting startling blue. "Why? Are you offering?"

Both Blondie and Mr. Dark laughed at that. "Would you take us up on it, if we did?" Mr. Dark wanted to know.

Ciara frowned. She reached past them, aiming for one of their forgotten glasses of ale. She took a deep swallow that left foam on her lip. "I –"

"Ah-ah-ah," Mr. Dark said. "Let me get that."

He lowered his mouth to hers, tongue tracing away the beer and teasing at the seal of her lips. With a soft moan, she opened to him. His tongue slipped inside her mouth, stroking gently. Behind her, she could feel Blondie nuzzling into the crook of her neck.

Being the meat in a man-wich was something she'd never done. But damn if it didn't feel good. The scrap of silk between her legs was soaking, they'd gotten her so hot. When Mr. Dark drew back reluctantly for air, his hand replaced his mouth, stroking her cheek. "I think this is the one, Seanan," he murmured.

Blondie – Seanan – lifted his lips from her throat. "I think you're right, Ardal."

Mr. Dark – no, Ardal – reached down to caress her breast, cupping it in one hand. She glanced around quickly, afraid that the barmaid might be watching, but no, she was busy with other customers. With the other hand, he caught her fingers and squeezed them gently. "Are you interested, little one?"

"It's Ciara," she said breathlessly. She knew she was ten shades of red, but she was an inch away from rubbing herself against Ardal like a wanton kitten. "And yeah, I'm up for it."

Frigid? She'd show Paul *frigid*. Out with the Madonna, in with the whore. And it felt *good*.

Something wicked made her reach down to cup Ardal's erection through his pants, hard as rock and twitching as if it knew how much she wanted it. Wanted it in her. "I think you're up for a little action, too."

Ardal bent down for another kiss, this one a little hungrier, more demanding. He tore his mouth away to whisper against her lips. "Then close your eyes. Seanan, take us back to the room."

Seanan bit gently on the smooth nape of Ciara's neck. "On our way."

Ciara shut her eyes. She felt a strange sensation of whirring, and then –

Chapter Two

"What the – how the hell?" Ciara blinked.

The smoke and noise of O'Dougal's bar had vanished in an instant, leaving behind only cool silence. When she opened her eyes, she saw that she, Ardal, and Seanan were alone in a vast room filled with softly cushioned chairs, vases of crimson roses, candles, and a bed... she swallowed. A bed more than big enough for three, draped in white linen, with hangings forming a canopy.

Ardal smiled at her. "Do you like it?"

"Like it?" Ciara stared around. She swallowed. "It's beautiful." *And made for seduction.* "But I don't remember leaving the bar. How'd we get here?"

"You don't remember?" Seanan's voice was teasing as he knelt at her feet. She realized that she sat in one of the plushest chairs, her sweater contrasting like a pauper's rags against its velvet richness. Come to think of it, she looked like a poor relation next to Ardal and Seanan in their leather and silk.

She crossed her arms over her breasts. "No. I don't."

"Ah, it'll come back to you," Ardal soothed. "Come, now. Another sample of what I tasted before." He bent to her, pressing his lips against her own. Despite her state of surprise and mild alarm, Ciara couldn't help herself. She moved back against him, her hands coming up to caress the silk of his shirt, to touch his chest through it. As his tongue swept her mouth, thrusting gently in and out, her core began to pulse in time with the rhythm. *Oh... oh, yeah.* This was why she'd come with the two men. They were sex, pure sex, on legs. And she wanted some of that. *Ugly little gnome with the bad hat was right,* she thought hazily.

Ardal drew back and reluctantly swept her bottom lip with a thumb. "Not so fast," he murmured. "Time for more, soon."

She gazed at him with wide eyes. "Really soon?"

He laughed. "Yes, little one. Really, really soon."

"My turn now." Seanan nuzzled one of her knees.

"You're too far down."

"Am I?" His eyes sparkled at her. "Bend to me."

Well, why not? Ciara leaned over, her hair falling in a curtain around their faces as she touched her lips to Seanan's. He raised up to meet her, eagerly clasping her cheeks between the palms of his hands. And oh, God, he moved like a master, his tongue just as skillful as Ardal's. "I can taste you both together," he whispered. "It's like nectar."

"And you know from nectar?" Ciara replied in a breath of a voice.

"I do." He laid one last kiss on the corner of her mouth, then sank back on the balls of his feet. "I want to see more of you, sweet lady. Will you let me?"

Remember the bar. How sexy these guys were, all over each other. How she'd wanted a taste of that. "Yes," she said bravely.

Both men laughed. "Such bravado!" Ardal sounded fond, but not at all patronizing. "Seanan, show her what you mean."

"With gladness." Seanan drew one of Ciara's feet into his lap. He studied her lace-ups, then turned to Ardal with a disappointed frown. "Sneakers."

"Nothing's wrong with those."

"But so clumsy, so heavy."

"You pay too much attention to the shell."

"They should be glass slippers," Seanan said, caressing her ankle with the ball of his thumb. "But perhaps you're right, Ardal. Let's see."

Ever so slowly, he unlaced her sneakers and pulled them off, pushing them to one side. She hadn't bothered to wear socks, and her feet were bare in his lap when he'd finished. "Ahhh," he breathed. "You were right. These are fine indeed."

Ciara blushed. She *did* have pretty feet, with a delicate arch and slender toes, but... "They're just feet."

"You give yourself too little credit." Seanan gave her a wicked look, then lifted one foot to his mouth. Twinkling at her, he slipped her big toe between his lips and suckled.

Ciara gasped. No one... no one had *ever*... A bolt of liquid heat shot through her pussy. Already wet, she felt her juices begin to flow anew as Seanan laved her flesh with his skilled tongue. He feathered his fingers under her sole, tickling ever so gently, and each touch was like a caress between her thighs.

He pulled off, licking his lips. "You liked that," he said, running his hand up her calf. "I can smell you. You're fragrant as one of these roses. Ready to unfurl for us. Yes?"

Ciara stared at him with wide eyes. *Remember the kink... remember the... oh, hell.* Screw the kink. She just wanted more of this. "I do. I am. More. Give me more."

Seanan and Ardal laughed together. "Then stand up," Ardal said. "Let us adore you." Each took her by a hand, pulling gently. "On your feet, pretty miss," he coaxed. "Between us."

When she was balanced upright, Ciara found herself sandwiched by the two men, both pressing against her, Ardal behind, Seanan before. Both men rotated lightly against her. She could feel the heavy weight of erections through leather, pushing at her mons and the curves of her ass. Her breath came in soft pants. "Oh. That's good."

"See how much we want you?" Ardal brushed back her hair to kiss her neck, trailing his lips down her shoulders. "But you're wearing too many clothes, little Ciara. Shall we do something about that, Seanan?"

"Oh, yes," the blond agreed. He brought his hands to the front of Ciara's sweater, tugging. "Put your arms up."

She obeyed like a child. He pulled the garment over her head and cast it aside. It fell into a pool of shadow in the corner of the room. Too late, Ciara realized she hadn't worn a bra. She was small enough to get away with it, her breasts barely a palm-full, though they were round and ripe, tipped with crimson areolae. Blushing, she tried to cover herself.

Seanan pulled her arms away. "No, don't. These little buds deserve to be tasted." He cupped one breast in his hand. "Ardal, can you reach?"

Ardal's bigger hand reached around, softly caressing her other breast. His fingers teased her nipple into a stiff peak, tweaking it gently. "I can."

"Good. You touch, and I taste." Seanan lowered his mouth, and drew her breast inside it. That tongue went to work again, rolling and licking, suckling her deep. Moisture began to drip down Ciara's thighs as he pushed against her, the weight of his cock so heavy and needy against her hungry center.

But wait. This whole show was under her control, wasn't it? And as good as that felt, she knew what she wanted. More of what she'd seen at the bar. She pushed at Seanan. He came away from her breast with a disappointed moan. "But I want," he pouted.

She gently peeled Ardal's hand away from her other breast, though it pained her to let that warm, exhilarating touch go. "I know. But I want to see you two together." She sank back into the chair. "Like you were at the bar," she ordered. "Undress each other."

Ardal and Seanan exchanged looks. "Very well," Ardal agreed. "But first, you let me do this."

He lifted her as if she weighed no more than a feather, standing her back on her feet. He reached for the zipper to her jeans and drew it down. Ciara blushed again as the aroma of her own desire rose to meet their noses, but Ardal only smiled hungrily. "So good, to find someone who wants us," he murmured. "Don't be ashamed."

Moving slowly, he drew the jeans down, over her hips to the ground. "Step out," he ordered. She obeyed, one foot after the other. A cool wind breezed through, tickling the smooth skin of her calves and thighs, chilling her wet center. She gasped at the sensation, almost like inquisitive fingers caressing her.

Leaning forward, Ardal was at just the right height to nuzzle into her sodden scrap of silk panties. "Forgive me this," he said, reaching for the sides of them. "You tempt me too much. I cannot wait."

He tore them neatly, as if they were paper, peeling them away from her pussy and casting them aside. He breathed deeply. "So delicious," he said, his voice like a kiss. "One taste. Just one."

Behind them, Seanan caressed his cock through his leather pants, watching them both with an eager hunger, as if he wanted to see it as much as she wanted to feel it.

So Ardal wanted a taste of her? Like she'd have denied him anything. Instead, reaching down, she threaded her hands through that dark hair and pushed him closer, bringing his mouth up against the thatch of wet red curls between her legs. He chuckled, the vibrations making her entire body tingle. His tongue flickered out, running along the seam of her cunt. "Sweet," he said. "So very sweet."

"More!" she demanded, spreading her legs a little wider.

Seanan placed his hands over her bare shoulders, rubbing gently. "You'll have plenty," he purred. "Ardal, show her what that mouth of yours can do."

"With pleasure." Ardal delved into her then, his tongue sliding between her folds. His fingers came up to pull them softly apart to give him better access to her core. He lapped up her juices, whispering things under his breath in a language she couldn't understand. Gaelic? With a soft chuckle, he lifted a little and found her throbbing bud. "This wants attention, doesn't it, now?"

Placing a hand underneath each curve of her ass, he lapped at her clit once, twice, again, then took it into his mouth and sucked *hard*. Ciara's body, already thrumming with tension, convulsed. She let out a short scream as she came, muscles shaking fiercely. Her hands clamped down on Ardal's hair, but he only laughed and licked at her, drinking her down like wine.

When she could breathe again, both men were there, pressing her into the chair. Boneless, hair tangled across her damp cheeks, she stared up at them. "Now," Ardal said, wiping his face with his fingers and suckling off the dampness. "You wanted a show, did you?"

She nodded dumbly.

"Then a show you will have." Ardal turned to Seanan, fingers running down his chest. "Love, let me show you to her. Every bit of you."

Seanan grinned, spreading his arms wide. "Do it. I want her to see."

Quick as a flash, Ardal's fingers darted down the buttons of Seanan's shirt. It parted like water and slid off his shoulders in a pool of silk, leaving his chest bare. Ciara's lips parted at the sight. So pale and perfect, like a marble statue. Muscles so defined that they looked carved. How could she possibly compare to that, with her soft curves?

"You're perfect as you are," Seanan said, as if he could read her mind. "No moving those hands to cover your tasty aspects. I want to see and smell your reaction as we do this."

Ciara stilled her fingers, which had been twitching to lift for her to hide behind. Lowering her hands to the chair, she watched as Seanan returned the favor with Ardal, peeling away his shirt with quick, practiced movements. Dark and delicious was no less perfect in his way. Broader, more solid, and just as hard and delectable. The men gazed at each other, hands roving over solid chests – then, as if they couldn't bear not to, came together in a harsh, bruising kiss. Ardal pinned Seanan's wrists at his stomach. His fingers splayed across his cock, the tip of it poking out the top of his leather pants, shining and wet.

Slowly, almost shyly, Ciara's hands crept to her pussy. She fingered herself carefully, just slipping one hand through the folds. "Now the leather," she said breathlessly. *It's my party.* "I want to see you naked. All of you."

The two men parted, licking their lips. Two sets of gleaming eyes turned on her. "Your wish is our command," Seanan said, reaching for his zipper. Ardal followed suit, gazing at her as if she held the world in the palm of her hand.

The leather scooted down their legs as smoothly as silk. They kicked the pants aside and stood before her, bare of any stitch, their erections flat against their stomachs. Pre-come bubbled out of the slits at their uncut tips, their foreskins drawn back and purple heads bulging.

Ciara inhaled deeply. She stroked herself a little more boldly, trembling. "You're gorgeous," she said, and meant it. "No one on Earth should look that sexy and live."

The two men laughed. "You're half right," Seanan said. He ran a hand down his cock, squeezing it. "Do you see this? I want to plunge it inside you, to feel you melt around me and press down tight. Do you want that, Ciara? Want to feel me deep within?"

"She's tempting as Hell itself," Ardal breathed. He moved behind Seanan and kissed his jaw. "But you may have her first," he said. "I cede my right. So long as I can take you at the same time."

All three of them... at once? Ciara shook hard as her second orgasm of the night hit her. The two men were there immediately, petting and caressing her. Seanan, the little devil, took advantage and plunged his face between her thighs, getting his own taste of her juices.

When he drew back, his lips shining, they were curved in a smile. "I'm doubly right. You do taste of nectar."

Ciara shivered, shook, and stared up at them. "You," she said slowly. "You."

"Yes. Me."

Ardal put an arm around Seanan's waist. "No more of this," he said, voice rough. "To the bed. The time for waiting and playing is over."

Seanan arched back against him, rubbing shamelessly. "Yes," he agreed. "Ciara? Will you?"

He lowered his hands to her. She gripped them, once again feeling lighter than air as he raised her to her feet. Despite her double climax, she ached and burned deep inside. She wanted that cock buried in her, and she wanted it now. "Bed," she said, reaching for Seanan. "Both of you."

Seanan chuckled. He swooped her up into his arms and laughed at the look of surprise on her face. "You're little as a posy," he teased. "Don't be so shocked."

"I'm not shocked. I just – I –"

Soft linens met her back as Seanan lowered her onto the left side of the bed. Oh, God. This was a wanton's bed, created for pure pleasure. Feeling as bold as a hustler, she spread her legs wide and beckoned with both hands. "Come," she invited. "You want me? Take me."

Seanan inhaled sharply. "Go on." Ardal gave him a slight push. "Then me."

The blond man climbed over Ciara, into the middle of the bed, rolling her onto her side facing him. His cock teased at her entrance, not quite penetrating but only nudging at her folds. She whimpered and pushed forward, but he held her off. "Not quite yet," he said hoarsely. "Ardal prepares me first."

"Ardal prepares…?" Craning her neck, Ciara saw and felt the weight of the man lowering himself onto the bed. He reached for an ornately carved box on the side table, rummaging inside. "What's that?" she asked, curious. "The toy chest?"

Seanan laughed and kissed her, all too briefly. "I don't need toys to make you come. Nor does he. It's lubricant, to ease his passage."

"Lubricant." Startled realization flashed over her. "So he's going to… while you and I…"

"He is." Seanan kissed her again. "Does that bother you?"

Bother her? Hell, the thought of being on the receiving end of that was better than being sandwiched in the middle. "No," she said breathily. "Not at all."

Ardal leaned up on one elbow. "Good." He smiled wickedly. "I would have done it to him if you had agreed or not." He ran his hand over the arch of Seanan's hip. "Look at him. So tempting. As fine a treat as you yourself, only different." He uncapped a small tube. The scent of sandalwood filled the air.

"Come," Seanan whispered. "Put your leg over mine. Yes, like that."

With her thigh draped over his, his cock nudging ever deeper into her folds, Ciara could feel Seanan trembling, could feel the ripples from Ardal's fingers penetrating him. "Does it feel good?" she whispered. "Would I like it?"

"You would love it," he promised, kissing her nose. "And sometime, we'll take you that way. But for now, we take this path."

"It's a good one," she said, putting her arm over Seanan's side to play with Ardal's chest, brushing his nipples with her fingertips. "Very good."

Seanan bucked and shook as Ardal's fingers twisted. "Oh, yes," he panted. "Very good."

Ardal put the bottle aside. Ciara caught one glimpse of his cock, gleaming with lube, before he lowered himself onto his side. "Open for me," he whispered. "We do this now."

"Are you ready?" Seanan asked Ciara. "Say no, and I'll forbear."

In answer, she pushed against him, spearing herself on the tip of his cock. She gasped at how good it felt, so slick and tight. "Ready."

Ardal's arm, long and lean, came over Seanan to grasp Ciara's bicep. "Then we make love," he said, his voice gravelly. He pushed forward with his hips, driving slowly into Seanan, pushing him deep inside Ciara. All three drew in a breath with the bliss of it.

"Tight..."

"Hot..."

"Wet..."

"Smooth..."

"Slick..."

"Mine."

"Mine."

Ciara echoed them, grasping Seanan tight, and brushing her fingertips across Ardal's chest. "Mine."

Then, there were no more words. Only Seanan, thrusting into her time and again, spurred on by Ardal's thrusts. His way grew smoother as she melted from within, and pre-come slicked its way down his cock. He writhed and groaned as he pushed into her, and Ardal pounded into him. Hands gripped tighter, legs wound round about one another, and they moved as one, push-pull, push-pull, gliding deep and fast.

Ciara's core throbbed. Seanan seemed to know just where to hit. Her internal muscles clamped down hard on his cock, milking it so that he gasped for breath. "Coming," she managed to stammer, kissing him full and open-mouthed. "Going to come again, Seanan."

"I – I too," Seanan rasped. "Ready for me, sweet Ciara?"

"So ready."

He slipped a hand between them and began to rub his thumb against her clit while thrusting. "Come," he panted. "Come, come, come…"

With another cry, ripped from her gut, Ciara exploded into the light. She felt her muscles squeeze powerfully, tearing the orgasm from Seanan. Hot pulses of seed hit her womb, triggering a fourth set of spasms. From the sound of Ardal's cries, and Seanan's shaking – God, she could almost feel that second cock, brushing against the lips of her pussy –– she knew that he felt the bliss, too. He saw the white light.

Coming down was long and slow, full of heavy breathing and lazy, sweeping caresses over bare skin. Seanan kissed her as if he never wanted to stop, tangling his tongue with hers in a languid post-coital dance.

Ciara felt as if she were floating in a dream. *This is kink*, she thought happily. *And God, but I could get used to it. Please, let them stick around for a while. I want more of this. More of Seanan and Ardal. I want Ardal to have his turn at me. I want… I want… more. Just more. Please?*

She laughed a little as Seanan slipped free of her in a gush of fluids. She felt his jerk as Ardal pulled out of him. Tugging harder, the darker man brought them together in a tight embrace.

"You are the one we've been looking for," he said, his voice gentle and slow. "We've searched for ages, Seanan and I. But you're woman enough for the both of us, little Ciara."

"Ages?" She giggled. "You're no older than I am. In fact, you –" She stopped. Her hand, moving on its own accord, had reached up to smooth the tangled hair away from Seanan's face. As she did so, it fell away from his ears. They weren't human ears. Elegantly pointed at the tip, pierced with silver hoops, and tattooed on the inside whorl with a Celtic design.

He blinked at her, and it was as if a haze cleared from her vision. She saw Seanan's eyes changed from human eyes to those of a cat, the pupils ovoid and pointed. He drew away from her. "Ardal, she sees!"

Ardal lifted his head. His eyes, too, had changed, and now that she looked she could see the pointed ears peeking through his hair. "Ciara, don't be alarmed. We mean you no harm. We only just –"

"Only just, hell!" she cried, scrambling out of bed. "Who are you? *What* are you?"

Chapter Three

Still naked, Ciara scrambled away from Ardal, Seanan, and the great big bed. She stopped at a safe distance and stared at them. God, how had she ever taken them for human? With their ears, and their eyes – the perfection of their skin and bodies –

She stifled a dry sob. *Figures. I can't get a normal guy to look at me twice. What do I end up with? Aliens!*

"Not aliens," Ardal said, putting out a hand as if to a frightened kitten. "Elves."

Ciara cracked up. "Elves? How crazy do you think I am?"

"What other explanation do you have?" Ardal slid out of bed. Now that her eyes were clear, she could see elegant Celtic tattoos curling down his chest and legs. Knots and bars and loops, each one gorgeously done. "Seanan and I are princes in Under-hill."

"Oh, God. Are you the insane one, or am I?" Ciara cast a frightened look around herself. "Under-hill, huh? Is that where we are? Did you do some kind of hocus pocus back in the bar and whisk us away to your home?"

"No, pretty one." Seanan followed Ardal. Tattooed like the other man, he slid to his knees in front of Ciara. "We're in a hotel just up the street. We've lived in this room for weeks now, searching for the right one."

"And that's me?" When the men nodded, Ciara let loose with another laugh. "Right one? For what? A three-way sandwich with a creamy center?"

"So crude," Seanan chided. "You have a mouth on you, but you're the one we've been waiting for. No one has dared to take on both of us at once before."

"And I guess you've been playing the field, huh? A new damsel every night?"

"Not every night." Ardal regarded her steadily. "But we have been searching, yes. And finally, we've found you."

Ciara put her hands on her hips, and realized she was still naked. Blushing, she reached for a hotel robe, hanging on a hook –

"Don't. Oh, don't," Ardal pleaded. "Let us look at you. So beautiful. So perfect."

Ciara let the robe drop. "See, that's what I don't get. I'm not beautiful. And perfect? Perfect for what? What is it you've been looking for that apparently I have?"

"You have the heart to love both of us," Seanan said gravely. "To accept us for what we are – lovers, friends, partners. If you let yourself, to believe that we are Elves, as we say. We have need of a mate, Under-hill."

"A mate." Ciara blinked. "Okay, that's it. I'm out of here."

"Stay but a moment more!" Ardal stood.

"Ciara, hear us out," Seanan added, as if he were the other half of Ardal's voice. "It's not what it sounds like to you, at first."

"It sounds like a whole bunch of St. Patrick's Day moonshine and malarkey." Ciara waved her hands at them. "I see it, now. Fake ears and contact lenses. The tattoos, okay, you might have had those covered with makeup that came off. But no way are you Elves. And there's no-how on God's green earth that you're going to convince me to be your *mate* based on one round of hot sex."

Ardal reached forward, managing to snag her hands in his. The feel of them, dry and warm, sent a tingle through Ciara's traitorous body. *Stop that!* she snapped at herself. *These guys are nuts!*

"Ciara," he said gravely, "Seanan speaks the truth. We need a mate. Elves cannot breed with other Elves, and our race is dying. We love one another, forming bonds close as the heart can twine, but we are coming to an end. We need fresh blood, mortal blood, to prosper again."

"Fresh blood." Ciara's mouth fell open as she realized something. "Condom! You didn't use a condom! You could have gotten me pregnant!"

Seanan's eyes lit up. He stretched out his hands toward her stomach. "A child," he whispered. "One born of love and fire. Could you deny us that?"

"Seanan, is she?" Ardal looked at him, expectant.

Seanan closed his eyes. "She is," he said, his face reflecting pure bliss. "Tiny as a molecule, but there is life."

"A baby," Ciara whispered. "How can you – you can tell, so early?"

"It's a gift we have." Ardal pulled her into the circle of his arms. "To Seanan go the rights of the firstborn, but I will claim the second. You have another egg waiting to be fertilized. Twins will grow inside your belly, one mine and one his."

"Now just wait a minute, buster –"

Ardal pressed his lips to her neck. "You want this, Ciara," he murmured. "You're unhappy with your life here on Earth. I can tell. I can read you. A dull job as a law secretary, men who treat you poorly, a small apartment without even the cat you long to have."

"How – how did you –"

"It is my gift," he said simply. His lips traveled up her neck. Gently, he pushed against her. His cock, hard and ready once more, nestled between her folds. "Come and love me, Ciara. Let me have you, and fill you with my child. The future of our world."

"I'm no one's future," she said, gasping at the feel of him, so close to her channel. "I'm just Ciara. And I can't be pregnant. It takes longer than that to know."

"Not with us," Seanan said. He stood, coming around behind her. "Go on, Ciara," he urged. "Love him. Let love increase." He slid a hand around to caress her flat belly. "You carry a son," he whispered. "My son."

"I… I don't… I can't…"

Seanan disappeared into the bathroom, and reappeared with a sudsy washcloth. Tender as could be, he washed Ardal's erect cock, finishing by brushing his hand down the length of it. "He's ready for you now, Ciara," he said. "Take him."

"There is no *don't*," Ardal murmured. "No *can't*. Just think. Just feel."

"Oh, God."

"Yes," he said. "I remember you crying the name. Now, cry for me again." With one thrust he entered her, her core still slick and wet from her own juices and Seanan's come. The power of his movement almost lifted her off her feet. She let out a low cry as she was speared. Ardal was huge, almost too big, but oh, it hurt so good! And then Seanan was behind her, steadying her hips.

"Take him in," he said softly into one ear. "Take all of him. Bear down with your muscles and milk him dry."

Ardal thrust again. "So tight," he said, his voice choked. "So hot. So wet. And getting wetter. For me, Ciara?"

Embarrassed, Ciara felt liquid pooling inside her. The powerful thrusts of his cock inside made her flow, coating him with honey. "It's not..."

"Oh, but it is." He bent forward, suckling on the curve of her neck. "Will you come for me?"

"Four times already," she said. "I can't. I don't –"

"Seanan," Ardal said. "Your hands."

Those slim, clever fingers slipped around to Ciara's clit, caressing it tenderly as Ardal thrust. They pulled and tugged, then stroked her. The pulse between her legs began to beat fiercely again, and she recognized the signs of a fifth mind-blowing climax coming on. She clamped down on Ardal, squeezing him tight. "You," she accused. "You've done this to me. Enchanted me."

"Nothing that you didn't want," Seanan said against her shoulder blade. "Deep down, if you look, you'll see that you wanted this all along. A man to love and cherish you. Now you have not one, but two."

Ciara writhed on Ardal's shaft. She could feel herself beginning to fall. Almost there... He thrust again, roaring out his pleasure, and with the sound, she collapsed across his chest, fireworks exploding in front of her eyes.

When she came to, they were on the floor, the three of them, Ciara draped across Ardal and Seanan's laps. They were petting and stroking her, neatening her hair and washing her down with a warm, damp cloth. "You," she said, blinking. "How did you do that to me?"

Ardal's lips quirked. "Do what, Ciara? Make you believe us?"

"Make you love us?" Seanan asked.

"All of it."

Ardal pressed tenderly down on her belly. "Seanan has read you. A daughter, my own daughter, tiny as his son, lives within you now."

"Babies," she whispered. "Two of them."

"Our children, and yours." Ardal bent to kiss her forehead tenderly. "You take to our seed as the hummingbird to nectar."

"I'm not a... not a breeding machine," she said. "I won't be a baby factory for you."

Both men laughed. "No one is asking you to be a machine, a thing," Seanan said, smoothing back her hair. "We know how to use protection. Only, once in a while, would we ask such a precious gift of you."

"For the good of your race."

"For us." Ardal's lips slid down to cover her mouth. His tongue tenderly traced her lips. "Say you'll come with us, Ciara. Home to Under-hill. Be one of us. Immortal while you bide there. Forever young and beautiful."

"And both of you... you'll be together?" she asked, turning red. "I can watch you love each other, as much as you love me?"

"Do you think you could part us?" Ardal ran a hand down Seanan's chest. "He is my heart's love, just as you are. Say you will, Ciara. Say you'll come."

Ciara closed her eyes for a long moment, thinking hard. Say that she did go with these men – Elves – to their land. Say she believed them about the babies. About the hope that together, they would be a unit. A family. Her heart ached to believe that it was true, just as her body trembled with the aftershocks of orgasm.

Why... why not? What did she have to lose, after all? Going with them might be a mistake, but it would be a glorious one. That she was sure of.

She opened her eyes. "Could I have a kitten?" she whispered.

Ardal laughed. "You can have as many of the pretty, furry, purry creatures as you want," he swore. "Is that a yes? You'll come with us?"

"Yes," Ciara said slowly. She dared to smile up at the men. Blondie and Dark & Delicious. Ardal and Seanan. Elves. Elves! Both of them, wanting her so much. "I'll go with you."

Seanan took one of her hands, and Ardal the other. "Then it's time for that 'hocus pocus' you mentioned earlier," he said with a twinkling smile. "Close your eyes, Ciara."

Obediently, she let her lashes fall shut against her cheeks. She felt a blurring, a whirling, and a sudden stop.

When she opened them, the three of them were in a forest glade. Night had well and truly fallen, and through a break in the trees she could see a glorious full moon high above. The sounds of music and dancing came from a short distance away, as well as the flickering light of a bonfire. Ardal and Seanan stood, helping her up.

"Garb yourself in the sky," Seanan said, waving a hand. A long dress of indigo fell around her shoulders, the skirts brushing the forest floor. He and Ardal made similar gestures, and were suddenly clothed in tunics and breeches of the same color. Hers, she realized, sparkled as if the stars themselves had come down to light on her skirts.

"Come and dance," Seanan invited, offering his arm. "Join us in the circle. Be one of us."

Ciara laughed in delight. "Forever young," she whispered. "Forever with you."

Ardal kissed her tenderly. "Always. Will you dance with us, to seal the pact?"

"Dance with you?" She took both their arms, and tugged them forward. "Have you ever seen the Electric Slide performed to drum and whistle?"

Ardal frowned. "No."

"Well, get ready for a surprise," she said, grinning broadly. "I have a few things of my own to teach you."

Ardal smiled; Seanan threw back his head and laughed loud and long. "Fiery Ciara!" he exclaimed, planting a kiss on her cheek. "Come and teach us."

"Others are waiting for us," Ardal said. "Are you ready?"

Ciara glanced down at her gown made from the sky and stars, and at the men flanking her sides. She laughed in delight. "Lead on, gentle sirs," she said gaily. "Lead on, and let's dance!"

It turned out to be the first time that the Boot-Scootin' Boogie had been performed Under-hill.

But it wasn't the last. Not by a long shot.

Willa Okati

Willa Okati is a long-time devotee of all things vampire and supernatural, but an even bigger fan of stories that feature beautiful men exploring their desires for one another. Physically, she lives in North Carolina, but mentally thrives in a world where each adventure is bigger and brighter than the next. She is also owned by far too many cats, but she insists that they serve as emissaries from the Muse and can't spare a one of them. You can visit her at her Web site, http://www.willsheornillshe.com.

Jolene's Pooka
Kate Hill

Chapter One

Jolene saw him for the first time on a brisk March night. She blamed it on being a bit tipsy from sharing one too many beers with a friend at the local pub. Still, she shivered and her heart pounded when he appeared as if from nowhere in the meadow across from her rented cottage.

Huge and black with fiery eyes, the stallion stared at her. He trotted closer and snorted, looking dangerous yet incredibly beautiful. Sleek muscles rippled beneath his glossy coat. There was something otherworldly about him that terrified her.

She walked faster and he easily kept up. She ran and he followed, those eyes of flame never leaving her.

Trembling, she reached her door and fumbled with the key. Just as it turned in the lock, she felt warm, moist breath against the back of her neck.

A deep voice rumbled, "Come to me, woman."

Jolene had never been easily frightened, but she let out a scream loud enough to shatter glass as she dove inside.

For several moments, she leaned against the door, her pulse racing. She heard his hoof beats on the cobbled walkway. Every now and then he snorted.

It's a horse. Just a horse. He didn't talk. Your mind was just playing tricks on you.

"Woman," roared the voice. "I said come to me."

"Go away!"

She was drunk. The voice and the horse were just figments of her imagination. When she gathered the courage to glance out the window, she saw nothing but meadows, trees, and the empty, moonlit road winding back to the town.

* * *

"It sounds to me like you've got yourself a pooka," Fallon said to Jolene, an amused glint in her eyes.

The women sat across from each other in the kitchen of Fallon's house two miles up the road from Jolene's cottage. They had known each other since high school when they had been exchange students. Ten years later, their friendship was as strong as ever. Jolene was vacationing in the small country town in Ireland where her old schoolmate resided.

"A pooka? What the hell is that?"

"It's a fairy that usually takes the form of a horse and goes around stealing crops and frightening people."

Jolene giggled. "Come on. Fairies are supposed to be cute little girls with wings and magic dust."

"Not all of them are like that. According to legend, most of them weren't very pleasant. Pooka is a shapeshifter, but he usually doesn't appear until autumn. You really must have caught his fancy for him to show his face now."

"You're laughing at me and I don't blame you."

Fallon reached across the table and patted her friend's hand. "I'm not laughing at you. Just having a bit of fun. You had too much to drink last night. That's all. Remember, if you see your pooka again, don't let him take you on a wild ride."

Jolene grinned, finally able to see the humor of the situation. Of course Fallon was right. Alcohol had conjured the fairy. He didn't really exist.

* * *

"Woman!"

Jolene awoke with a start, her heart pounding.

"I said come out here. You belong with me!"

The deep, masculine voice filled her room. A glance at the window revealed the silhouette of a horse's head against the shade. Jolene shivered, yet sweat beaded on her brow and upper lip. *This is not happening!*

"I know you hear me. Come for a ride with me."

Slowly, she inched her way toward the phone to call for help – not that it would do much good. She was miles from her nearest neighbor.

The line was dead!

Hoof beats clacked on the cobbled walk and the horse snorted. "I can smell you. Soft perfume. Womanly musk. Come outside so I can enjoy your face and form along with your scent."

Jolene tightened her fingers on the sheets. If she had a gun she might be able to scare him off.

"Fine, then," he said, a note of disappointment in his voice. "I can wait."

The silhouette disappeared from the window. Hoof beats clattered above the howling wind, then faded.

Unable to go back to sleep, Jolene sat in bed, her entire body tense, the pooka's velvety voice echoing in her mind.

Chapter Two

Larkin's hooves thundered over damp earth. He raced for miles, challenging even his magical physique. The woman had turned him away yet again, but he was more determined than ever to win her heart.

For more centuries than he cared to remember, Larkin had endured a half existence in his beloved homeland. When other magical folk faded into a realm just beyond mortals' reach, he refused to admit there was no place left for his kind. The world changed, and he stood by and watched until he alone traveled the countryside, the spirit of an age long forgotten and invisible to humankind.

He watched from a distance as strange wonders sprang across his island. Devices that jingled, roared, and filled the air with smoke. Lights that glowed without flickering flames. Even the people talked and dressed differently.

The longer he watched, the angrier he became, then his anger turned to sadness. No matter what the world had become, he wanted to be part of it again. He missed the hum of mortal voices and the sensation of a warm, fleshy woman wrapped in his arms.

While so many of his brothers had enjoyed teasing and tormenting humankind, Larkin had relished the pleasures of sharing their enjoyment. He missed flinging an unsuspecting mortal onto his back and galloping across the countryside. By the end of the ride, their fear had always changed to excitement. Maidens in particular seemed to appreciate the thrill of riding a towering black steed.

Gradually, he faded from their view. The people no longer believed, so they could no longer see. Sometimes one or two of the more superstitious – the very old or the very young – would catch a glimpse of his shadow flying across a meadow or hear his whispered voice on the wind, but that was all.

Until *she* came.

Larkin knew the minute he saw the chestnut-haired foreigner with fathomless hazel eyes that she would be his link. The longing inside her cried out to him, begging for something old fashioned and powerful to sweep her into its protective embrace. So great was her need that when she'd glanced across the meadow, she had *seen* him.

He'd terrified her, as his kind had always done to humans, but he'd also sensed her desire. He excited her and he knew without a doubt he could give her the love and pleasure she craved.

Unfortunately, she was taking much longer than the maidens of old to accept him. Usually a woman would have already tumbled into the hay with him. He reminded himself that in spite of her connection to the past, she was still a child of the present.

Leprechauns, banshees, merfolk, and other magical creatures no longer existed in her world. Therefore he expected her to deny his presence as much as she craved it.

Larkin slowed to a walk, catching his breath as he approached the ruins of the castle where he and his brothers had once dwelled. With scarcely a thought, he changed into his human form. The damp grass chilled his bare feet and the night wind lashed his naked flesh. Gazing at the moon, he drew a deep breath.

A long, mournful cry disrupted the peaceful night. Again it rang out, carried by the wind, a familiar lament that brought a slight smile to his lips.

Only another fairy or a dying mortal could hear the banshee's cry. It had been too long since that sound echoed across this land.

The wail grew louder, then stopped suddenly. Soft, cool arms slipped around him and breath tickled his ear.

"It's been a long time, Larkin. Aren't you ready to join the rest of us?"

He turned, gathering the beautiful, milky-skinned, black-haired woman into his arms. She didn't feel quite solid, rather like embracing a thick yet velvety fog.

"I like it here."

"We no longer belong. Come home."

"I am home."

"Larkin," she placed a gentle hand to the base of his throat and gazed at him with sorrowful eyes, "I fear one day you will hear my cry for a reason other than your fairy blood. That you will bind yourself permanently to this world."

"That is my hope."

"It might also be your undoing. Come with me. Make love to me like you used to."

In spite of her beauty and the knowledge that they were more alike than he and a mortal could ever be, he had no desire to bed her. She would feel cool and practically weightless. Her lips would have no taste and her skin no scent.

At least when he took human form, he was solid with warm flesh and a wild, musky aroma that women relished – or so he had been told by the maidens he had lain with.

"I won't come again," the banshee continued. "Please don't stay here alone in a world that remembers us as they do a children's story."

He shook his head and brushed her cold lips with a kiss before disentangling his body from hers.

Jewel-like tears glistened on her pale cheeks as she backed slowly away, her gaze locked with his and her lips parted in a sorrowful cry.

Then she was gone.

Larkin was alone again, left with the bittersweet taste of desire.

Her invitation of lovemaking had stirred him, but he wanted a warm, human woman. He wanted to feel the heat of her lips and tongue, hear the throbbing of her heart, and catch the scent of her honeyed sex, drenched and awaiting his cock.

His pulse quickened and his staff swelled, aching with need. He considered returning to the mortal woman's cottage and trying to persuade her again. A glance at the sky told him it was too late. The sun was about to rise. His power faded by day. Until she fully accepted him, he could only appear to her after dark.

Slipping into the bowels of the castle, to the dank stone chamber dug belowground, he stretched out on his back and curled his hand around his cock.

He closed his eyes and imagined the mortal's hand caressing him. Her touch would be softer than his, her hand far more delicate. Slowly, he eased his grip and stroked, the foreskin rubbing deliciously over the ultra sensitive flesh beneath.

In his imagination, the woman's warm, moist lips slipped over his cock head, sucking and caressing, the tip of her tongue teasing the tiny eye. He could almost feel her licking his shaft with wet, swirling strokes.

Forcing his breathing to remain slow and steady, he swept his hand up and down his cock, rubbing fast, then slowing the pace. He kept himself hovering on the brink of climax, savoring the fantasy of the mortal woman until he thought he could bear no more.

The mortal had such lovely breasts, full and swaying slightly beneath the rather clinging tops that were fashionable nowadays. Her lovely bosom bounced slightly when she walked, a most pleasing sight. The flare of her hips beneath the faded blue trousers she usually wore beckoned for him to undress her, free her from the somewhat masculine garb and fling her naked onto her back. He sensed that she wanted to be possessed, taken with passion, but also loved.

Larkin could give her exactly what she needed, and she could be his companion. He would guide her in the ways of love, and she would teach him to understand the modern world.

If not for this woman, he might have succumbed to the banshee's call to rejoin his brothers in the world beyond. He could not go, not without tasting the lips of this flesh and blood woman whose soul called to him.

Closing his eyes tightly and arching against the hard stone floor, he let his hand fly. His hips thrust hard and he came, his entire body straining, a groan trapped in his throat.

Self-pleasure felt good enough, but couldn't compare to what he would experience when he joined with the woman. He would not wade alone and cold in the aftermath of passion, but have the pleasure of a soft, warm body pressed close to his.

Patience, Larkin. You must have patience. Eventually, she will come to you.

Chapter Three

In the morning, Jolene was almost afraid to leave the house, but she had to go to town and speak to the police. Common sense told her that horses didn't talk, so a man must be stalking her.

After a policeman heard her story, he looked at her like she'd lost her mind, but followed her home and searched for signs of her midnight visitor.

No hoof prints or even footprints were found, but her phone line was mangled.

"Maybe you should find a place to sleep in town instead of staying all alone out here," the policeman suggested.

"I came here to be alone."

Having spent all year in a noisy city, subjected to the constant anxiety of her corporate career, she wanted to enjoy her vacation in solitude, except for occasional visits with Fallon. Even then, she'd turned down her friend's invitation to the St. Patrick's Day party at her family's pub.

"Suit yourself. Anyway, it was probably just a teenager trying to scare you. Keep your doors locked, and if it happens again, let me know."

The policeman left her staring at the torn phone line.

A frightening realization dawned on her. Letting the authorities know if she had another visitation would do no good. In spite of all Fallon's teasing and wild stories, Jolene knew she had a genuine Irish fairy on her hands.

* * *

He came again that night, and the one after that.

Jolene's fear of him slowly turned to fascination. Excitement coursed through her when she looked out the window and saw the magnificent fire-eyed stallion galloping toward her cottage. Desire slid down her spine like supple fingers when his deep voice called to her. Every night he said the same thing. *Woman, come to me.*

The sound of his voice alone was almost enough to make her climax. It filled her with more passion than she wanted to admit, even to herself. Soft yet powerful, it remained in her head long after he'd gone. When she managed to drift into an uneasy sleep, even her dreams were filled with the echo of his voice.

Still, she continued ignoring him, but he seemed more determined than ever to lure her from the cottage.

A few mornings later when Fallon stopped by to see her on the way to work, Jolene guided the conversation toward Celtic folklore. "When a pooka visits you, what does he usually want?"

"Oh, Jolene. Not the pooka again."

"Your story caught my interest."

"I guess, like most fairies, he wants to cause mischief of some sort."

"Oh," Jolene sighed. How very disappointing. Ever since learning that her particular fairy was a shapeshifter, she had been imagining him changing into a sexy, half naked guy and sweeping her off her feet.

"If you want to get rid of one, show him a little interest and he'll get bored. Once he knows you're not scared of him, his fun is over."

Damn. Jolene had imagined that once she showed him a little interest, their fun would just begin.

"Are you sure you won't change your mind about coming to the party tonight? I hate to think of anybody spending St. Paddy's day alone."

"Yes. I just want to stay in and relax."

Fallon raised an eyebrow. "You're sure you're okay? You look tired."

"I'm fine. I haven't been sleeping very well, that's all."

"Is there something you want to talk about?"

She longed to discuss her strange nightly experiences with someone, but she thought it best not to mention seeing the pooka again. Her friend was already looking at her like she was crazy.

Perhaps she was. After all, what sane woman believed a talking horse stalked her by night?

Worst of all, she was starting to enjoy the pooka's visits. Even if he was just an illusion, he was a damn interesting one.

That night when the hoof beats thudded outside her cottage, Jolene was wide awake and ready.

Her entire body tingling with anticipation, she waited by the door. There was only one way to prove she wasn't crazy and that was by confronting the creature itself.

"Woman!"

"I'm here," she said, her voice steadier than she felt.

"Come to me."

"What do you want?"

"What does any man want?"

His rumbling, sexy tone tightened her nipples and made her heart thrum.

"But you're not a man," she breathed.

"Clever girl. I am much more than a man."

That powerful, velvet voice enveloped her. As if in a trance, she opened the door and stepped outside. A breeze stirred her hair and caressed her face as she made her way down the cobbled walk.

Without warning she was hurled in the air and landed astride the stallion's back. She gasped and clung to his neck as he galloped off.

Wind lashed tears from her eyes. Her knees clamped his sleek sides and her heart pounded in time with his hoof beats. His scent, musky yet herbal, filled her. Beneath her, his giant muscles flexed. It was like riding a storm, yet for some strange reason she felt safe.

Finally he slowed and she loosened her grip so she could stroke his neck. It was sleek, glossy, and incredibly strong. In the distance stood the ruins of a castle. Moonlight bathed its crumbling gray sides, yet there was something majestic about it.

"You feel as good upon my back as I imagined," he said. "I watched you for many nights, woman."

"My name is Jolene."

"Jolene," he repeated softly.

"Who are you?"

"I am the past. My kind once ruled this land, but with the coming of the new religion we were driven out. People believed in us once. Now we are but stories told to visitors and children."

"Is that why you came to me, because I'm a tourist?"

"I came because your soul cried out for the simplicity of a time long past and because –"

"Yes," she whispered, running her hands down his powerful neck and sifting her fingers through his silken mane.

"Because I am lonely. I no longer need to be a magical creature wooing mankind, but I long to live as a man myself. My people abandoned this place. I do not know enough about the modern world to integrate myself…"

"You want to fit in?"

"Help me," he whispered, "and I will help you find what you've been looking for."

"I just want peace and quiet."

"No. You want a man."

She laughed. "Oh really?"

"Not just any man, but one who knows how a woman should be treated. One who is not afraid to act as a man should. One who has not been tamed."

Though his words stirred her anger, they also ignited her passion.

"Close your eyes," he ordered.

For some reason, she obeyed. She gasped, feeling as if she were floating on air.

When she opened her eyes, she was no longer on the stallion's back, but in the arms of an absolutely gorgeous black-haired, green-eyed man. His chiseled face was shadowed with a hint of stubble. The neck she clung to was powerful and the arms cradling her were thickly muscled.

Hesitantly, she slipped a hand across his bare chest, loving its warmth and the sensation of hair against her palm.

"Fallon said if I acknowledged you, you'd be bored with me and leave."

"Many of my kind once played such games, but that was never my way. Friends and lovers I keep for life."

"Lovers?"

He nodded, his penetrating eyes fixed on hers. The rise and fall of his chest as he breathed comforted her, yet at the same time incited her passion.

Good sense told her she should be absolutely terrified. She was in the presence of a creature that should not exist. He had just changed from beast to man in a blink. Things like that simply didn't happen.

"You're trembling," he said. "Are you cold?"

"Aren't you?"

"We'll soon be warm."

He carried her to the castle and into a bedchamber. In spite of the dilapidated state of the rest of the place, the room was clean and beautifully furnished, from the canopied bed to the rug in front of the huge fireplace where flames crackled and leapt.

"What is this place?"

"It was my home once. Every autumn my brothers and I would haunt this land, feasting on crops and tempting maidens. I can still taste the sweetness of both." He closed his eyes for a moment, an impassioned look sweeping his handsome features. "But that was long ago. The world has changed much since then. Sometimes, if I think hard, I can still catch the scent of the villagers' fires. I can hear their voices and see their lanterns aglow with candlelight. But those are just memories. I can't truly touch them, as I'm touching you now."

He placed her on her feet in front of the fire and cupped her chin in his hand, tilting her face up to his. His hand moved to her cheek. Caressing it gently, he leaned forward the slightest bit and brushed a kiss across her forehead. His lips were moist and soft, yet at the same time firm. She could just imagine how good they would feel against hers.

"Will you share yourself with me, woman?" he asked close to her ear, his warm breath caressing her neck. "Will you let me pleasure your body and mingle your spirit with mine? Give me a taste of what I once had."

"In return for introducing you to the modern world?"

"It's long past time for me. What do they say? Out with the old and in with the new."

Jolene swallowed, stepping back slightly and staring at him. He was tall, powerfully built, and hairy in all the right places. The cock jutting from the black, curly nest on his groin was long, thick, and magnificently veined. She could almost feel its smooth, bulbous head against her lips. His hair-dusted thighs looked as if they had been carved from rock. Even his long, rather bony feet looked sexy.

He grasped a handful of her hair, not painfully, but roughly enough to excite her.

"You are a rare beauty, a treasure that I never dreamed of uncovering in this world that I no longer recognize."

"Listen. I don't –"

His mouth covered hers in a warm, tender kiss. His tongue gently parted her lips and slipped between them, exploring with sweeping strokes that soon had her melting against him. Her eyes closed, she concentrated on the wonderful sensations flooding her. He tasted of herbs. His skin and hair carried the aroma of meadow grass and musky male.

Slowly, his fingers loosened in her hair and he wrapped his arms around her, holding her even closer. Jolene's hands slid up his back and gripped the powerful muscles. All the while his tongue continued teasing hers until he trapped it and sucked gently before breaking the kiss.

"Look at me," he commanded.

She met his gaze. Tiny reddish flecks glistened in his green eyes, revealing the magic of his nature.

"I have waited ages for you, Jolene. You've waited for me, too."

"I didn't even know you existed."

"You wanted me to. I can see in your eyes the kind of life you lead and how much you want to abandon it. You need not return to that cold white cell surrounded by the dreaded machines of your modern world."

"Cold cell? You mean my office? How do you know about that? And what do you mean I need not return? How am I supposed to support myself?"

"I see images of your life in your eyes. It's one of my gifts. As for support, I will care for you."

"With what?"

"With my riches that are buried beneath this castle."

"I like being self-sufficient."

"Then go to your cold cell," he snapped, "but it will be because you choose to, no longer because you must."

Jolene's head spun. This was all too much. Yes, she was attracted to him. Yes, he made her feel like a rescued maiden from a medieval legend, but did she really want to get serious so quickly with a –

"You still do not trust what you see with your eyes and touch with your hands. Then no more delays. I must give you what you cannot deny."

With a sweep of his hand, her clothes vanished. Her face flushed, but before she could move, he swept her into his arms and carried her to the bed.

Placing her upon it, he sat beside her and touched a finger to her lips when she tried to speak.

"Silence. Just feel, Jolene."

She watched, her heart fluttering, as his fingertips stroked between her breasts. He cupped one and squeezed gently, then swept his thumb over the nipple until it hardened. A slight smile on his lips, he stretched out beside her and flicked his tongue over her nipple.

Jolene gasped with pleasure.

His lips fastened on the sensitive bead and he sucked, intermittently flicking with his tongue.

"Oh," she moaned softly, threading her fingers through his hair.

"Umm," he purred, releasing her nipple, then giving it one last lick before moving to her other breast. "That's right, woman. Sing to me. Sweet melody of lust."

His mouth covered her other nipple, licking and sucking until Jolene thought she might come from the sheer delight of his teeth and tongue on the little bud.

Her clit ached and her muscles tightened with the marvelous beginnings of orgasm.

Leaving her breast, he trailed his tongue down her belly, dipped it into her navel, then lapped her ribs with wet, sweeping strokes. Hauling her legs over his shoulders, he covered her clit with his mouth.

"Oh! Yes, yes!" she cried, his enthusiasm taking her completely by surprise. His skilled tongue and lips teased her sensitive flesh. Several rhythmic upward strokes of tongue were followed by wonderfully tugging lips. All the while he clutched her bottom, kneading and caressing the full globes.

Jolene's legs trembled as she neared her peak. At any moment she was going to explode. He licked over and over, soft wet flesh upon soft wet flesh.

"Ah!" She convulsed, writhing and moaning, her heartbeat filling her ears.

He held her steady, his tongue never leaving her until she lay still.

Panting, she kept her eyes closed, lost in a haze of sensation. Before she could fully recover, he started licking her again. She arched, her heart hammering as passion engulfed her once more. One of his hands slipped from behind her so he could explore her pussy. A long, lean finger slid inside her sheath, searching while he sucked and licked her clit.

Faster than she imagined, she felt the wonderful tightening that preceded explosion.

"Please. Yes. Please!" Somewhere beyond her excitement, she realized she didn't even know his name. It would be nice to call him something at such an intimate moment. Before she could contemplate further, she climaxed.

When she descended, he had moved alongside her again and began stroking her hip.

She opened her eyes and gazed at him. "What's your name?"

"Larkin."

Smiling, she caressed his face. "I like that. So you picked me because I wanted an untamed man, huh?"

"You're a woman of passion and need a man who can match you, but part of you also wants to be protected and loved. Your soul beckoned mine, Jolene. Even if you don't believe it now, one day you will." He kissed her mouth, then his lips traveled down her torso, pausing only long enough for him to circle her nipples with his tongue.

Jolene closed her eyes and stroked his hair and shoulders. Rather than chilly as she'd been earlier, she felt warm all over. His powerful body exuded heat and his kisses could melt a glacier.

His stiff cock brushed against her leg. At that moment she longed to please him as much as he had pleased her.

"Larkin." She pushed against him, but he was too strong. "Stop. Let me touch you."

"You are touching me."

"Not where I want to."

He chuckled, a masculine sound that made her burn with lust, and lifted his head to gaze at her.

"It's my cock you desire, my wanton Jolene?"

"Yes. Oh, yes," she purred, gratified to see the passion burning in his eyes.

Giving her belly one last lick, he rolled onto his back and spread his long, sinewy legs. Her heart pounding, she crawled between them and stared at him for a moment. He was gorgeous with his broad, hair-dusted chest, thick biceps, and washboard abs. Though he now appeared like a normal man, he exuded supernatural power that thrilled her to the core. A short time ago, he had been a magnificent black steed carrying her on his back. Like the leprechauns this land was famous for, he possessed ancient treasure. He had existed since the Pagan age, but was choosing to reenter the world at her side.

"Are you going to keep me waiting, woman?" he breathed, his handsome face tense with desire.

A glance at his steely cock told her that she aroused him as much as he aroused her. Licking her lips, she bent and clasped his staff. For several seconds she breathed on its head, then gently flicked her tongue over it. With her eyes closed so she could better enjoy his taste and scent, she began licking his cock from base to crown. She swirled her tongue around it, then sucked on the tip.

"Ah," he groaned, burying his fingers in her hair. "That's right, Jolene. There. Ah."

She listened intently to the rhythm of his breathing and paid careful attention to the way his body tensed and strained. Quickly, she learned that he loved having the underside of his cock head licked. He also seemed to get a particular thrill when her mouth briefly left his staff to lick and suck his balls.

"Yes, oh, yes," he murmured, caressing her head. His hands trembled a bit, yet he didn't clutch her hard or tug on her hair.

When she began kneading his sac while sucking his cock deeply into her mouth, his entire body tensed. His hips thrust gently. The knowledge that he was restraining himself to keep from hurting her made her want to please him even more. She sucked faster and deeper, one hand stroking his shaft while the other squeezed his balls.

A shudder ripped through him, and he pushed her away.

"That's enough," he panted, his chest heaving and the ridges of his sharp cheekbones flushed. "Mount me, woman, and ride."

Jolene didn't have to be told twice. Straddling him, she grasped his cock and lowered herself upon it. Inch by inch the satin skinned rod slid into her passion drenched pussy. Goodness, he filled her perfectly. Never in her life had anything felt as amazing as this.

Her pulse racing, she began riding him, slowly at first, but the painful pace didn't last long. Flinging her head back, she bounced upon him.

Larkin clutched her hips and grunted with passion, his hips thrusting upward, following her rhythm.

"Yes, oh, Larkin! Oh, this is so, so..." Overcome with sensation, she trailed off, panting hard and bouncing wildly atop him.

With a swift motion, he rolled her onto her back and pinned her beneath him.

For a moment they lay still, their bodies joined and their panting breaths mingling. Jolene opened her eyes and gazed into his. They looked so fierce, like when he was the steed, but also tender. At that moment she knew that no matter what happened, a portion of her heart would always belong to this spirit, this mythic creature, this untamed man.

"Sweet Jolene," he whispered against her lips before claiming them in a kiss filled with raw passion. His tongue explored every moist corner. Hers met it in a sensual battle that neither could lose.

He began thrusting, pulling out until he nearly slipped from her completely, then swooping down and filling her with his thick, hard cock. Slowly, he increased his rhythm, his powerful body trembling with need.

"I love how you feel inside me," she murmured, clinging to him. "You're so big and you touch me exactly where I want to be touched."

"I am here to please you, Jolene," he said, thrusting faster. By the harshness of his breathing, she sensed he was almost on the verge of climax – or so she thought.

She came, moaning and thrashing, her legs wrapped around his waist and her pussy clenching his cock, but he remained hard within her.

His powerful rhythm never ceased, but continued driving her toward yet another orgasm. To Jolene the entire world seemed to stop turning. All that mattered was the climax she was striving to reach and the gorgeous man pounding into her lust drenched body.

He seemed to know exactly what she wanted.

"I need you, my beautiful Jolene."

"I'm right here," she gasped, her hands soothing his back. It would be mere seconds before she came, but she wondered if he could hold out that long. The tension emanating from him seemed almost unendurable. His breath rasped in her ear and tremors of desire shook his steely frame.

Several more fast, hard thrusts and she burst into an orgasm that was, miraculously, as powerful as the last three.

With a savage cry, Larkin came. He collapsed upon her, soaked in sweat, his breathing ragged.

After a moment, he lifted his head and chuckled. "Jolene, love, that's the first pleasure I've had with a woman in longer than you can imagine."

His words touched her more than she thought possible. He'd said he'd been lonely. For the first time she noticed the years of solitude glistening in his eyes and had the sudden urge to comfort him.

"You already have, Jolene," he whispered, as if reading her mind. Perhaps he was. He'd said he could see her life reflected in her eyes.

If she was starting to feel attached to him after one night, she was bound to fall in love with him if they spent any length of time together.

"That's the idea, my Jolene."

"Fallon said you'd lose interest."

His brow furrowed and his eyes flashed. "You'd better stop listening to this Fallon. She might think she knows the legends about my kind, but she certainly doesn't know me."

"We'll just have to educate her."

His irritated look faded to a smile and he stroked her face with his fingertip.

"Speaking of Fallon, as much as I hate to leave this lovely room, I know the perfect place to start *your* education in the modern world."

"Where?"

"First we'd better get you some clothes. You'll look gorgeous in a T-shirt and jeans."

"T-shirt?" His brow furrowed. "Jeans?"

"You'll see." Standing, she grasped his hand and tugged until he appeased her and rose from the bed. He kissed her chastely this time, but the gesture still managed to excite her. If she didn't get him out of the castle soon, she'd fall right back into bed. As much as she relished the idea of making love with him all night, she could hardly wait to get to the St. Patrick's Day party at the pub. When Fallon finally saw her "imaginary" pooka, she was going to be shamrock green with envy.

Chapter Four

Jolene walked alongside Larkin, her arm looped through his. She couldn't keep from staring at him. Here she was in the company of a real fairy. If not for the solidity of his body against hers and the memory of their wonderful lovemaking, she would have thought she'd imagined him.

Glancing at his lean, muscular body clad in a black leather jacket, T-shirt, jeans, and boots, she sighed with delight. The shops in town were closed, but using his magic, he had duplicated an outfit she'd shown him in a magazine and he looked fantastic in it. Just as she'd suspected, the taut curve of his backside was made for snug denim.

He turned to her, moonlight glinting in his eyes and shining upon his glossy black hair now bound at the nape of his neck. "Is something wrong?"

"It's hard to believe all this is really happening."

He paused, tugging her into his arms. "But you *do* believe. Tell me you'll never stop believing, Jolene." A hint of desperation shone through his rugged veneer. "You have no idea how much you mean to me."

"I still don't understand why you decided on me. You've lived here all your life. Surely some women must have caught your –"

He took her face in his hands and kissed her to silence. "For years I've been ignored, no longer feared or desired. The magic means little to me anymore. I want human touch. The closeness shared by a man and woman. I've missed that more than you know. Finally I've met the woman who is meant for me alone."

His words warmed her and raised soft, feminine emotions she'd never felt before. "Don't you think we're moving a little fast?"

"Love, I've awaited you for centuries, and you've waited for me all your life."

Oddly enough, he was right. Until she'd met him, she'd never realized how much she craved male companionship. The men she'd dated had been decent enough, but they didn't arouse her like he did. Most of them were attractive with good careers and respectful to her, but they bored her. When she looked into their eyes, she knew they were completely civilized, molded by their culture's constant search for wealth and political correctness to the point of losing their individuality.

Larkin's wild spirit and self-confidence intrigued her. The way he took her in his arms and called her his woman did things to her libido that she never imagined possible.

"Here we are," she said, tugging him toward the pub, grateful for a reason to end a conversation that unsettled her too much to continue.

"Just remember, Jolene, you belong to me and I belong to you. Nothing can change that."

Before she could reply, he grasped her shoulders and kissed her. His lips moved gently against hers. His tongue slipped into her mouth, both asking and demanding.

Splaying his hands against her back, he warmed her with sweeping caresses. The party and everything except his kiss faded from her mind. Completely absorbed in the marvelous sensations coursing through her, she thought only of making love with him again.

The pub door creaked open and someone cleared her throat loudly.

"Jolene, do you and your friend plan on coming in?"

Jolene jumped with surprise and tried to pull away from Larkin, but he kept one arm wrapped firmly around her.

Rather than struggle against a position she liked so well, she settled against him, placed a hand lightly on his chest, and smiled. "Fallon, this is Larkin."

"Pleased to meet you." Fallon extended her hand which he kissed.

A charming gesture, but it sparked a bit of jealousy within Jolene. She'd have to teach him a modern handshake.

Fallon didn't seem to mind in the least. She smiled, a dreamy expression in her eyes. "I don't believe I've seen you in town before, Larkin."

"I usually keep to myself. Besides, you might have passed me by and not noticed."

Fallon's appreciative gaze swept his handsome face and athletic build. "Somehow I doubt that. Jolene, what kind of friend are you, keeping a secret like this from me?"

Feeling mischievous, Jolene grinned and said, "I didn't really keep a secret. I told you all about the pooka."

Fallon laughed and gently squeezed Jolene's hand. "You always had a fine sense of humor. I suppose if a fairy took human form to woo a mortal woman, he would look just like this."

"Thank you." Larkin bowed slightly, a gleam of amusement in his eyes.

"Well, tonight if I see you ride away on a big black horse, I'll believe your story," Fallon said. "Anyway, I'm happy you decided to come to the party after all. Come inside."

Larkin cocked one of his wickedly arched eyebrows. "What party?"

Fallon glanced at him like he'd just sprouted another head. "The St. Patrick's Day party."

Jolene felt him stiffen a bit. His jaw tightened visibly.

"Uh, we'll be in soon, Fallon."

"Fine, but you two better behave yourselves out here." She grinned and slipped back into the pub.

Jolene turned to Larkin and caressed his face, startled by the defensive look in his eyes. "What's wrong?"

"St. Patrick's Day. Your friends will not accept me. They are of the new religion. I should not have come here."

"Don't be ridiculous. Be as charming to them as you are to me and they'll like you. Did you see how Fallon couldn't keep her eyes off you?"

"That cannot be avoided. Most women are helpless when faced with my virility."

Raising her eyes to heaven, Jolene bit her cheek to keep from laughing. "How can a man with an ego this big have a rejection complex?"

"I know where I'm not wanted, woman. My kind were driven off long ago."

"Your kind are the stuff of legends. Stories about you make people happy. If you want the world to accept you, Larkin, you need to accept it as well."

He balled his fists and turned away, gazing skyward. "Perhaps you're right. I do want to become a part of your world, but –"

Jolene rested her hand on his back, feeling the tension in his powerful muscles and longing to comfort him. "Don't be afraid."

He spun, his eyes flashing. "I fear nothing, woman."

"Then prove it." She took his hand and tugged him into the pub.

* * *

Larkin's heartbeat quickened when he stepped into the pub. He chastised himself for being concerned with what mortals thought of him, yet deep inside he understood the importance of fitting in tonight.

The small pub was crowded with locals and visitors. Music and conversation filled the room, and the aroma of ale stirred memories of gatherings long ago.

After a few uncomfortable moments, he began to relax. Times had changed, but in many ways people remained the same. They still enjoyed good food, drink, and company.

Fallon and Jolene introduced him to their friends. The females looked at him with customary appreciation. While Larkin found their attention flattering, he made sure Jolene remained close to his side. She was his woman and he wanted the world to know it.

Several of the men watched him with a hint of rivalry in their eyes, but his charms, which worked as well on men as on women, soon disarmed them. They clapped his back and drank with him like he was a brother.

Fallon's grandfather, a lively old man with glistening blue eyes, began telling stories about fairy folk to a group of tourists huddled around the bar. At first Larkin stiffened, offended by the way the stories seemed to amuse rather than awe the people.

"You see," Jolene whispered close to his ear. "They enjoy hearing about that stuff."

He relaxed a bit and tightened his arm around her shoulders. "Perhaps you're right. There's still a place for us after all."

"I bet you could tell them some fascinating stories."

"I could probably spin a few tales."

"Mr. O'Neal, would you care to share the spotlight?" Jolene called when he finished his story.

"Jolene," Larkin warned.

The old man's eyes twinkled. "You have some stories to tell?"

"Not me, but Larkin knows quite a few."

Mr. O'Neal's captive audience now turned to Larkin. The awkward feeling from earlier reappeared, but only for a moment. Soon he was telling tales of times long past. As he talked, old memories became more vivid. He spoke of his brothers' mischief, stealing crops as well as maidens' virginity. He reminisced about the many fairies who had once inhabited the island and the surrounding sea. The humans listened with fascination in their eyes and the last shred of discomfort faded completely from Larkin. The tourists seemed particularly interested in leprechauns and gold. Jolene later explained that those images were associated with St. Patrick's Day, particularly in her homeland, America.

When all the stories had been told, one of the pub's workers brought out a harp and played.

Jolene melted against Larkin as they enjoyed the music. He could not find the words to describe how good it felt to be among people again and to have a woman he cared about in his arms.

"It's getting late," Jolene murmured, glancing at him. "Want to go to my cottage and finish celebrating by ourselves?"

He nodded and kissed her cheek.

After saying goodnight to their companions, they left the warmth of the pub and stepped into the chilly outdoors.

Jolene smiled. "I can hardly wait to get home and make love."

"Neither can I. It'll be a short run."

In a blink Larkin changed into his horse form and magically flung her onto his back.

"Hold tight, my Jolene," he said, then whinnied playfully, his hoofs dancing on the cobbled walk.

Before he galloped off, he caught sight of Fallon staring out the pub's window, a look of utter shock on her face.

Moments later, they reached Jolene's cottage. Before stepping inside, he changed back to his human shape, not bothering to create clothes. He magically discarded hers as well so that she rested, naked, in his arms.

Snuggling against him, she shivered. "Larkin, it's too cold to be out here nude."

A moment later they were cuddling in bed with a fire blazing in the hearth across the room.

Raising himself on his elbow, he gazed at her and gently circled her nipple with his fingertip. His thumb swept the hardening peak. He rolled the pink bead between his thumb and forefinger, then bent and captured it in his lips.

Drawing a sharp breath, she buried her fingers in his hair and arched against him. He loved her scent, taste, and little gasps of passion.

"Larkin, please keep touching me," she panted.

His tongue continued sweeping her nipple. Every now and then he bit the plump flesh ever so gently, making her writhe. While his mouth teased her breast, his hand stroked her inner thigh, inching higher until he reached her pussy lips. Using one finger, he began exploring her, thrilled to find her completely drenched with lust. He slipped his wet finger from her and used it to circle her sensitive bud.

She moaned softly, her hips squirming. He rubbed faster while at the same time sucking her nipple.

"Oh, yes. Oh!" she cried, her breathing harsh.

Just before she came, he covered her body with his, supporting his weight on his hands, the tip of his cock pressed against her slit.

"I want you, Larkin," she murmured, gazing at him through half closed eyes. She clutched his shoulders, trying to force him nearer, but her strength was nothing compared to his. "Please."

He slid into her slowly, enjoying the sensation of her soft, wet sheath around his cock.

Finally buried to the hilt, he remained still, his pulse racing. Her eyes were closed, a passionate expression on her lovely face.

"Jolene, look at me."

It took her a moment to open her eyes, and when she did, he was pleased to see the first glimmer of affection mingling with lust.

"No matter what happens, you will always have my gratitude, woman."

"Is now the time for this conversation?" she panted, her pussy tightening around his cock.

"There's something I must tell you."

"What?"

"Without you, I was fading from this existence, becoming a legend like the others of my kind. I know that is still my fate. Change cannot be stopped, but through you I can remain connected to this world."

"Through me?"

"You believed in me. You wanted me."

"I do want you, Larkin." She tightened her arms around him.

"Just for tonight?"

Holding his gaze she shook her head and smiled slightly. "No. I doubt I could let you go after just one night."

"Jolene." He kissed her mouth, then touched his forehead to hers, their faces so close that their breaths mingled. "I swear to treasure you for all our lives. I will make you happy."

"I'll do the same for you." She hugged him tighter.

"You already do. Now don't let go of me."

His muscles tensed as he drove into her with fast, powerful thrusts.

Closing her eyes tightly, she clung to him, her arms locked around his neck and her legs wrapped around his waist.

She came, a sexy, feminine cry of fulfillment escaping her lips. Her wet sheath pulsed around his cock.

With several more quick thrusts, Larkin joined her in ecstasy. Panting, he rolled onto his back and cradled her against him.

"Larkin?"

"Yes, love?"

"You'll always have my gratitude, too. I never imagined feeling this wonderful."

"This is just the first of many wonderful nights to come. You have my word on that, Jolene."

She smiled and kissed his chest. "Happy St. Patrick's Day."

"Yes, my love." He squeezed her gently. "It definitely is."

Kate Hill

Kate Hill was not available for an interview at the time we were wrapping up this lovely tale... Last we knew she was making travel arrangements for Ireland. Heard she's rented a cottage off in the woods...

For an updated status report, visit her online at www.kate-hill.com.

Chemistry to Burn
Lacey Savage

Chapter One

Angelina Moore's beard itched.

Like the turtleneck of her least favorite fuzzy sweater, the furry bristles she'd picked up at the costume shop tickled every place they touched, especially the sensitive spot right beneath her chin. She swatted at the thick, bushy beard, and for a moment, sighed with relief when it no longer scraped against her skin. The respite was short lived, as the mere act of breathing made her bend her head and the maddening fake hair swept the hollow of her throat.

She growled her frustration between gritted teeth, well aware that her best friend could hear every murmur through the microphone she'd hidden beneath the lapel of her jacket.

"This is by far the dumbest thing you've ever done." Eve Benning's exasperated tone resonated clearly through the earpiece hidden in Angelina's left ear. "What possessed you to think you could get away with it?"

"If I had another choice, do you really think I'd be here?"

"Couldn't you just ask someone for a glamour spell? Your cousin, Trixie, or your Aunt Dora?"

Angelina toyed with the zipper dangling at the bottom of her leather jacket. "Look, it's bad enough to be the only fairy in the family with no real magical abilities. No wings, no glamour spells. Nothing. I'm not going to make a bigger fool of myself by asking for help, especially when I got myself into this in the first place."

Eve was silent for a long moment. "I'm glad you trusted me enough to tell me you were going to do this," she whispered at last.

"I don't think I had much choice. You would have found out about it one way or another."

From the moment the two girls met in fifth grade, they'd watched out for one another, no matter how hare-brained their schemes became. Together, they'd gotten proof of Eve's ex-boyfriend's cheating, managed to get a tenured professor fired for sexual harassment, and had even indulged in a threesome – and a very memorable foursome – one night on a cruise ship.

Over the years, they'd learned there was no one else they could count on. They'd been in some dire situations together, but even Angelina had to admit that this brilliant idea of hers could well be the last adventurous thing they ever did.

Eve snorted, a decidedly unladylike sound. "I still say you should have let me come with you. I'd be of more use to you out there than I am in here."

"We've been over this a hundred times. I need you in the van in case I have to make a quick getaway. If Griffin has guards with him, and they spot me, I may need you to drive up to the gate on very short notice."

"Hopefully not before you land a few solid kicks to the bastard's balls. After you're done with him, there'll be no doubt in his mind that he shouldn't have messed with Angelina Moore."

Angelina grinned, her self-confidence boosted by her friend's encouraging words. "Good to have you along."

"Yeah, well, don't get used to it. Are you sure you won't reconsider and go after Griffin the old-fashioned way? With cops and a warrant?"

Angelina opened her mouth to protest, but Eve cut her off before she could begin to launch into the same explanation she'd given her friend every day for the past two weeks. "I know, I know. This is personal. How's it look in there?"

From her hiding spot behind a tall pine tree, Angelina could see the entire sprawl of the Hard Delights amusement park. "Busy."

A Ferris wheel shone brightly against the night sky, and beside it, a long dragon in a curiously phallic shape swung from side to side, its bulbous head revealing a slithering tongue. Twenty feet away from where she'd taken cover, two men stood on either side of a black metal gate, greeting the huge crowd continuing to pour into the park.

Located an hour's drive outside Vernon, Connecticut, the park had managed to keep away the media circus that usually accompanied adult ventures like this one. Since it was far enough away from town, children mistakenly wandering in and getting an eyeful weren't likely, so the government didn't bother to turn up the heat on the festivities.

"A gay carnival, huh?" Angelina could picture Eve shaking her head. "Wish I could see it."

"After I'm done here, you can borrow the outfit," Angelina suggested, not bothering to hide a smirk.

"And speaking of outfits, how are the pants holding up?"

"Barely." Angelina tugged at the waistband of the leather pants she'd picked up at the costume shop. There'd been only a few full disguises in stock from which to choose. Her options had been limited to a pirate's outfit that definitely didn't look like anything Johnny Depp would wear, a biker, and Santa Claus. Considering she was trying to pass for a man, not win the prize for best costume at a masquerade, she'd gone with the biker. Scratching at the irritating beard, she was beginning to wish she'd picked the pirate. At least he only had a moustache. And a wooden leg.

"Okay, hon. Go get 'im."

Angelina took a deep breath, then another, her palms digging into the hard bark of the tree. Eve was right. She had to go in there, and soon. If Griffin managed to launch the firework shells before she had a chance to sabotage the fuses, this would all be in vain.

"Stay with me," Angelina whispered as she broke free of the cover of the forest and started walking toward the gate. Eve gave an assenting grunt.

The park was even busier than usual tonight, since Hard Delights was celebrating its third year of operation. There were all kinds of activities planned, most of an adult nature, including Angelina's – Griffin's – fireworks display. Angelina cringed at the inward slip. Those fireworks hadn't been hers for a long time. Not since her former business partner decided to steal her formula and create his own batch of physics-defying black powder.

Unlike regular fireworks, which could only be designed in simple shapes, Angelina's formula made it possible to create intricate images and set them free against the backdrop of the clear dark sky. Also, unlike the usual sparkling lights and colors, her fireworks had the power to come alive, to be animated and flicker and move in any way the designer chose before gradually fading into the star-studded midnight velvet behind them.

They said it would never work, of course. The most brilliant minds in chemistry had called Angelina a lunatic, a misguided fool. Even Griffin, the only man she'd trusted with her formula, had scoffed and tried to talk her into creating something more useful, more profitable. That is, until he stole every last note she'd ever made on the explosive powder and disappeared.

I guess even small sums of profit seem bigger when you don't have to split the take.

"You there. Where do you think you're going?" The harsh male voice stopped Angelina dead in her tracks. She turned slowly to face one of the guards standing outside the metal gate.

"I thought the park was open to everyone," Angelina said, deepening her voice and praying she wouldn't attract any unwanted attention. Though she knew that the park officials wouldn't turn away a woman just because of her gender, she also knew that ninety-nine percent of the people there tonight would be men, which would make a five-foot-nine redhead much too easy to spot.

"You gotta buy a ticket. Twenty dollars."

"Twenty dollars?" she echoed. "That's absurd."

"It's a special night." He moved in closer to stand just an arm's length away. Angelina ducked her head and stared at the ground as she dug her hand into the back pocket of the leather pants, digging for the bills she remembered Eve sliding in there. *For cotton candy*, Eve had suggested.

After exchanging the bill for an orange cardboard ticket, Angelina avoided meeting the man's eyes and walked inside.

She hadn't known what to expect, but the cacophony of light and noise that surrounded her as soon as she slipped through the gate was beyond even her wildest imaginings. The aroma of popcorn, hot dogs, and sweet cotton candy blended with the spicy musk of aftershave and raw sex.

To her right, two men leaned against a lamppost, the harsh neon light spilling over their dark skin. Arms around each other's waists, they watched her, an amused smile on their sharp features.

Across from them, another couple sat on a bench, their tongues entwined, hands skimming across each other's ribs. Angelina watched their fingers trail over tight shirts encasing hard, flat stomachs. The one sitting on the right took things one step further, tugging on his companion's belt. Angelina caught a brief glimpse of sweat-matted hair and glistening pale skin before forcing herself to tear her gaze away. Desire poured through every vein, making her acutely aware she hadn't had sex since Griffin left.

This park, oozing sexual energy from every neon-encrusted ride, was definitely not the place for a horny, oversexed fairy. As a woman, she might have been able to withstand the sensations flowing through her body. As a magical being attuned to every nerve ending, it was all she could do not to find a public washroom and relieve some of the tension thrumming in her loins.

Pulse pounding, she urged herself onward and moved through the throng, taking care to avoid eye contact with anyone who seemed likely to call her on her sorry excuse for a disguise. Gum stuck to the bottom of her shoe and she swore softly as she pulled her foot up from the sticky mess.

Eve chuckled in her ear. "See anything interesting?"

"Men. Lots and lots of men." In fact, Angelina had never seen so many good- looking men gathered in one place. All skin colors, body types and nationalities mingled with one another in front of rides with names like "The Big One," "One Eyed Monster," and "Long and Lean."

"I guess it's true what they say," Eve offered in a playful tone. "If they're not taken, all the good ones are definitely gay."

"Suddenly, I'm starting to think that's not such a bad thing." Only inches away, two of the most delicious men Angelina had ever seen engaged in a passionate kiss. Their lips parted, allowing their tongues to sweep and come together in a dance that lit Angelina's already flustered libido on fire.

"It's been too long since anyone's kissed me like that." Her voice held a hint of melancholy she tried to mask without much success.

"Griffin was a fool."

Angelina had trouble disagreeing with Eve when she had a point. Yet, she couldn't help the way her gut twisted at her friend's words. "He wasn't all bad."

Reluctant though she may have been to admit it, Angelina couldn't hide the fact that she still cared for him, especially not from Eve. Seeing his smiling, arrogant face in the Sunday paper when the announcement for tonight's fireworks display made the news had brought back all kinds of memories she wished had remained buried.

"Sure he was," Eve argued. "How else do you explain the fact that he took everything? He's taking credit for your work, Angelina, even now."

"He had the most perfect ass," Angelina countered. "No man with such a hot ass could be all bad."

Eve laughed, shattering the tension that sizzled through their small communication device. "And a really big cock."

"Hey!"

"What?" Eve asked innocently. "You bragged."

"Yeah, maybe once or –"

The rest of her words caught in her throat and disappeared on a sharp intake of breath. Standing outside the dark opening to a ride called "Blow Me Away," Griffin Taylor looked surprisingly comfortable in dark pressed pants and a soft white shirt that clung to his muscular shoulders like a second skin. Six-two, broad-chested, and built like a football player, Griff had never really blended in with the scientists and chemistry professors they'd hired to work for Incendiary Enterprises. Yet here, among a multitude of stunning men who mercilessly teased, fondled, and brought each other to the heights of flirtatious ecstasy, her former lover seemed to have found his niche.

Desire swept through her, quickly burrowing between her legs. Her pussy throbbed with recognition.

Griff looked up, his eyes scanning the crowd. Full, sensual lips pursed in concentration. Angelina's breathing stilled, though she knew there was no way he'd recognize her from that distance, especially in the biker outfit and the damnable beard.

"Eve," Angelina murmured, trying to keep her lips still as she spoke into the tiny microphone, "we're on."

Chapter Two

From his vantage point atop the "Blow Me Away" roller-coaster platform, Griffin watched Angelina stroll into the amusement park, her determined stride only wavering when she caught sight of him. He made a show of letting his gaze wander over the heads of the multitude of men, but his eyes remained fixed on the gorgeous redhead he'd gone to such absurd lengths to draw to his side.

Too bad she looked so little like herself now.

Griffin tried to hide a smirk as he watched her. The leather pants were definitely not her size. They hung down around her waist and trailed on the ground, their shapeless form hiding her luscious long legs. The oversized leather jacket wasn't much better. Shapeless and bulky, it only served to mask all hints of femininity he knew to be lying beneath.

He remembered every inch of her stunning body. The pale, creamy skin, taut brown nipples, flat stomach, and the mound of red curls he loved to run his fingers through as he nudged at her clit. He could even recall her scent, so different from that of other women. She always smelled and tasted sweet, like he'd just dipped his tongue in a jar of honey. There wasn't a hint of spice to her. No musk, no pungent aroma of arousal. Just nectarous, syrupy cream, like melted sugar.

He shivered at the memory, forcing himself to look past Angelina's unflattering clothes. Biting the inside of his lip to keep from grinning, he wondered what had possessed her to go with the outrageous disguise. Even if the costume fit properly, her feet were a dead giveaway. The shiny black pumps had tall, narrow heels.

Not to mention the wig and beard. A disaster. The mound of stringy brown hair sitting ruffled atop her head barely hid the long corkscrew curls she'd stuffed beneath.

As for the beard... well, it hardly seemed fair to call it that. The thick patch of fake fur resembled something she'd picked off the side of the road, and it looked like it irritated her skin just as much. She tugged and scraped at it, her face twisting with aggravation. The last yank pulled the beard off altogether. Far from angered, Angelina seemed relieved, staring at the guise for only a moment before dumping it in a nearby trashcan.

That was more like it. Angelina's fine ivory skin always shone with an internal glow, perpetually dewy and silky smooth to the touch. Her strawberry-red lips parted as the tip of her tongue swept out to moisten them. Gripping the jacket's collar, she turned it up, hiding half her face behind it. Her green eyes darted in his direction. Griff looked away, pretending not to notice.

Only when she turned her back and marched off in the direction of the fireworks did he jump off the platform to follow her. Keeping his distance, he made sure she didn't realize she had company, signaling security to let her "slip" past them. Angelina pressed forward with all the confidence he remembered. It didn't seem to matter to her that she'd just walked into a gay fiesta. Though he saw her glance at a particularly amorous couple, she didn't halt her stride, or shiver with revulsion. In fact, if he knew Angelina, she'd be enjoying the show later, after she'd accomplished what she'd set out to do with that silly disguise and her purposeful gait.

In a place like this, the pyrotechnics were set up about a hundred and fifty feet behind the main stage. The park management hadn't booked a concert tonight, preferring instead to engage the crowd's attention with the exclusive fireworks display Griff had promised them.

Angelina neared a closely parked group of three flatbed launch trailers, where Griff had personally placed round shells, each containing a specialty pyrotechnic marvel.

Her shoulders tensed as she took a cursory look around her. A few feet away, two men were engaged in more than conversation, their groans filling the night air. Across from them, thirty-five pound steel mortars held the shells in place. A top-of-the-line computer sat well back from the crowd, waiting for the command to launch.

Angelina didn't hesitate. From her right pocket, she pulled out a pair of pliers and knelt before one of the trailers, evidently meaning to get to work as quickly as possible. Each flatbed held a hundred and ten charges. Angelina was a whiz when it came to chemistry, physics, and anything in between. If she'd planned on snipping the fuses on each charge, Griff knew she wouldn't waste a moment of unnecessary time looking for the right spot to cut. She'd tackle the task methodically, rapidly destroying the display in less than half an hour.

If only she'd lavished that kind of attention on him when they were together, Griffin wouldn't have had to go to such extreme measures. Instead, she'd preferred her lab, her powder, and her microscopes to everything he ever had to offer.

The couple's passionate groans masked Griffin's footsteps as he approached Angelina from behind.

"I'm here, Eve. Stay close." Angelina's soft murmur made Griff halt in his tracks. He hadn't seen an accomplice, but that didn't mean Eve wasn't there. Angelina's best friend was never far behind.

Content with his quick perusal of the surroundings, and not giving Angelina a chance to destroy even one of the fuses, he gripped her arm and pulled her to her feet. Clamping his hand around her mouth, he yanked her back and held her close to his body.

Her reactions were quicker than he'd expected. A muffled cry reached his ears a moment before a sharp stab from her elbow brought a stinging pain to Griffin's ribs. Her teeth embedded themselves in his palm.

"Fuck!" He hissed an indrawn breath and released his grip on her arm. "What is wrong with you?"

"What is wrong with *me*?" she shrieked, drawing the attention of the nearby men. Griff waved them away as they started to approach. "I wouldn't be here if it wasn't for you."

"Still upset about that?" he challenged in a light, bored tone. "Couldn't you just lock yourself up in your lab for another week or two and design some other crazy concoction the scientific community would never take seriously?"

Angelina gritted her teeth, her jaw tight. Anger flashed in her emerald eyes for only an instant before she lunged for him. It was all the opportunity Griff needed. He gripped her wrists with one hand and spun her around so her back was against him. Lowering his head, he nibbled at her earlobe. She squirmed, but her pulse quickened beneath his thumb, sending a shiver of arousal straight to his groin. "Did you really think you could sabotage my work, Angel?"

She struggled in his hold. "Don't ever call me that again. And it's *my* work, you thieving bastard."

He chuckled, nipping at the tender skin at the side of her throat. "Come on, now. Other than that grimy lab in your basement, you wouldn't have a thing if it wasn't for me."

Her body stiffened. "You gave me your money. I gave you a lot more than that."

"Angelina? Talk to me, honey. Has he hurt you?" The voice came from Angelina's jacket. He trailed his fingertip beneath the hard leather until he found the small hearing device that had fallen out of Angelina's ear. A delicate plastic cord had kept the miniature contraption from falling to the ground.

"I'm fine, Eve," Angelina said. "No need to send out a search party."

"She's not here, is she?" Griff asked, following the cord to the microphone hidden lower beneath the jacket. Angelina gave an almost imperceptible shake of her head.

Not loosening his hold on Angelina's wrists, Griff tossed both snooping devices to the ground. "What did you hope to accomplish here? Once you'd sabotaged the display, then what?"

She shrugged, the gesture a barely discernable lifting of her shoulders. "You could never do this without me either, Griff. It's my work that got you this contract, and whatever profit you're gaining from it. How much did they offer you? Ten thousand? Twenty?"

"Fifty."

She sighed and slumped against him. "Was it worth it, Griff? Stealing from your partner?"

It was his turn to shrug as he struggled to find a way to explain. Angelina was so certain she knew all about him. For the most part, she was right, but there were things she'd never understand.

Pulling off the cheap wig, he inhaled the fruity scent of her shampoo as her tresses spilled down her back. Damn, but she even smelled as good as he remembered. He wondered briefly if her pussy would, too. "I didn't do it for the money, Angel."

"Why, then? The glory?" Anger and bitterness clung to her mocking tone.

He supposed she had every right to both those emotions. The longer he held her against him, the more his reasons didn't seem to matter. Guilt knotted in his stomach, along with shame. Neither was a feeling he was accustomed to, and both left a bitter taste in his mouth.

Angelina's lithe, slender body trembled beneath his touch as he grazed the base of her neck with the tip of his finger. "What if I told you I did it for you?"

Her bitter laugh mingled with the animated voices around them. For the moment, they were alone behind the stage, but that wouldn't last long. Someone was bound to wander back here and find them, and then he'd have to let her go. His cock stirred, pressing against her back.

No. He'd made that mistake once already. He'd never let her go again.

"Come on, Griff. You don't expect me to believe that."

"Believe what you will, for now."

"Nothing you say is going to make me change my mind about you."

He slid his palm beneath her jacket, brushing it over the tip of a hardened nipple. The realization that her body thrummed with the same level of arousal as his made his breath catch in his throat. "What if I show you instead?"

With one last tweak of the stiff bud, he freed her wrists. Angelina stumbled forward, caught her balance, and spun around to face him, her chin thrust out, shoulders squared. "You shouldn't have released me. I'll leave, but I'll come back the next time you decide to use my work for your own gain. And the next time, and the time after that. You'll never be free of me, Griff."

The smile that broadened over his features must have surprised her, because her eyes widened. "I'm counting on it."

Angelina's brows furrowed over her startling green orbs. "What game are you playing?"

Her jacket gaped open, revealing full, ripe breasts encased in a silk shirt. Griffin's balls tightened in their sack. He *had* to have her, but it had to be her choice. "No game. Just a simple proposal."

She huffed and planted her hands on her hips. "I'm listening."

"You'll get your work back."

"In return for?"

"Some of your time."

She shook her head. "I don't understand."

"Spend an hour with me, in there," he said, indicating behind him to a roomy trailer.

The camping gear had been part of his contract. He'd agreed to launch the fireworks himself, if they let him spend the night on the premises. His request must not have been as odd as he'd thought, because the park's management didn't hesitate. He had three signatures on the contract a few minutes later.

Comprehension flickered over her features as she stared past him at the camper. He could almost see her weighing up her options, deciding whether fucking him would be worth the return of her formula.

"One more romp for old times' sake, and then you'll be gone? Forever?"

"If that's what you want."

She lifted her chin and held his stare. "That's what I want."

Disappointment jutted through Griff. The force of the emotion unnerved him, even though it was no less than he'd expected, and certainly no more than he deserved.

For now, her decision would have to do.

"After you," he said, sweeping his arm out in an overly elaborate gesture.

Angelina brushed past him, not meeting his eyes as she crossed the distance to the camper.

Griff flexed the muscles in his back, trying to dislodge some of the tension that had settled there. Puffing out a long breath, he watched her disappear through the door of the RV.

He glanced at his watch. 9:05 pm.

He had less than an hour to prove to Angelina she needed him as much as he wanted her.

Chapter Three

"You planned this," Angelina said, pointing an accusing finger at Griffin.

They stood in the middle of what the outside proclaimed to be a SportsLux Recreational Vehicle. Cherry cabinets lined the walls of the fully equipped kitchen, complete with porcelain sinks, a stainless steel refrigerator and copper pots and pans hanging from a specially designed hanging pot rack.

The living and bedroom area were each separated by a retractable wall, which allowed the living space to be expanded on a whim, or drawn to an enclosed space for added privacy. Currently, all the wall separators were pulled back, exposing every inch of the trailer as containing the high-quality, lavish elegance Angelina had been accustomed to when she was with Griff. He'd spared no expense on the camper, but instead of awe, anger pierced Angelina's gut.

Griffin had been a silent partner in Incendiary Enterprises. Using the hefty inheritance he'd received as sole beneficiary after his father's death, he'd provided the money she couldn't obtain through the government or grants funded by the scientific community, in exchange for a share of the profits. He didn't work for the company in any significant way, but his money ensured that Angelina could continue to develop the formula that would put Incendiary Enterprises on the map.

Which was why it had hurt so much when he stole her work and disappeared with everything she'd had to show for years of slaving over chemistry sets. It wasn't as if he needed whatever paltry sum the new fireworks would bring. Sure, fifty thousand dollars was a lot of money for anyone, but to Griffin, it was still mere pocket change.

"You knew I'd come here," she whispered, trailing her fingertips over a pair of velvet-covered handcuffs that lay on the bedside table. No sign of use marred the perfect lining, but Angelina remembered the feel of the heavy restraints around her wrists. She rubbed the bridge of her nose, trying to remember if they'd used them more than once.

"I knew you couldn't resist," Griff confirmed, taking a step toward her.

Angelina lifted her arms to keep him at bay, desire and fury twisting in her chest. She didn't like the game he played. Whatever his sweet words and sweeter smiles had to tell her, she knew there had to be another reason for bringing her here besides mind-blowing sex. He could have that with any woman. Why would he need to return to the former lover whose heart he'd ripped out when he took the papers lying unattended on her desk?

"I trusted you," Angelina said softly.

For years, she'd locked her work away in a fireproof cabinet before leaving the lab. An identical safe stood in a corner of her apartment, and that night, she'd taken her notebook home with her, intending to scribble more notes over the weekend. Yet, instead of storing it safely away, she'd left it lying on the dining room table and gone to sleep. She remembered Griffin's body curled up beside hers as she drifted off.

In the morning, he was gone. And so was her formula.

"But I wanted more than that." His gruff voice startled her. She looked up from the crimson velvet lining to find him only inches away.

"What –"

Before Angelina could finish her thought, Griff lunged for her, pressing his mouth against hers in a fierce, passionate kiss. Her lips parted almost of their own accord, granting him entry. Their tongues met in a ravaging, possessive thrust, sending a flutter of excitement into Angelina's stomach.

This isn't happening.

She couldn't be doing this with him. Until an hour ago, she'd thought him the enemy. The man who had betrayed her trust. She would have done anything to destroy him, and now her pussy hummed with desire, indicating that with a mere kiss, a touch of his expert fingers over her breast, he could make her forget all that.

Well, it *wasn't* happening.

Fury reared inside her and she bit down on his lip, hard. He pulled out of her grasp, his hand flying to his mouth. It came away bloody, and his eyes widened. "What the hell did you do that for?"

She smirked, feeling a little better. "You deserved it."

Her victory was short lived. With a growl, Griffin grabbed both of her wrists and wrenched her arms over her head even as she tried to twist free of his grasp. The handcuffs snapped into place with a loud metal clang.

A sliver of trepidation rose in her throat, but the overwhelming arousal flooding her pussy eradicated the weak argument she considered making. He reached into a drawer and pulled out a black silk scarf, which he quickly turned into a blindfold and wrapped around her eyes.

Her breathing turned ragged as a shiver ran down her spine. "Griff?"

He didn't answer. She felt his hands caress her breasts, tweak at the hard nipples beading through her shirt. He twisted one between his fingers, almost painfully, and she hissed in a breath. Warmth flooded her nipple, chasing the sharp pleasure-pain. She recognized the feel of his mouth, wet and hot around her tight bud. Moaning against him, Angelina's knees weakened. She stumbled back and leaned against one of the walls of the trailer, thankful she hadn't hit anything on the way there.

She thought she heard him chuckle as he broke away. He pulled the bottom of her shirt out of her waistband, ripping buttons as he yanked it open. Cool air played over her breasts. She hadn't bothered to wear a bra under the thick leather coat. Now she questioned whether that had been a good idea.

The oversized leather pants came off next. Not a shred of light penetrated through the overbearing darkness of the blindfold, but the rest of her senses attuned themselves to every action Griff performed. She felt the rough texture of his palms as he pulled down her panties and let them pool around her ankles. Her skin broke into goose bumps as his lips touched her mound, the tip of his tongue delving briefly inside her slit, and she could smell him, the masculine scent of spicy aftershave mixing with the tangy aroma of sweat.

"Oh, Griff." She brought her hands down, ran them through his hair as he licked her pussy. Without warning he pulled back roughly.

He gripped her shoulders and positioned her so that her thighs hit something solid. "On your back," he commanded, shoving her lightly. She landed on a feather-soft bed.

Grabbing her ankles, he spread her legs apart. She felt her pussy lips open and her arousal drifted up to her nostrils. Heat flooded her cheeks at the thought of being on display before him. She tried to bring her legs together, but his grip was too strong.

"No. I like seeing you this way. I thought about having you like this every day while we were together."

She shivered at the ragged depth of emotion in his beguiling voice. "You did?" The words stuck in her throat. Her cunt throbbed, and her thoughts fluttered aimlessly around her mind as she tried to focus on what he'd just told her. "But you could have had me any time you wanted."

"Not like this." He licked the inside of her thigh, eliciting a shudder. "You were always too busy. Your experiments came first. When I had a few minutes of your time, sex was quick and dirty."

She chuckled, but the truth of his words made her squirm. Had she neglected him when they were together? Was that why he –

No. It was impossible even to contemplate. Griff took the formula for the money, the profits he wouldn't have to share. Yet he'd told her there was more to it than that. Could he have meant that he did this to get back at her for some perceived slight?

"Now you're mine." He released her ankles and moved away. Angelina felt the loss of his presence as a physical blow. She arched her back, needing his touch, unsure of where he was in the room.

When he returned after what seemed to Angelina like an eternity, he lifted her ankles over his shoulder. She took a deep breath and held it as her pussy flooded with her slick cream. Some of the wetness dripped from her cunt to slither down between her ass cheeks and, she assumed, pool on the bed. In her apartment, she would have never allowed her moisture to flood the crisp white sheets. But here, in this trailer, with Griffin poised above her, the physical manifestation of her arousal seemed like the perfect complement to their surroundings.

"You've always had the most magnificent pussy," he whispered, trailing a finger over her cleft. He dipped in for only a brief moment, then removed his hand. She heard a slurp and a pop, and she imagined him licking her juices off his finger. "Sweet. I bet you're the envy of every woman on the planet."

She grinned. Her fairy heritage had its advantages. Though her cream tasted like melted candy, she wished she didn't produce quite as much fairy dust.

"And these sparkles," he said, inserting two fingers into her greedy cunt. Her inner muscles sucked him in and she squirmed, pulling him deeper. "I always wondered what kind of lubricant you used."

"It's not lubricant," she said before she could think better of it. Explaining her magical race while he had her in such an intimate position didn't seem like a good idea.

Thankfully, he didn't seem inclined to pursue the issue. "Well, whatever it is, it's delicious."

His fingers moved in and out of her, slowly at first, then faster. When he added a third, she thrust her hips up to meet his powerful motions. He flicked her clit with his thumb and she cried out, her muscles clenching with the onset of her climax.

Something nudged the entrance to her ass. Before she could protest, Griff brought his free hand to her lips. "You're wet enough for me to use your own juices as lubricant. Trust me."

She shook her head. *Trust him?* How could she?

He pushed the tip of his cock deeper and she felt the thick head slide past her anal ring to invade the depths of her ass. She hissed out a breath as the pain drifted to mingle with the delight his fingers brought her cunt.

"Relax." His voice was soothing, but the hoarse tone told her he was as anxious to come as she was.

"I don't know if I can," Angelina admitted.

He ceased his thrusts. "Do you want me to stop?"

Her body trembled, her pussy crying out for the much-needed release. "No."

Griff nudged his cock in another inch. "Good."

He took his time, making the process excruciatingly slow, but giving her inner muscles time to adjust to the unfamiliar length and girth inside her anus. "You're so tight. Oh, God, Angel."

This time, the nickname didn't irk her. Instead of anger, she felt an absurd sense of delight as her name rolled off his tongue in the heat of ecstasy. The handcuffs clanked as she brought her hands up to run her fingers through his thick dark hair, forgetting for a moment she was being restrained.

Griff's cock entered her ass balls-deep, and she rocked against him, trembling slightly as she became accustomed to the pleasure-pain. He found his own rhythm, his cock matching the thrusts of his fingers inside her slick passage.

Release hovered just a breath away, but she had to know. "Why, Griff?"

He stilled his motions. "Because I love you."

Tears stung her eyes. Unlike the day he left, she didn't fight them, and the fat drops of wetness spilled out from beneath the blindfold and trickled down her cheeks.

He really hadn't betrayed her for the money. She remembered the countless nights she spent in the lab. Sometimes, they'd go weeks without seeing one another, and when they did, she was often too exhausted to care whether or not they made love. She cancelled dinners, missed movie dates, forgot Valentine's Day all three years, because her formulas were more important than her lover.

Now, with him filling every space within her body, she couldn't imagine how anything could be more important, more outstanding than this. "I'm sorry," she murmured.

He bent his head and kissed her cheek, the gesture more intimate than even the hard thrusts inside her ass or his fingers claiming her pussy. Warmth flooded her belly, initiating a shudder of gripping convulsions. Light burst behind her eyelids as the orgasm built from her stomach and flowed through her body, ending in the tips of her toes.

Her inner walls tightened around Griff, milking him as she came. He groaned, spilling his seed deep inside her ass. Their cries mingled in the still air of the trailer, bouncing off the walls, carrying Angelina to unimaginable heights of ecstasy.

Griff untied the blindfold and pulled it off before he drew his cock away from her body. He slid out almost as slowly as he entered. Angelina watched his flat, rippling abs, the hair on his strong chest matted with sweat. His fingers left her body last, and he smeared some of her juices along her waist, leaving a trail of golden sparkles blended in with the moisture.

After uncuffing her wrists, Griff disappeared into the bathroom to clean up. Angelina waited until he returned and lay beside her before asking the question that had been on her mind since the last shuddering traces of her overwhelming orgasm subsided. "You don't have much time, do you? Before your fireworks launch?"

His soft chuckle quickly turned into a full-fledged laugh. She stared at him, unable to comprehend what was so funny. When his mirth subsided, he turned to her, his wide grin extending from ear to ear. "Oh, baby, don't you get it? Your formula doesn't work."

Chapter Four

Angelina's frenzied anger was a wonder to behold. She leapt off the bed in her full naked glory, body sparkling with a soft golden glow, her long curly tresses a tumbled mess falling around her shoulders.

"You're such an ass," she whispered, her quiet tone a startling contrast to her body language, which indicated she'd like nothing more than to punch Griff in the groin. "I should have known this was all an act," she continued when he didn't argue. "The furious lovemaking. The kiss on the cheek. The declarations of love. Do you really think I'm that stupid?" She held up a hand. "Don't answer that. It's obvious I am. I fell for every one of your idiotic tricks."

Griff raised an eyebrow. Try as he might, he couldn't wipe the amused grin off his face. Angelina's deepening scowl told him she didn't find the situation nearly as enjoyable as he did. "A few minutes ago, you certainly seemed to be enjoying my... *idiotic pursuits.*"

"That was before I knew you wanted something from me."

Griff propped his elbow on the bed and lifted his head from the pillow. "All right, I'll bite. Other than the obvious, which I already had, just what exactly do you think I want from you?"

The blazing fury in her green eyes dimmed slightly. "You want me to look at the fireworks. Figure out why they're not working. We both know the formula is solid. I tested it in the lab."

Griff shrugged. "Testing something in a controlled environment and having it work in a real-life application are two very different things."

Angelina slammed her fists into her hips. "The formula is flawless, Griff."

"Believe what you will, babe. When I realized you didn't even have enough interest in me to pursue me for your work, I thought I should at least benefit from this in some way or another. I followed your formula to the letter. The fireworks do nothing more than splatter sparks all over the sky in the same tired shapes as always. There are no frolicking, naked men. No couples fucking each other's brains out. No animation."

The dejected sigh that broke free from Angelina's lips settled straight into Griff's chest. Her shoulders slumped, she sat on the edge of the bed, her back turned to him. "I really thought..."

"I know you did." He slid up behind her and wrapped an arm around her waist, drawing her close. The warmth of her silky skin pressed against his stomach made his cock stir. "I was wrong for taking your work, Angel. We'll go back to the drawing board, work on it together."

Angelina's spine stiffened. "You want to come back with me?"

"I do. But only if you'll have me."

She turned to face him. Her mascara had run, leaving a dark streak over the span of one rose-dusted, flawless cheek. "Things will be different this time. I was just as much to blame for your foolish act as you were." The brief smile on her face took some of the sting out of her words. "How frustrated you must have been to feel you had no other way to get my attention."

Griff raked a hand through his hair, suddenly unable to meet her eyes. "That's no excuse, Angel. I'm sorry."

She pressed her palm against his cheek and lifted his head so their eyes met. The understanding he saw in the depths of her emerald eyes took his breath away.

Their lips met with a shock of electricity, but the kiss was tender, slow this time. Griff ran his hands over Angelina's ribs, her flat stomach, the curvy underside of her full breasts. The shiver that ran through her found its way into his body, tightening his balls. Her mouth tasted almost as sweet as her pussy, and the way her tongue swept against his in a passionate dance ensured that his cock strained, rock hard, against his belly.

Griff reached down to part her legs, but found her thighs already spread, her pussy gaping eagerly for his touch. Her cunt, slicked with her juices, welcomed his finger as he nudged at her core. She moaned against his mouth, thrusting her hips up to meet his hand.

One finger slid easily inside her tight hole and she gasped, biting down on his lip. He stilled for a moment, expecting another rush of blood to break its way to the surface, but her nibbles were gentle as she squirmed against his hand.

Relaxing, Griff thrust another finger into her wet cunt, and a third. She rocked back and forth on his hand, deepening the kiss, her groans making his cock twitch in anticipation.

Angelina broke away first, wild lust glistening in her eyes. "If you don't fuck my pussy, I can't be held responsible for what I might do to you."

Griff chuckled and withdrew his hand. "Yes, ma'am."

The delicious juices beckoned to him, and he brought his fingers up to his lips for a brief taste. Angelina joined him, their tongues lapping her moisture off his hand, flicking against each other as they wiped it clean.

Swinging a leg over his hips, she straddled him. Plunging down in one hard thrust, she impaled herself on his cock, the motion eliciting a soft gasp from her throat. Her velvety cunt enveloped his rod, sucking him in with tight, rhythmic convulsions of her inner walls.

"I missed you," Griff murmured against the side of her throat as her hips rose and fell while she rode him.

"I know."

She understood, but it wasn't enough. It would never be enough. He could spend the rest of his life making it up to her. "I'm sorry."

"I know."

He took her earlobe between his teeth and tugged gently. "I love you."

She leaned back, meeting his eyes. A smile tugged at her lips. "I love you too."

Her cream ran down over his balls, her scent enveloping them both in its candied aroma. He buried his face in the side of her throat, nuzzling the tender skin, and sped up his motions inside her. Angelina met him thrust for thrust, all talk forgotten, their groans and the slapping of skin against skin the only sounds within the confines of the small room.

He dug his fingers into her hips. Angelina bit his shoulder as he slammed into her, his balls tightening in their sack, his cock eager to spurt inside her.

"Come in me," she whispered in his ear. That was all the encouragement he needed. The charge that had been steadily building in his cock released in an explosion of cum.

Angelina arched her back, her body convulsing with small shivers as her climax overtook her. She dug her fingernails into his shoulders as she rode him, milking him for every ounce of seed he could spill inside her.

Her heaving breath came in harsh, ragged gasps when she finally slumped against him. Their sweat-coated bodies stuck to one another and he gripped her ass, holding her down on his softening cock.

Not wanting to break free from the confines of her sweet cunt, Griff gripped her tighter. "Stay with me tonight."

"Sure," she murmured in his ear. "There are so many things I want to do to you."

The promise sent another charge to his cock. Angelina grinned and wriggled against him. "But first things first," she continued. "Let's see about making those fireworks work."

Chapter Five

Angelina held the sheets of formula in her right hand while she stared at the assembled shells, fuses, and powder before her. Everything looked fine. According to her calculations, Griff had done everything right. By all accounts, the fireworks should perform exactly as they had in the lab, lighting the night sky with a myriad of sparkling sexual encounters.

She frowned and glanced down at the paper. "What are we missing?"

Griff thrust his hands in his pockets. He stood so close that when he spoke his lips grazed her earlobe. "We've been through this. I followed your instructions to the letter. Black powder, fuse, tube. It's all there."

"How did you make the powder?"

"Just as you instructed. Charcoal, sulfur, potassium nitrate." He tapped the notes. "In exactly the right measures."

Angelina spun on her heel, excitement building in her chest. "That's all?"

Confusion flittered over his sharp, angular features. "What more is there? I took all your notes, didn't I?"

Gripping her lower lip between her teeth, she pointed to a fourth ingredient. "What about that one?"

Griff's eyes widened. "You don't actually mean –"

Angelina laughed. Her formula really *was* flawless. If all the ingredients were applied properly, at any rate. Fairy dust wasn't hard to come by... if one knew where to look. "Of course I do. Why do you think I wrote it down?"

"Fairy dust?" His nose crinkled as he uttered the words. "There's no such thing."

Angelina's grin widened until she thought her cheeks would split with the effort. "Oh, baby. You have a lot to learn."

They didn't have much time. The fireworks were scheduled to go off in a little under ten minutes, and Angelina intended to see the first preview of her formula got all the attention it deserved.

She rushed back into the trailer, Griff close on her heels.

"And just what do you think you're doing?" he asked when she stopped to stare at the bed sheets. "We could go for another round, but I don't think that'll help with the fireworks."

"On the contrary. That's exactly what the fireworks need."

He took a deep breath and exhaled it slowly, but didn't press for more answers. Angelina stood on tiptoes and planted a firm kiss on his lips. "I'll explain everything," she promised before brushing past him.

Still holding the papers with her scribbled formula, she leaned over the bed, letting out a relieved sigh when she found what she was looking for. A mound of golden powder sat in the middle of the bed, and aother, smaller one, on the edge.

"What is that?" Griff asked, peering over her shoulder.

"Fairy dust."

She scooped both piles onto the paper, using the edge as a level. When she was sure she had every speck of fairy dust, she took it outside, careful to keep the wind from blowing any away before she could sprinkle it over the top of the shells.

The formula called for one speck of fairy dust per shell. As her Aunt Dora had told Angelina for as long as she could remember, science and magic weren't mutually exclusive. Instead, they coexisted. When blended in the right way, they created some of mankind's most potent inventions. Like electricity. And the ability to imprint an image onto a sheet of paper in the photographic process.

"Fire it up," Angelina said, pointing to the computer hooked up to the shells.

Griff still looked skeptical. "Let me see if I understand this. Your…"

"Cum," she supplied when he seemed at a loss for words. "My cream, juices, moisture... whatever you'd like to call it. It produces fairy dust."

"Which would explain the sparkles."

She nodded. "Exactly. When it dries, it leaves the dust behind in its natural state. It's a bitch to remove from bed sheets, though. Dry cleaning only, and that can get expensive really quick."

Griff threw up his hands in a gesture of puzzled surrender, which only made Angelina laugh again. "We'll talk more about this later." He handed her a set of safety gear – ear plugs, safety goggles, and a hard hat – and punched in a few keys on the computer keyboard. Angelina held her breath as the first burst lit up the sky.

Gold, silver, and red hues tinged the midnight velvet, and a hushed awe fell over the park. The bright image showed two men, one on his hands and knees, the second kneeling behind him, his cock pounding rapidly at his lover's ass. The detail astounded even Angelina, who breathed a heavy sigh of relief as she perused the image. The man's thick hair, the splayed fingers gripping the other man's ass.

"Gorgeous," Griff said, admiration tingeing his tone.

The first volley of sparkles was followed by a second, and a third. Men engaged in every possible lover's technique glittered above the park. The astonished silence quickly turned into lustful groans as the park's visitors started to duplicate some of the activities being depicted across the dark sky.

Angelina yelped as Griff's hand gripped her ass and squeezed lightly. "You didn't bewitch me, did you?"

She laughed. "Trust me. There were times I'd definitely wanted to. You can rest easy, though. My fairy abilities leave a lot to be desired."

He tilted her chin up and brushed his lips softly across hers. "The rest of you is pretty damn perfect."

She gripped his firm ass in return and thrust her hips against his body, feeling his erection hard against her stomach.

His wicked grin mirrored her own. "You'd do well to remember that."

Epilogue

Men sandwiched Eve from all sides as she stood in the middle of Hard Delights, gaping up at the brightly-lit sky. Any other time, she'd have enjoyed being pressed up against hard bodies with solid erections prodding her flesh. Now, however, all she could think about was Angelina.

"Come on, hon. Answer me." She'd tried to get through to her best friend countless times over the past hour, but as before, no response echoed through her small earpiece.

Another burst of fireworks lit up the sky. This time, the sharp image of a man on his knees filled the midnight velvet. The animated face grinned around a mouthful of cock. His partner's hips thrust wildly, meeting the man's fevered sucking with passionate motions of his own.

Eve looked away, scanning the crowd for Angelina's biker outfit. She couldn't have gone far. The park only had one exit, and that was heavily guarded. Although the men patrolling the gate remembered Angelina's ridiculous beard, they swore they hadn't seen her come out.

She must be here. Somewhere.

Shoving her way through the zealous crowd, Eve emerged onto a thin stretch of dark pavement. She caught a few stares being cast her way, and knew that in her short red sundress and four-inch scarlet heels, she didn't exactly blend in. Right now, her appearance was the least of her worries.

"Damn you, Griffin," she murmured, scanning the area around her for the hundredth time. She'd searched half the place already. The shells were being fired from the other side of the park, but as soon as the first burst had lit the sky, men blocked her way in their enthusiasm to reenact some of the activities going on overhead and Eve found herself looking for another way around.

Her shoe caught in a crack in the asphalt, and she stumbled, regaining her balance by gripping the edge of a trashcan. A barrage of profanity settled on the tip of her tongue, but she swallowed it back as her gaze fell on an unmistakable mass of brown, fuzzy hair.

Fear reached inside her chest, gripping her heart. Angelina's beard. Her friend's plan had failed. That much was certain from the glittering sparks filling the sky. But what if Angelina never even made it to the fireworks? What if someone stopped her before she ever got that far?

Think, Eve. Where could she be?

She surveyed her immediate surroundings, slowly this time, analyzing everything in her path. A sign close to the trashcan proclaimed the "Blow Me Away" roller-coaster standing only twenty feet away offered a gut-churning good time. At its base, a structure that housed all the mechanical innards of the ride looked more like an old-fashioned shed, complete with a red barn door.

Taking a deep breath, Eve hurried toward the place. If Angelina's disastrous disguise had fallen off, either by accident or on purpose, Griffin could have recognized her. It stood to reason he'd have locked her away until he could launch the fireworks.

Groans penetrated through the entrance to the shed-like structure. Eve paused, pressing her ear to the smooth wood. The passionate moans sounded male, but she couldn't be sure. One was high-pitched and muffled, making it possible the sound could be a woman's voice. Or a scream.

She shuddered and pushed the door open. Darkness shrouded her senses, enveloping her in its solid, shadowy warmth. The door swung closed behind her with a squeak.

A single overhead light bulb spilled dim light over two men. At the sight of the slick, manly physiques, Eve's hand shot out to grip the wall for much-needed balance.

Wide hands with long, slender fingers gripped a man's ass cheeks, spreading them open. The thickest cock Eve had ever seen entered his puckered hole, and the screams she'd heard from outside filled the room. Whether from pleasure or pain, Eve couldn't tell.

As she watched, the man doing the fucking began to change. His shoulders widened, hair sprouted from his smooth, dark chest. His already slender fingers elongated further, claws unsheathing from rounded fingertips, digging into his companion's tender flesh. Angry red welts sprung up in their wake.

A terrified cry gripped her throat, but it was choked to silence when the beast turned toward her. His jaw sported thick stubble, and his teeth – or were they fangs? – glistened wetly as he grinned. Brilliant blue eyes bore deeply into hers.

"Well, well, if it isn't Little Red Riding Hood." His voice was deep, masculine, without a hint of the slur she'd have expected from the misshaped mouth. "This isn't grandma's house, babe. And here, the big bad wolf will definitely eat you."

Eve's mouth fell open, and she did the only thing she could under the circumstances.

She collapsed in a dead faint at his feet.

Lacey Savage

Lacey Savage began her love affair with romance at an early age. In high school, she checked out steamy romance novels from the public library and would often be found reading them in the middle of class. Lacey still reads more than she cares to admit, and probably more than her husband would like, considering how many books she keeps bringing into the house. Her favorite genres have always been erotica, romance, fantasy, science fiction, and mystery, so she tries to incorporate a little of each into her writing.

Lacey initially majored in Marketing, then went back to school to major in English Literature. After earning her degrees, she decided to turn her efforts to her true passion: writing. A hopeless romantic, Lacey loves writing about the intimate, sensual side of relationships. She currently resides in Ottawa, Canada, with her loving husband and their mischievous cat. You can learn more about Lacey by visiting her Web site at www.laceysavage.com or she can be reached via email at laceysavage@rogers.com.

The Troll Under The Bridge
Shelby Morgen

For my "Daughter," Chas, the Blue Faerie, who keeps me young.

The Troll Under The Bridge

"What is the world coming to?" The Cop stood staring at me, shaking his head.

Oh, I knew what he saw. It was just after dark, but there were enough lights in the park to show me off to my best advantage. Long, tall, lush body. Curves in all the right places. Perfect skin, dusted a light powder blue tone. Bright burgundy hair – mounds of it, sculpted in a very artistic Mohawk. Yeah. He wanted me. And that embarrassed him.

It was the legs that did them in. I'm 6' 4". And in this short black leather miniskirt, that means I show off about an acre of legs. They're my best feature. Well, unless it's the boobs. God was good to me there, too. I flashed the Cop my best grin.

He blanched. "Are those tusks?"

"The better to eat you with, my dear."

"What?"

"Don't you get it?" I stretched, showing off a bit more leg. The park bench was getting a tad hard. Long evening. I waved an arm in the general direction of the huge span overhead. "Bridge, you know? Bridge?"

He just stared at me uncomprehendingly.

"I'm the Troll under the bridge."

He blinked.

I stretched again, giving him a nice shot of cleavage from the straining upper hem of my tank top. "Don't you want to be eaten by the Troll under the bridge?"

He had the look. Not sure whether to unzip his pants or call social services.

So I decided to help him a bit. "It's not like I *live* under the bridge. I have a great apartment on the east side, just a couple of blocks from here. But it's hard to meet guys who appreciate Trolls when you're stuck in an apartment, and the Internet is just full of wackos. I like to hang out here in the evenings. Seems appropriate." Cops like "normal" conversation. Makes them feel all is right with the world, even when it clearly isn't.

He took a deep breath, straining the fabric of his uniform shirt where it buttoned over his chest. He didn't actually move, but the long, corded muscles in his arms flexed. He was thinking of moving. Just couldn't decide which way to go. I wanted him to think harder. As in seriously consider jumping me.

"It isn't illegal, is it? Being a Troll, under a bridge?"

"Depends on what you do under the bridge."

"Maybe I lay in wait, trying to catch nice, juicy cops to eat."

"Right."

"Don't you want to investigate further, officer?" I offered, running a finger between my breasts, where the slight sheen of perspiration the afternoon heat inspired left a rivulet of sweat. He blinked again, in that slow, stunned way men have when they can't decide whether they want to fuck me or run for their lives. But he was a cop. Cops don't run.

OK. Yeah. I have a thing for cops. Especially big, strong, beefy cops with muscles that jump when they even think about moving. Big, strong, beefy cops who can't take their eyes off my boobs. The muscles in his arms weren't the only things twitching. His cock fought layers of fabric to get to me, though apparently he was doing his best to ignore that message. Well endowed, too, from the looks of that bulge. I wondered what he'd do if I ran a nail over his crotch. Yum.

"Would you like to see my apartment?" OK, that lacked finesse. But I was getting horny just watching him getting hard for me.

Uh-oh. I must have pushed him a bit too far. He had that cop look on his face now. Remote. Detached. "Look, Miss, there's no law that says you can't sit on a park bench under a bridge. You just can't eat the tourists, OK? You can't even *offer* to eat the tourists, no matter what your getup. That's soliciting, and that is illegal."

Soliciting? What the fuck! "Tourists? You think I'm a fucking prostitute? I'm a Troll, damn it! Trolls sit under bridges, waiting for unsuspecting victims. Victims to EAT. When did that turn into sex?"

He cleared his throat, looking a tad embarrassed. "Well, you did say 'The better to eat you with,' but I thought..."

"You thought I was offering you a blow job? Why would I do that? Don't get me wrong. I love sex, but I don't do blow jobs with strangers. I mean really. Did I ask you for money? No. So what's in it for me? What are you gonna do for me if I give you a blow job, hey, Mr. Cop?"

More than a little pissed off now, I stood, meeting him eye to eye, running my nice, sharp nail down the seam of his zipper. Even the feel of that hot, hard cock jumping at my touch wasn't enough, now. "You got a problem with Trolls, Mr. Cop? Not good enough to hang out with you humans, are we? Can't possibly be doing anything as innocent as just sitting on a park bench. Must be doing something illegal. Why not prostitution? All Trolls are inherently evil anyway, right? Must be doing something wrong. Let's all pick on the Troll."

The sight of my bared fangs, fully exposed now and rather close to his face, should have sent him running, screaming for help. Instead he did what I'd wanted him to do in the first place – he grabbed me and kissed me.

Did I mention the man was built? No lesser human could have pulled an enraged Troll against his chest, held her there, and practically bruised her lips with a kiss like that. Damn he was good. Hot and angry and questing, his tongue battled with mine, fitting nicely between the tusks, raking over my teeth and stealing my breath away.

He clawed at me, bunching my skirt up, gripping the firm cheeks of my ass, grinding my pussy against the growing tent in the front of his pants. Oh, God. It was hard to remember why I was mad at this cop while his cock was driving me wild. I shoved my hands between us, tearing at his zipper, but there was too much cop stuff in the way. He released my ass long enough to reach for his gunbelt and I shifted my stance, widening my legs to give him better access. Taking advantage of his momentary distraction, I pulled my mouth back from his and bit him - hard - on the shoulder.

"Damn, you taste good," I muttered.

"Let me get this shirt off and I'll taste even better."

"Why should I, Cop? What are you going to do for me?"

"How about we flip a cuff key to see who eats who?"

Oh, yeah. I could play that game. "Aren't you afraid of me?"

"Oh, fuck, yeah. Just shaking in my boots."

I had to laugh at that. Especially since he wasn't wearing boots. "What about being out of uniform while you're on duty? That's bad, right?"

"Not ON duty. On my way home. Just came by here to watch the fireworks out over the bay."

"Well, OK, then. Maybe we can make our own fireworks." Working quickly, I helped him undress, trying my best not to shred his uniform. God he was hot! And his cock - at least nine inches, and thick enough to satisfy even a Troll like me. I raked my claws down his backside, glorying in the strength of the man. He didn't even yelp. My pussy flooded with moisture, oh so ready for that bad-ass cock.

As if he knew what I was thinking, he dropped to his knees, pulling my skirt down with him. I'd complain about that later, when I found out how much it would cost to repair a black leather miniskirt. For now I was all about the feel of his tongue pushing my lower lips open, lapping roughly over my aching clit. Oh, fuck. How was I supposed to maintain my Bad-Ass-Troll posturing when the man hummed "God Bless America" while he sucked my clit?

Fuck, fuck, fuck! The fireworks were starting. He fumbled for something on his discarded belt and pulled out a mini-baton, thrusting it hard into my empty, waiting pussy while his tongue and teeth worked me like a pro. Oh, damn, that was good. I hooked my claws on his shoulders, trying hard not to shred the fragile human skin. He worked the baton like a dildo, each thrust pushing me harder, higher, till I screeched in time to the rockets, so hard, so fast, so bright, the lights flashing, the colors bursting, yes, yes!

"Fuck me!" I screeched, pulling him to his feet, wanting, needing his cock. He obliged, lifting me, sliding my cunt down over his thick, throbbing cock as if I weighed nothing. No finesse here. Just one long, hard slide right into home base.

Damn he felt good. I bent my head, licking his shoulder where I'd bitten him not long ago. Oh, yeah. Just the lightest trickle of blood. I bit again, harder this time, though careful even at a time like this not to do any permanent damage. I just wanted to taste him. Lick him. Consume him.

No. Must not hurt the human. Bad Troll.

As if the feel of my teeth on his skin excited him, he pulled out, thrusting hard, his hands pulling me down roughly over his cock, then lifting me. It wasn't enough. Not near enough. He backed me over against the bridge tower thingy, whatever it was called, where the rough concrete held me as he thrust, ripping at my skin like hundreds of claws. Yes! Oh yes! That was it. Pain. Pleasure. The scent of blood. His, mine, mixed together. Fireworks exploding everywhere.

He bit me. Small, human teeth, but teeth, latching hard onto my neck at the base of my shoulder, while his hands fisted around my breasts, his thumbs crushing my nipples against his palms. Pain that went almost beyond pleasure assaulted me from every direction, and still he thrust on, his cock going harder, deeper, his balls slamming against me with every thrust. Oh, damn, oh, God, oh fuck, yes! Yes! I came like the fireworks, pulling, clawing, flashing lights, explosions all around.

"Fuck me, damn you, Cop!" I screamed as I bit his ear.

"Fuck me, Troll!" he screamed back.

And I did. I tightened my muscles around him like a fist, squeezing, not just his cock, but my legs around his waist, my hands fisted in his short cop hair, my teeth buried in his neck so close, so close to where they could do real damage. I knew the danger of it turned him on, felt it in the way his cock swelled impossibly harder, his balls no longer slapping, because they'd drawn up tight now. Desperate, I clawed and scratched, taking as much as he could give me, trying for one more orgasm before I ran out of time.

A little more, just a little more... another thrust, and another. Short, hot, a staccato merger of pain and pleasure, his nails scraping my skin, his mouth sucking the small bite mark, and his cock, that glorious, powerful cock, thrusting deep into my wet, aching pussy. I fought him desperately, wanting more, more, needing that final release, that last wash of color before...

He slid his arms down under my knees, pulling them from around his waist to raise them up, giving him better access as he slammed into me. Groaning, he thrust frantically now, his pace signaling the end as he closed his eyes, the muscles of his neck standing out in heavy cords, the force of his thrusts grinding his pelvis against mine with a power that would have shattered a human.

But I'm not a human. I reveled in the pain, the power, of him, but mostly in the sheer trust this man had that nothing, *nothing* he could do with his body would *ever* be too much. He knew what I wanted, and he wanted it too. As he groaned out his warning, I came, the last wash of color filled the night, the last burst of fireworks signaling the end.

God but it was good. Wave after wave of ecstasy washed over me, leaving me weak and trembling in his arms as he came, shooting his searing heat into me. Damn. Damn, damn, damn. "So good," I whispered. "So fucking good."

"Oh, yeah." He tried to move, but he couldn't, any more than I could. The weight of our bodies kept us leaning against the bridge thingy. Post. Whatever. I threaded my fingers slowly, absently, through his hair. His short, cop hair.

Did I mention I have a thing for cops?

"So how'd the interview go?"

"I got the job."

"Really? Great! Congratulations!"

"How could they not hire me? I have the perfect credentials. I'm a Troll."

"When do you start?"

"Monday night. They were thrilled I wanted to work night shift."

He laughed, even though he knew I wouldn't really turn to stone in daylight. I'm just not fond of the heat. "So, do you get a uniform?"

"Oh, yeah."

"I like uniforms."

"You like Trolls."

"Just one Troll."

"Good. Cause Trolls don't share well."

"Neither do cops."

"I get a badge, too. Know what it says?"

"*Mine*?"

"No. Department of Highways, Toll Collector."

We laughed together, slowly unwinding our bodies as he helped me back to my feet. "Maybe I'll have to run my motorcycle through your toll gate one night and see what happens when the bad-ass guy in leather doesn't pay his toll."

I shivered with anticipation. Oh, yeah. Even after seven years together, I still loved these games. "I'd love that. But I'll never get tired of playing Troll under the Bridge."

"You're a natural," he agreed. "We're being issued new handcuffs, special Troll-proof ones. Maybe I'll arrest you next time."

My pussy flooded thinking about it. Damn. This man could get me horny with just a word. Did I mention I have a thing for cops? Or maybe just this one. But I warn you, he's mine. And Trolls don't share their toys.

Shelby Morgen

Shelby Morgen is insane. What else would have led her to start her own business – as a small online publishing company? Bill, her business partner and husband of 23 years, shares the dream with Shelby. Perhaps the insanity is contagious.

When you can catch her awake and not buried up to her eyebrows in work, she assures you this is the best job in the world – she's the keeper of dreams.

Changeling Press E-Books
Quality Erotic Adventures Designed For Today's Media

More Sci-Fi, Fantasy, Paranormal, and BDSM adventures available in E-Book format for immediate download at www.ChangelingPress.com – Werewolves, Vampires, Dragons, Shapeshifters and more – Erotic Tales from the edge of your imagination.

What are E-Books?

E-Books, or Electronic Books, are books designed to be read in digital format – on your computer or PDA device.

What do I need to read an E-Book?

If you've got a computer and Internet access, you've got it already!

Your web browser, such as Internet Explorer or Netscape, will read any HTML E-Book. You can also read E-Books in Adobe Acrobat format and Microsoft Reader, either on your computer or on most PDAs. Visit our Web site to learn about other options.

What reviewers are saying about Changeling Press E-Books

Lena Austin – Unicorn Valley: Gryphon's Heart

"Readers beware once you have started reading any of the books in Lena Austin's "Unicorn Valley" series you will want to read them all! This magical land that she has created in her books is beyond imagination. Having elves, vampires, unicorns, werewolves and many more all in one place will have fans of paranormal and fantasy drooling with envy."
– *JoAnn, Fallen Angels Reviews*

Stephanie Burke – A Man Called Lust

"Ms. Burke has given us yet another great story to sink our teeth and imaginations into. The world she has created is full of magic and love. If you have never read a Stephanie Burke book, then I suggest you grab this one, you won't be sorry that you did."
– *Donna, Fallen Angel Reviews*

Ciarra Sims – Possession Obsession

"I found myself unable to put this story down, until it was finished. If I could give it more hearts, I would have, it is that good! You will not be disappointed when you pick-up this must read adventure."
– *Janalee, The Romance Studio*

Aubrey Ross – Mystic Keepers: Cayenne

"If you love Christine Feehan and Sherrilyn Kenyon, you're going to absolutely love Ms. Ross. Her men are right up there with the Carpathians and the Dark Hunters."
– *Donna, Fallen Angel Reviews*

Isabella Jordan – Eyes of the Leopard: Discovery

"Jordan packs sensual, lust-filled steaming erotica into an all-too-short story. The plot always stays on focus and never becomes overshadowed by the sexual encounters of the main characters – who hold their ground and never fail to hold our interest."

4 1/2 Hearts! – Romantic Times BOOKclub

Angelina Evans – Paladin's Pride: Out of Sight

"*Paladin's Pride 1: Out Of Sight* is a very original science fiction erotica story. Angelina Evans has done an excellent job of world building with this one. The danger surrounding our hero and heroine is ever present and constantly in their thoughts. The sex is hotter than hot and the hero is every woman's fantasy come to life. I really liked his invisibility. I highly recommend this one to all lovers of hot sex in their science fiction."

– Chere Gruver, Sensual Romance Reviews

Elayne S. Venton – Bonds of Justice: Blade's Decree

"A fabulously stimulating read; I found myself bouncing in my seat as I tried to figure out how to rush to the next page without skipping anything... Ms. Venton does a fantastic job of bringing the over-protective alpha male to life while giving him a tender side."

– Keely Skillman, Coffee Time Romance

Ruth D. Kerce – Undercovers: Lady of the Night

"Renee and Sam have a delicious sexual relationship. They are both completely open to their thoughts, feelings, and desires. Ms. Kerce has done a fabulous job writing a love story for two people who always have to be on top, in the bedroom and out of it. Who wouldn't want to get *Undercovers* with sexy Sam?"

– Ansley Velarde, The Road to Romance

Jonathan Wright – In The Belly Of The Night

"When these two finally decide to come together the sparks fly and the world seems to catch on fire. Sex between them is a liquid heat and a race of endurance. I am normally very leery of reading romances that are written by men but Mr. Wright has written a great story with romance, suspense and a big helping of the supernatural. What more could you ask for?"

Five Stars – *Oleta Blaylock, Just Erotic Romance Review*

Shelby Morgen – C.H.A.S.E. 1:
All I Want For Christmas

"Candy and Brook have chemistry together that nearly explodes off the page. The sex between them left me needing lots and lots of ice water. Shelby Morgen's *C.H.A.S.E. 1: All I Want For Christmas* is a dynamite story that had me captivated from beginning to end."

– Mireya Orsini, Just Erotic Romance Reviews

Changeling Press, LLC

www.ChangelingPress.com

Printed in the United States
43016LVS00002B/131

9 781595 962805